PRAISE FOR RICHARD B. SCHWARTZ

Proof of Purchase

It's like this guy is just channeling Raymond Chandler on every page. . . . The ending . . . would make Mike Hammer proud.
— Jochem Steen, *Sons of Spade*

In this engaging hard-boiled mystery, one of three in Schwartz's Jack Grant series (Frozen Stare; The Last Voice You Hear), the seasoned California PI looks into the disappearance of an ex-girlfriend at the request of the woman's husband. When her mutilated body turns up in the woods, Grant makes it his mission to track down her murderer. With the assistance of Lt. Diana Craig, an attractive fast-riser in the San Bernardino police department, Grant follows leads that point to his client, as well as to a consortium of underworld bosses who are branching out into a mega-real estate project. The pair find time, between car chases and gun battles, to begin a relationship. . . . Fans of Robert Parker will enjoy encountering Grant . . . .
— *Publishers Weekly*

The Last Voice You Hear

It's not often that an author's second book is as good as the first, and even less frequent are the instances when an author . . . top[s] it with an extraordinary second . . . deliver[ing] a walloping good tale as well. Richard B. Schwartz has done just that. In *The Last Voice You Hear*, Mr. Schwartz places himself on par with our finest contemporary murder-mystery writers. This is a book you won't want to miss. . . .
— Alan Paul Curtis in *Who Dunnit*

The author . . . writes vividly, putting the reader right into the scene. Schwartz explores the meaning of right and wrong, crime and justice.
— Mary Helen Becker in *Mystery News*

The story rockets along . . . a fast-moving, well-told story with a surprising conclusion that blurs the line between crime and justice.
— Joseph Scarpato, Jr. in *Mystery Scene*

Jack Grant, the Vietnam vet and Pasadena-based PI who debuted in Frozen Stare (1989), returns in this engrossing sequel by Schwartz, author of several scholarly studies of Samuel Johnson. Schwartz knows his London, but surprisingly he evokes California with equal ease, mainly with vividly etched strokes. An apparently maniacal killer is on the loose in London, someone strong and very practiced at impalement. So far, so nasty. But when a victim is dispatched in similar fashion in Disneyland, of all places, Jack Grant is called in. He discovers the killer's identity, but there's a problem: there's a method to the killer's madness. Moreover, Grant has an ethical problem of his own: he's plagued by his conscience, since he understands and even sympathizes with the murderer's cause. The cinematic climax takes place high above the floor of the California desert, and Schwartz squeezes every last drop of suspense from his setting. . . . The result is a high-tension thriller awash in sanguinary detail. Paper towels, anyone?
— *Publishers Weekly*

Frozen Stare

I welcome Richard Schwartz to the club. It's been a long time since I've seen two more engaging characters entering the series scene.
— Sandra Scoppettone

Grant and White play nicely off each other and the switch-on-a-switch works well.
— *Kirkus Reviews*

This tale, in the California private eye tradition, has a rousing finish and is an enjoyable read.
— *Publishers Weekly*

A new author devoted to the hard-boiled tradition. . . . Schwartz has the hard-boiled formula down pat. . . . Schwartz does not break any rules in Frozen Stare. . . . He writes crisply. The narrative moves at a slam-bang pace as bodies pile up. . . . As a dedicated student of the hard-boiled school of detective fiction [Schwartz] has learned his lessons well.
— *The Washington Post Book World*

Gives a whole new meaning to the phrase 'cold-blooded murder'. . . . This is a quick read with plenty of action. Schwartz's first novel is a winner!
— *Sarasota, FL Herald Tribune*

This is a delightful tale, full of amusing touches, and the relationship between Grant and his good cop friend, black Frank White, is a joy. I hope that Schwartz can keep this standard up for a long time to come.
— *The Armchair Detective*

Nice and Noir: Contemporary American Crime Fiction

Opinionated but always fascinating, shrewd and smart, but always readable. . . .
— *The Thrilling Detective*

A GWEN HARRISON NOVEL

THE LAST TEMPTATION

RICHARD B. SCHWARTZ

THE LAST TEMPTATION

Published by Dark Harbor Books
First Edition 2025

Cover design: Luis J. Medina Torruellas
www.Torruellasarts.com

ISBN: 979-8-9899271-6-6 Paperback Edition
          979-8-9899271-7-3 Hardcover Edition
          979-8-9899271-8-0 Digital Edition

Library of Congress Control Number: 2025913036

Author services by Pedernales Publishing, LLC
www.pedernalespublishing.com

10 9 8 7 6 5 4 3 2 1

Printed in the United States of America

v8

For Lexi

All change is of itself an evil, which ought not to be
hazarded but for evident advantage.

Samuel Johnson

The house of delusions is cheap to build but drafty to live in.

A. E. Housman

ONE

After a particularly difficult assignment that entailed a significant shoulder wound, a period of extended bed rest and multiple forms of medical tinkering, the Director persuaded me to extend my R&R at a location that was both upscale and off-grid. (Transl.: more than 1500 miles from the District of Columbia.) He dipped into an obscurely-labeled fund and financed my stay at *The Broadmoor*, a century-old five-star resort in Colorado Springs. Director Gradison always preferred large venues because they offered ample space in which to reduce his agents' exposure. Since the *Broadmoor's* grounds and 'wilderness experience' properties encompassed approximately five thousand acres, that particular box was satisfactorily ticked. He also preferred to low-key the accommodation (I didn't really need a suite anyway), but his assistant, Peggy Chapman, scored me a room that contained a mini-conservatory. Just off the bedroom, it was a glass-enclosed reading nook that was bathed in natural light that warmed the room in a lovely fashion, particularly at 6,035 feet. In late winter it's good to be closer to the sun.

That is why you can drive through that portion of the Rockies and see frozen rivulets in the rock face while sitting in your car in your shirt sleeves. It's also why Pikes Peak seems modest in its height. When you start your journey a mile above sea level the surrounding landscape becomes a topographic map with unanticipated shapes providing unexpected perspectives. I hadn't explored too much of it yet, but I did make a point of a brief day trip to the nearby Air Force Academy, where I hoped to encounter some exotic wildlife. I had to settle for a 12-point white tail with his accompanying harem of five. The Academy chapel is an architectural must-see but the feature that captured my particular attention was its stunning, three-dimensional rendition of the Shroud of Turin. I thought of it again and again during my modest morning runs and afternoon swims.

Most of my down time had been spent reading techno-thrillers and southern California crime fiction and (of course) exploring the offerings of the hotel's 20-odd restaurants, cafes and lounges. So far my favorite had been *The Grille*, a less formal adjunct to the golf course. I was surprised that the much-heralded trout and bass were too bland for my taste but delighted to discover a pepper steak and cajun shrimp linguine which were, as my MI5 counterparts would say, right up my street. There was also a Berkshire pork chop done up in a southern style that was beyond memorable. I'm not a serious foodie and was interested to learn that the original black and white pigs actually did originate in Berkshire, just 5,000 miles down the road and across the sea. Their provenance/heritage remains important, but this particular example served up at the *Broadmoor* was actually from a supplier in the Ozarks.

Tonight I was checking out the *Ristorante del Lago*, the hotel's pasta/pizza emporium that also offered some pricey main courses. It was going to be a tough night choice-wise, because there were so many of my favorites on offer (continuing with the British slang). Would it be Buffalo Ricotto salad or a Wagyu beef concoction? A selection of cheeses or salami (the River Bear bresoala sounded appetizing)? Cacio e Pepe or Lobster Pappardella? Lasagne or whole, roasted, herb-stuffed Branzino?

The only thing I was sure about was the gelato with a double espresso. There would be no room for a side order of vegetables (probably heaped on a porcelain trough that would serve at least three people); the wine or wines I would leave to the sommelier. With luck there might be just enough room at the end for a glass of Sambuca with 3-4 (5-6?) dark coffee beans for contrasting nibbles.

I should mention that I had had a modest breakfast, had skipped lunch, and did a brisk 45-minute stint in the two-lane, heated lap pool, my partner a matronly senior citizen with a white swim cap, vintage one-piece and a surprising degree of muscle tone and personal stamina. I wanted to earn that dinner and I believed that I actually had, but there was far more on the evening's menu than I had originally anticipated.

TWO

The first lesson that one learns in the Bureau is to dress conservatively, which is to say, invisibly. The Director occasionally wears a black suit with tiny white pinstripes (when he is not wearing his still-fitting general's uniform), but Edgar's order of the day had always been Bureau gray. Peggy Chapman spent the bulk of her time in a single suite of offices in the successor to the Hoover Building next to the DOJ but confided to me that she still limited herself to a ten-outfit rotation that varied from light gray to (a single instance only) of charcoal gray. The goal is to merge with the wallpaper and conduct systematic, often extended surveillance without attracting any to yourself. In a restaurant setting that meant that you opted for remote tables that provided some protective covering and reduced lighting. When Wild Bill died with a handful of aces and eights he had been forced to sit in the only seat available, one without his preferred backing wall (a story told early and often at Quantico, with the accompanying fact that Wild Bill suffered from glaucoma and ophthalmia, the corollary lesson being that you should be in proper uniform as well as top physical form when you embarked on a dangerous assignment).

I had opted for a cream-colored blouse, but one that blended with the wall treatments of the Ristorante. This was mostly from sheer force of habit, since I hadn't expected any dramatic occurrences beyond my need to make difficult menu choices and make sure that I wasn't so carried away by the carb overload that I accidentally ordered a wine that would shatter my per diem cap to an even greater degree than I had previously budgeted.

All of these plans dissolved when I accepted the waiter's offer of a cocktail and ordered an ultra-dry Bombay Sapphire martini on the rocks with a generous twist of lemon peel. His next mini-derailment of my dinner plan was to suggest that I try the soup-of-the-day, a *pasta e fagioli* (for which I am always a total sucker). The waiter noted that the preparation included a special step in which a portion of the broth is blended with a portion of the beans to produce what he termed a 'delicately creamy' result, which (along with the special Tuscan kale) takes the dish several steps above its simple, canned counterparts.

It was a very fine choice, particularly given the fact that it was all that I was going to eat (along with some freshly-baked bread with chilled butter). My long-planned meal was curtailed by the presence of an unexpected individual three tables to my left. He drew attention with his *Brioni* suit and *Audemars Piguet* watch. I'm no expert, but I figured the suit to be a blend of cashmere and silk. Entering that neighborhood will cost you a tariff in the $15,000+ range, half or less of the cost of the watch, unless, of course, that putative stainless steel is actually white gold or platinum. The haircut probably ran him $250 and the shoes peeking beneath the tablecloth at least $20,000, assuming that they *were Ferragamo's* calf, etched to obtain the embossed crocodile effect. His single-day wardrobe probably exceeded the total value of a reasonably well-heeled couple's entire clothes and jewelry cupboard.

His dinner date ('niece'?) was half his age, dressed in a simple outfit from the *Nordstrom Rack*. She looked eager and hopeful; perhaps this was some form of job interview, perhaps some instance of inter-generational collusion. I didn't recognize her, but I knew who would: Special Agent Mike Liu, a master techie from the Salt Lake City office who could be counted on to maintain confidences and produce quick results. I looked at the remaining portion of my soup wistfully, adjusted the close-up setting on my cell camera, caught the two in the act of being themselves and sent the picture to Mike on a secure line. He responded in twelve minutes.

"Looks like a nice restaurant, Gwen. Too bad these two disrupted your meal."

"I'm in mourning, Mike, but duty calls."

"Duty is a bitch," he responded. "By the way, you still owe me a steak dinner from our last collaboration."

"I haven't forgotten."

"Well, you know who the swarthy man is; how could you not?"

"Just wanted to run him through your facial rec software to be sure."

"Well, he *has* had a little work done on his eyelids (doubtless the result of his well-known vanity) but you can't move your eyes, nose, ears and other appurtenances around without using Photoshop. That is Hassan Darvish, international arms dealer extraordinaire."

"Specializing in middle eastern and European terrorist customers. But that's not his real name, is it?"

"Nope, his birth name was Azimi. Haven't checked in awhile, but if I remember correctly the Darvish connotes holiness and spirituality while the real name, Azimi, means something like 'mighty' or 'magnificent'."

"And possibly delusions of grandeur?"

"No doubt," Mike said. "He's tried to soften his image—preparing himself to fit in at the embassy parties with the good white Burgundy."

"Instead of playing his real role of oleaginous slimeball slinking around in alleyways with blood dripping from his fingernails."

"Perfectly accurate," Mike said.

"So who's the dinner date?"

"Allyson Barry," Mike said, "the daughter of some superannuated hippies from the redwood country. Bachelor's degree from UC-Santa Cruz with a double major in Sociology and Political Science, or, as they say there, 'Politics'. You can sometimes escape the long arm of the law, but you can never detach yourself from alumni/ae rolls and yearbook pictures."

"I don't like it," I said. "What are those two doing having dinner together in the shadow of Cheyenne Mountain?"

THREE

The Cheyenne Mountain complex is now known as Cheyenne Mountain Space Force Station. The construction began in 1961 and was completed (to the degree that such facilities are ever really 'completed') in 1967. Its purpose was to withstand a nuclear strike and enable the country to continue its key military operations before, during and after an apocalyptic event. It originally housed all of the principal NORAD functions until NORAD moved its day-to-day operations to Peterson Space Force Base, a set of facilities adjacent to the Colorado Springs Municipal Airport.

If you Google these matters you will be told that Cheyenne Mountain is now used as an alternate command center and a training site for a number of military entities. If you believe that that is a full and complete summary of its function you would probably be an enthusiastic bidder on the sale of one or more of the country's larger bridges.

The Cheyenne Mountain complex occupies over 5 acres, contains at least 15 buildings, required the excavation of 693,000 tons of granite, with a mountain height of just under 10,000 feet. It was built to survive a 30-megaton nuclear explosion; its blast doors weigh 25 tons. It is the only DOD facility certified to withstand a high altitude electromagnetic pulse attack. And remember, once again, that this is what you will learn from Googling within that totally unclassified area known as the public domain. While I am not privy to the detailed, eyes-only operations of the Space Force I find it very difficult to imagine that the site is a semi-mothballed backup facility with a few classrooms and flight simulators.

What is far easier for me to imagine is that an Iranian arms dealer could have a side hustle in the general area of strategic espionage. He would surely have the means to purchase information from those in need of some serious walking-around money. The question was: is Allyson Barry such a person and was she disrupting my dinner by showing her wares to Darvish?

I texted Mike and asked him what he could find on little Allyson's form of gainful employment.

"Political consultant," Mike replied. "At least that's what it says on her LinkedIn page. It also says that she hasn't posted in awhile. If she actually has a formal operation it is unincorporated and there is no link to a larger organization of which she is a participating partner or everyday employee. You want my best guess…?"

"Always," I said.

"This is just some post-graduation bullcrap. She had to think of something and she wrote down what she aspired to be rather than what she actually was—a barista whose previous courses of study prepared her for a logical next step in life, for which she lacked interest or aptitude: law school."

"Works for me," I said.

"Anyway, your key question has been answered. She doesn't work as a civilian or uniformed member of the Space Force. I checked the federal records and there is no one/each Barry, Allyson there."

"So the next question is: if she's not attractive or important enough for him to invest his very expensive time, what is it that she is actually offering for sale?"

FOUR

"Good question," Mike said. "Let me come at this from another direction. I'll check out her parents and try to see if they're still supporting her."

Since Darvish and his dinner companion were still working on their pasta courses I had the time for a double espresso. I sipped it slowly, waiting to hear from Mike. Twelve minutes later my cell vibrated gently.

"Got the rundown on the parents," Mike texted. "Mom's name is Marianne, but her birth name was Mary Ann. This is probably some form of homage to the recently-departed Ms. Faithfull. Dad is 'Ted'. They met at Humboldt State, amid the redwoods. BTW, their alma mater now carries the honorific title of Cal Poly Humboldt. Marianne is a special ed teacher in a sketchy section of Sacramento. Ted is a titular 'community organizer' but he actually works as a custodian at Marianne's school. I suppose that's what happens when you major in Art History and Museum Studies. Their (very) humble abode is in Del Paso Heights, which should probably be called Del Paso Depths. And I know what you're thinking: in Cali a school custodian probably makes as much as a lawyer in rural Arkansas. The problem is that you can easily pay 300K for a shack in Sacramento, along with your Cali income, sales, property and gasoline taxes. Bottom line: it doesn't look as if Allyson is drawing any heavy allowance from mommy and daddy. Therefore, as we thought, she has no visible, discernible means of support. I can, however, offer you some tangential personal information. I saw a notice in the *Sacramento*

Observer concerning the family's 'activism'; back in the day Allyson's twelve year-old *nom de guerre* was—get this—'Bluebell'."

I thanked Mike and he asked me if I needed anything else. Since Darvish was dawdling with his fettuccine, gesticulating with his fork and generally enjoying holding court before a wide-eyed acolyte, I ordered a second double espresso and asked Mike to bring me up to date on Darvish's life story.

"'Shadowy' is probably the operative word," Mike wrote. His early days are clearer than his more recent ones. He comes from serious money. His parents in Tehran sent him to school in England. He started out at Winchester College—not quite Eton or Harrow, but quite reputable and very pricey. It's been around since the 14th century and was established as a feeder school for New College, Oxford. For some reason or other Hassan went to Cambridge, perhaps because of their strengths in science and engineering? Anyway, he went to St. John's, probably the closest he ever got in his life to anything that was remotely religious. It's reputed to be good in engineering, but not in the league of Trinity, with faculty whose sometime predecessor was Isaac Newton.

"Ater graduation he did some work at Princeton, but left before taking a graduate degree. He returned to Tehran for five years (about which nothing significant is known) and then was able to score a job at *General Dynamics*. The rumor was that some congressman paved the way for his negotiation of the immigration hurdles. There was no suspicion concerning any compromise of our national security, just the usual backhander from his parents' (or some Imam's) coffers to the always-open palm of what his protocol-observant colleagues termed 'the gentleman from New Jersey'.

"He spent several years at *General Dynamics* and then went to the corner of the medieval maps where it says 'Here be dragons'. His name pops up in places like Belarus, Qatar, Pyongyang, Bangalore, et al., but he generally flies sufficiently far under the security systems' radar to escape attention or indictment. There is only one exception: a paper in the Ukraine compared his growing wealth with Adnan Khashoggi's, the billionaire arms dealer. The brave reporter took what was termed a 'sabbatical' shortly after the article's release and promptly disappeared into the ether.

"AK was a Saudi, of course, and departed for his eternal reward (or damnation) in 2017. Funny side note: back in the day AK was funding a sports center at American University, but the plan received a black eye when the students appeared in scarves at a basketball game, holding signs saying 'Adnan's Army.' That was in the days when there was still such a thing as academic humor and a modicum of actual shame. Anyway, Darvish now has homes in Zurich, Malibu and, of course, Washington D.C. and Manhattan. He's stayed clear of the law, in part because he's generally not associated with sales of multiple cargo containers filled with row upon row of small arms, rifles, mortars, light anti-tank weapons, rocket-propelled grenades and such. His forte is the sale of high tech, often exotic parts for guidance systems, including sensors, navigation and control systems, and—these days, of course—algorithms. Sometimes his wares are contained on a single thumb drive. That means that he has to walk the line between selling generic hardware and carefully-guarded state secrets. In other words, he's trying to stay in his pre-war palace on East 64th Street and avoid a single-bed, half-bath place with iron bars in lieu of plaster walls. His subspecialty is information on submarine warfare. We usually think of large, airborne missile systems to take out cities and smaller, ground-based ones to take out bombers, drones, et al., but for the moment submarines represent our only significant, comparative advantage against China, which makes them a pivotal part of our nuclear triad. Their torpedoes and, more important, their missiles, all have guidance systems, something of which Hassan is highly knowledgeable."

"Very serious stuff," I responded, "and a weaponry system whose functionality would be an important part of Cheyenne Mountain's portfolio."

"Yes, indeed," Mike said.

"So how does Bluebell fit into this picture? And how important is it that she and Hassan have taken the opportunity at this time to break breadsticks together?"

"That's what you need to find out," Mike said. "The only thing I can tell you is probably of no use: a person like Darvish would not be meeting with the daughter of a Little-League level set of superannuated activists whose sole continuing operation is the occupation of a house in a ghetto nearly 3,000 miles from the Puzzle Palace. Now if she had been a graduate of MIT or the Engineering school at the University of Illinois… or a current employee of *Raytheon, General Electric, Honeywell, Boeing* or *General Dynamics*…but she's not. She's the person who marched in the tenth row of the demonstrators disrupting lunch in the cafeteria of a school whose mascot is the banana slug."

FIVE

I couldn't disagree with Mike's assessment, but (still grasping for any information I could obtain) I asked him to check the registries of local hotels to find out where Hassan and Bluebell were staying. I wondered if they were meeting momentarily before returning to parts (as yet) unknown or conducting an extended series of meetings. I also said a prayer of thanks to the Bureau's guardian angels for allowing the two scuzzballs to cross my path and arouse my curiosity, as well as for giving me a highly-skilled colleague like Mike Liu. I knew that I would be checking in soon with the Director and I wanted something more interesting to give him than the fact that Hassan and Bluebell had both opted for the dessert of Vanilla Panna Cotta and a pot of hot tea.

This time Mike returned a text in six minutes. "Noblesse does not necessarily oblige," he said. "Bluebell is ensconced in a mundane room at the *Cheyenne Mountain Resort*, a *Hyatt* property. It's not a dump but her room runs about the same amount as it would at a well-positioned *Hilton Garden Inn*. Hassan, on the other hand, is luxuriating in one of the named suites at the *Broadmoor*. They don't list the tariff; you have to call, probably so that they can negotiate with you to your considerable disadvantage. Their website does warn you that the cost will begin at a grand a night. It's like the British train system; they don't like to list the rates so that they can change them every few minutes."

"How long are they staying?" I asked.

"Each for one night. My guess is that they bopped in sometime this morning, Bluebell on one of those regional jets with the low ceiling and the hard seats, Hassan on something private, spacious and cushy. And before you ask: there are only a few nonstop flights from the Springs to places of significance—Chicago, e.g., and on the east coast, BWI. Of course, a lot of people drive to the Springs from the Denver airport, a major *United* hub, as you well know. Anyway, I've accessed the security cameras at both hotels, from the front doors to the parking facilities. I'll get back to you in the a.m. with any information I can turn on their next stops."

"As always…" I said.

"Just don't forget my steak dinner," Mike answered.

"I wouldn't think of it," I said.

I called the Director right after I heard from Mike the following morning, bringing him up to speed on the unexpected diners and their next destinations. "Darvish had a Dassault *Falcon 8X* waiting for him at mid-morning."

"Long range puppy."

"Yes, sir, but he only flew to New York."

"He could fly from Manhattan to Beijing on a *Falcon*," the Director said. "He does have a place in the city, however. He may just be stopping over, committing a capital crime or two and then taking off again. What about the Barry woman?"

"She had a modest rental car, drove to Denver and flew from there to San Francisco."

"Hmm. Give me a sec. OK, she could have flown Southwest to Sacramento for $119. Obviously she's not stopping off to see mommy and daddy, at least not yet."

"Is she on our radar, sir?"

"Not in any significant way; she was picked up at one of the pro-Hamas demonstrations at Columbia and near the 3rd police precinct building in Minneapolis, which was burned during the George Floyd riots. In each case she was questioned but not arrested. Apparently she was nicely-dressed, unmasked, and able to persuade the local authorities that she was an innocent bystander whose curiosity got the better of her…that it wouldn't happen again…that she supported the local police, etc. etc."

"Two cities, what?--1,200 miles apart? Too much of a coincidence for me, especially for someone who's not a fundraiser, admissions officer or pharmaceutical rep. In fact, she's not anything as far as we know."

"Right. And the local police were not exactly locked arm-in-arm with the Bureau, DHS, ICE, et al. To be fair there was nothing that they could actually use to frog-march her to the county jail. Did I ever tell you what my grandfather used to call the local lockup in his native Kentucky?"

"No, sir," I said.

"Well, it's not so much the jail proper as it is one of its prominent features. He referred to temporary incarceration as 'spending the night under the clock'."

"I like it," I said.

"You would have liked him. He had little patience for law breakers."

"My natural compadre," I said.

"So, Gwen, what are our next steps?"

SIX

"I'd like to follow her and try to determine who her playmates might be."

"You're on R&R, Gwen."

"It would be light duty, sir."

"Let me think about that for a day or two. Meanwhile, ask Mike Liu to see if he can pick up her trail in Rice-a-Roni land."

"Still waiting on word from Mike concerning Bluebell, but he was able to tell me that Hassan went to the University Club for brunch. After some Eggs Benedict he went to their library and worked his way through a stack of legacy-media newspapers."

"Alone?"

"Yes."

"Interesting that they have such an extensive CCTV system; I wonder why. Probably to protect their books. Nobody steals Hollandaise sauce, but you can cut the plates out of a Renaissance folio and sell them piecemeal for hefty sums. Or maybe Hassan's an intellectual. He could afford the entry fees at the Aman Club and chooses instead a place with a great private library."

"For what, Sir, a couple grand?"

"Yep. The Aman Club, on the other hand, will set you back 200 large to get through the door and an annual fee of 15. Not that I've ever been there…well, at least not in person."

I smiled to myself as my phone twitched. "Incoming from Mike, Sir…."

"Hold on at your end," he said. "Peggy's making a fresh pot of coffee. I'll be back in ten to twelve...."

"OK, Sir," I said. "Info on Bluebell. When she landed at SFO she got a cab into the city and had some overpriced pastries at a *Starbucks* on Mission Street near Market."

"How many *Starbucks* are there in that neighborhood alone—a dozen?"

"More like 9-10, I think. Mike commented on that fact. Anyway, she was soon joined by a woman who was more or less her own age. They embraced (nothing romantic, just an old friends-type move); the other woman got a cup of exotic liquid, sprinkled some cinnamon on top and settled in for a 15-minute conversation."

"Who did most of the talking?"

"They shared the time. Bluebell wasn't issuing orders or interrogating, at least not that you could tell from the inaudible visuals. It was more like they were catching up with one another. Nothing exchanged hands and no one was shown content from a cell phone screen."

"Any i.d. on the other woman?"

"Yes, as a matter of fact. The other woman was a student at Santa Cruz, so a couple years younger than Bluebell. They wouldn't have known each other from school but maybe they have mutual friends. The woman was a math major, an undergrad from Bahrain. Birth name: Noor Ali."

"Liberal place, at least as far as the Middle East goes," the Director said. Island kingdom. Lots of islands, actually. Lots of commerce. Many of the locals are bilingual in English."

"Noor was the name of the King of Jordan's wife."

"His fourth, if memory serves. Former American citizen. Beautiful woman. In her 70's now. International figure; works for peace, understanding and all the good things. Husband was often helpful to us, as is his son. Hashemites. Direct descendants of the prophet but not usually seen converting by the sword."

"Not studying politics," I said. "That's probably a good thing. Math would be important in Bahrain; maybe they support students around the world who specialize in certain specified areas."

"Yes," the Director said. "I was on a train to London many years ago and the hottest topic among the young was the fanciful rumor that then Prince Charles would move to Scotland, assume the Scottish throne and commandeer the North Sea oil. Utterly preposterous, of course, but the fervid politicos couldn't get enough of it. I struck up a conversation with a foreign student and all he could talk about was the subject he had been required to study: Agronomy."

Again, I smiled. Walter Gradison knew the world of warfare, espionage and security better than anyone I had ever met, but he always leavened the facts with personal stories that brought the facts to life and made them more human.

"We'll keep looking," I said, "and Mike will do some lip reading. If you could keep me posted with any relevant information on Darvish, I would appreciate it."

"Of course," he said. "I would love to know how we get from Cheyenne Mountain to Mission Street. And how about a personal address for Bluebell? A very preliminary search at our end still had her in Santa Cruz."

SEVEN

"Just checked in with the General," I told Mike. "He's grateful for your labors. He was wondering if we had a home address yet for Bluebell."

"Getting close on that; back in a few," Mike said.

"Tell you what…I'm going to have a swim. I'll check back with you in an hour and a half. Get some coffee; take your time. See what you can find."

"Will do; thanks for the break."

Knowing Mike, I checked back in an hour on our secure line. He had a long message for me.

"First off, I've got her address. She made the mistake of making a contribution to a so-called women's health organization. As expected, they shared her contact information with a gazillion comparable groups and I was suddenly inundated with solicitation lists carrying her address. Suffice to say, she and Hassan are actually neighbors, but with a significant difference.

"They're both on the upper east side of Manhattan, and she's even in what appears to be a nice building. The problem is that her apartment is less than 300 square feet. It's the kind that shows up in those clips on *Facebook*, the ones designed to either attract you to the idea of living in NYC or running away from it in horror. This one's access point is below ground level and the front door looks like something you would find between the hallways in Cheyenne Mountain—very thick, very industrial and very secure.

"The apartment was clearly fabricated with an eye on existing realities and maximum cost-cutting. I figure it might have been a maintenance man's digs back in the day. You enter a small hallway and the minimalist bathroom is within the entryway. It's the kind where you could sit on the toilet and wash your hands or turn on the shower at the same time. (Being careful not to bump your head in the process.) That's followed by a single room which contains a kitchenette with an array of miniaturized appliances, space for a foldout love seat that's too small for any significant romance, a side table containing a tiny TV, a rack for a pair of TV-dinner trays and a single clothes closet.

"The closet is wide but it's so shallow that you would have to position your hangers at a tight angle. If you wanted to store a bicycle you'd have to put it in the entryway and go on a heavy diet of *Wegovy* so that you could scoot your skeletal frame around it for purposes of ingress and egress. I don't have any idea where you'd put your luggage…maybe on its side in the clothes closet or on the floor beside the love seat."

He paused and I checked to see if he was still online. "And for this munificent shoebox you would pay how much—2 grand a month?"

He was there. "Actually a mere $1,850."

"Secure, in a nice neighborhood, without too many rats or brown crawlies…that may be a reasonable rent, at least in a place where the word *reasonable* has little relevance to the normal expectations of those living beyond its borders."

"True," Mike responded. "So why do neighbors travel nearly 2,000 miles to have dinner with one another?"

"Good question," I answered. "Maybe they don't want to be seen together back on the block. Maybe they were each in transit and the Springs represented a good rallying point. Bluebell was heading to San Fran. Darvish may have been returning from the west coast. Maybe there was something in the Springs they were each interested in seeing…."

"Keeping that aside for a moment, I do have some other information."

"Shoot," I said.

"Financial stuff…."

"Excellent," I said.

"OK, it's interesting. Her banker is B of A. She's basically living hand to mouth with her checking account. The balance would carry her through a second month but not much further. She also has a small savings account for walking-around money…less than $5K."

"New York is an expensive habit."

"Indeed," Mike said, "but that's not the really interesting part…."

"Which is?"

"The checking account. Most of the monthly income is automatically deposited from other investments."

"You mean like CD's, stocks and such."

"Yes, with the money coming from foreign sources. Haven't yet tracked them in detail. There are also cash deposits. Actual cash, not checks or money orders."

"She's concealing the actual sources."

"Yes," Mike said. "She could be paid in commodities…gold, silver, jewelry, high end watches, guitars…whatever. You pop into your local pawn shop, walk out with your cash, head off to the bank."

"So what do you conclude? There is no real job with a salary, social security payments, 401K payments, and so on; and what she's doing is dodgy. She doesn't want anyone to know the sources of her income."

"Yes, and there's probably some tax criminality involved. The Feds are being shorted and so is the city of New York. Haven't checked the city or IRS records yet, but that's my guess. (And I haven't yet checked on other possible addresses.) If I were her I would be very careful. NYC is committed to filling their coffers; I've heard of people who live in upscale places like Armonk who commute daily into the city. Some have *pied `a terre* apartments there. Suddenly they find out that the city's counters of beans are monitoring their toll payments and seeking beaucoup taxes because of the relative time they are spending there. 'You don't really live in Armonk, buddy; you live in SoHo'."

"That's how they caught Alphonse, Michael--on charges of tax evasion. That's how they actually curtailed his operations."

"The syphilis didn't help him either."

"Point," I said.

"But wait…(as they say in the infomercials), there's more."

EIGHT

"I'm always ready for more," I said.

"It's about Queenie."

"Queenie?"

"Noor. My new nickname for her."

"The mathematician from *Starbucks*."

"Bingo. I've been looking into her finances also."

"Dodgy, like Bluebell's?"

"Not so much. Her government covers her tuition and her parents send her some pocket money every month. Nothing grand. $125. Enough for an occasional change of clothes and some noodle cups. There was one more interesting item: Noor has a brother: Khalid. He's been a naughty boy. His student visa was revoked and he was sent back home a few months ago."

"What school?"

"Columbia."

"Lots of radical activity there."

"Yes, but Khalid was sent down (as we Anglophiles say) for sexual assault. Not sure about the specific details. He claimed that everything was consensual, but as the Secretary of State always says, 'the visa is a privilege, not a right,' and he withheld some of the details of the case to protect the young woman involved. Anyway, Khalid has bid a fond farewell to Morningside Heights and returned to Bahrain."

"I wonder if Noor is seeking some help from Bluebell's Consulting Service to reinstate his visa."

"A possibility," Mike said, "or perhaps seeking some of Hassan Darvish's coin to buy his way back to white Harlem via some political back channels. Perhaps in return for some shady services?"

"Not likely that the Secretary would sit still for any of that."

"True, but Darvish has more to trade than dollars, dinars or rials. His information could be priceless to the SecDef and the government's intelligence operations."

"Mr. and Mrs. Ali would have to call in some serious markers for that kind of help."

"True, and unfortunately there's nothing in the public record or the layers just beneath it to suggest that the Alis have any connection with our international man of mystery and arms dealing. To him, old man Ali would be a face in the crowd, keeping mundane records down at the docks…but then Hassan likes docks and could call in a marker of his own when he's preparing for an off-the-record delivery."

"All possible," I said, "but we're not talking about anything all that exciting. Khalid's been bounced from school; how many other institutions of higher learning throughout Europe would be happy to collect his tuition?"

"Beaucoup," Mike said. "And you haven't asked me the $64,000 question…."

"What was he studying at Columbia?"

"Not Nuclear Secrets or Chemical Warfare," Mike said. "He was in the MESAAS program."

"Middle Eastern and…?"

"Middle Eastern, South Asian and African Studies," Mike said. "He has 14 institutions to choose from in his own country if he is actually intent on studying such things. Columbia has a better reputation than any of them, of course, but we're still not talking about anything highly technical or potentially subversive, just undergraduate boilerplate."

"We're probably just chasing our tails on this one, Mike, particularly if there's no indication of untoward behavior on the part of Noor."

"Which there is not," Mike said, "at least not that I've been able to find. As far as I can see from her transcript she's been more interested in stuff like vertex operator algebras and symplectic geometry than espionage and international evildoing."

"Keep an eye on her," I said. "You never know what these crazy kids are getting up to these days."

"Will do," Mike said. "In the meantime…wait a sec. My radar is talking to me. Give me an hour…."

"You got it," I said.

I hit my *Keurig* cup stash and followed my new avocation: finding espresso grinds and using them for mid-sized regular coffee. My new fav was *Café Bustelo*; it tasted good and it was also cheaper than Charbucks (as a cynical friend used to call it).

I had rearranged the clothes in my top dresser drawer, deposited some miscellaneous detritus in the hotel's recycling and trash baskets, began formulating a shopping list and was on a second cup of *Bustelo* when Mike came back online.

"Ms. Bluebell is on the move," he said. "Tracked her from *Starbucks* to SFO, where she boarded a flight to Seattle."

"And you'll tell me whether she's headed to the Space Needle, the mothership/*Nordstrom* store, the original *Starbucks* or the *Boeing* factory…."

"I will indeed," he said.

In just under three and a half hours he gave me some updates on her landing and her securing a taxi, gave her time to settle in and then continued with his narrative.

"She's at the University—the U of W—in a coffee shop alcove. Something called the *City Grind Espresso*. It's on the bottom floor of an art gallery. I've been trying to run some facial rec on her companion, but so far no luck. Hold…."

"Description?"

"I pulled up the video feed for you. Uber nerd. Short in stature but with a slight paunch. Bushy brown hair. Wire-framed glasses. Everything but the pocket protector and the holstered slide rule."

"You're really dating yourself, Michael."

"Sad, isn't it? Anyway, I would usually be able to access some yearbook photo sites, but so far I've been drawing blanks. Wait a sec…ok, some fuzzy, side shots…oh, nice, here we go. Story in the *Seattle Times*. Human interest stuff. Local boy makes good. His name is Lawrence Andreeson and he published a scholarly article as an undergraduate."

"On?"

"The San Juan Islands."

"Nearby archipelago," I said.

"Yes, good tourist draw. A top place to see Orcas."

"Big-brain guys," I said. "Complex social behaviors."

"His article had to do with their declining numbers. Fortunately they'll eat anything and they're highly-skilled hunters."

"The newspaper probably liked the fact that his piece was both politically correct and tourism friendly."

"Very observant, Special Agent Gwen."

"It's not that complicated, Michael, but thanks."

"Here we go," he said. "Trying to get you some personal stuff…."

"How did the two relate to one another?"

"No hugs or kisses. A nervous handshake from Larry. Bluebell looks like she's about to do an interview with him for her high school paper."

"His age?"

"Just compiling…."

I sat quietly, giving him time to write.

"OK," he said. "He's twenty. A senior at the U."

"Probably skipped a grade along the way. Fast learner."

"He's not really a local boy. He was born in Corvallis, Oregon. Parents both teach at Oregon State. Dad teaches modern philosophy and Mom teaches something called environmental studies in the English department."

"What do people in English know about the environmental sciences?"

"I think the answer to that is that they now teach everything, so long as they can do it from the same point of view."

"Got you," I said.

"One other little tidbit. Larry's birthname was Lars. He must have changed it so that it would be more acceptable to the Clints, Biffs and Jasons in his current classes."

"Interesting," I said. "Andreesons are thick on the ground in Scandinavia, but also in other parts of Europe. It ultimately tracks back to the Greek *Andreas*. It means 'manly'. From the angles you've shown me, I can't say that I would choose that word to describe him."

"So you'd say he's more Greta Thunberg than hammer-wielding Thor?"

"Not sure I'd saddle him with the Greta handle," I said, checking again on the video feed, "but a name change is always interesting. Back in biblical times it meant you were preparing yourself or being prepared for some kind of special mission, though it does seem more likely that his special mission involves a weathered backpack, No. 2 pencils and mornings, afternoons and evenings in a library carrel."

"Right. Unfortunately, I'm not seeing any body language that might suggest the nature of their relationship or her reason for being there. He's munching on a muffin and the crumbs are falling into his lap. She's taking a more dainty route, with a croissant. Eating it in tiny nibbles. From the size of her cardboard cup I'd bet she's doing a simple coffee, while he's sipping something cold from a clear plastic cup."

"She *is* taking notes…again, she looks like she's interviewing him. He's shuffling his feet but it looks like he's simply burning nervous energy. He doesn't appear to be agitated or emotionally-involved. This is his go-to posture. Anything untoward in the public record?"

"Not that I can see," Mike said. "He's too small in stature to have a rap sheet for anything physical. He *was* stopped for a minor traffic violation when he was 17, but my guess is that he was so wrapped up in his own world that he accidentally strayed into somebody else's lane. Yes, that would be a good word for him: *otherworldly*."

"So…like a monk, a scientist, or maybe a permanent grad student."

"Something like that," Mike said. "Wait a sec…he's jotting something down on a 3x5 card…he's showing it to her…she's taking a note in her tablet…."

"An order for some AR-15's?" I asked, "or, much more likely, a crude picture of a seal about to become an orca's lunch."

"That's where the smart money will be," Mike said. "Anyway, it looks like the meeting is coming to a close. He's looking at his watch and she just slid the power/off bar on her tablet."

"Which one do you want to follow?" I asked.

"Her, I think," Mike said.

NINE

"Well," Mike said, "don't ask me to reveal any trade secrets, but I was able to follow both. As expected, Larry returned to the library. I was able to home in on the Dewey decimal numbers on the shelf; he was in the local history area for Seattle."

"No surprise there," I said. "How about Bluebell?"

"Bluebell is still on her more austere budget. She's staying at something called the *College Inn Hotel*. A mere $87/night. I didn't think that was possible these days. Oh, wait…you have to share a bathroom with the adjoining room."

"Deal breaker," I said. "Big time."

"That may be why so many people prefer living on the streets in Seattle," Mike said.

"Roger that," I said. "My guess is that she's heading out as early as possible in the morning."

"Don't know the time," Mike said, "but she's only booked for one night."

"And you'll be watching closely…."

"Like a chinook salmon looking over his shoulder at a grizzly's claws and open mouth."

I was right. She was about to spend most of her day en route to Madison, Wisconsin. With the connecting flight via O'Hare, it would be well over six hours before she was walking on Bascom Hill, assuming that she was headed to the university.

I was wrong. She was headed to a 'farm-to-table' fern bar just off the Capitol Square. Mike was especially happy because it had good CCTV and her dining companion was positioned perfectly for his facial rec software.

"Grad student in Sociology," he said. "One of the university's long suits. Back in the day when they did serious, intelligible ratings, Madison's Soc department was often numero uno in the country."

"Name, address and other vitals?"

"We're back among the Larrys," Mike said. "This is one Lawrence Heinrichs. He lives in one of those old, cut-up, frame roach motels on Mifflin Street—the kind where your Victory garden is 5% tomatoes and 95% weed."

"Academic specialty?"

"Something euphemistically called Social Stratification. Probably more like Envy 101."

"Agent Liu, your conservatism is showing."

"I know. Sorry."

"Anything else of interest?"

"Not really. Born and bred in Milwaukee. Actually in Brown Deer. Upscale neighborhood. Undergrad at Oberlin."

"I always thought of Oberlin as a place to study music."

"Yeah, me too, but they're very socially conscious around those parts."

"So what is Bluebell up to?"

"Hard to say. Trying to organize something? A conference? A journal board? A new professional organization? A riot?"

"There you go again," I said. "What's the physical dynamic?"

"Copacetic. There's no gesticulating or table pounding. They're both nibbling their salads like very polite rabbits. If there's any correlation between the place's website menu and their actual offerings they're eating very generic. Or should I say *generically*? Looks like endive, goat cheese, tiny tomatoes, maybe a few strawberries. Pleasant enough, but nothing that would make my mouth water."

"Anything exchanged by hand?"

"Nope. They look like people who were placed at the same table at rush hour and who are making the best of a bad bargain. She's not taking notes; he's not passing note cards. I will say this…"

"Yes?"

"He looks a lot more manly than nerdy Lars, who's probably sitting on the dock of the bay on Bainbridge Island, counting the seals."

"Otis Redding died in Madison," I said. "He drowned in Lake Monona."

"Wow. Forgot that. Points to the lady with the little *SigSauer* in her purse."

"Anyway, how would you describe Bluebell's dinner date?"

"I'd say the look is more 'working-class chic' than 'library dweller'. I was also surprised that he's clean-shaven. Back when I was in college the Soc grad students all tried to look like Old Testament prophets, often to cover their acne scars. Reminded me of the old physiognomy joke…."

"Why do some grad students have long chins and high foreheads?"

"Right. Because when you ask them a question they tug at their beards and when you tell them the answer they hit themselves in the forehead with the palm of their hand."

"Shouldn't they also say 'Uff da' in that neck of the woods?"

"Probably," Mike responded.

"Where's Bluebell staying?"

"At the *Red Roof Inn*. Two stars, but this time with a bathroom."

"Maybe she's on some sort of fixed per diem and she gets to keep all the money she saves," I said. "Either that or she likes to go slumming. I'll tell you this…whatever her job is…include me out. I prefer some creature comforts."

"I didn't expect her to be in a suite at *The Edgewater*," Mike said, "but there's a colony of hotels out on the west side of town in Middleton that are reasonably priced, close to restaurants, and decent enough."

"Agreed. Maybe she's being micro-managed by a savage bean counter or trying to build street cred with the radical left. Either way…include me out."

"I was able to hack into the hotel software. She's only at the place for one night."

"That kind of travel is a hell of a grind," I said. "Half the time your body's still in motion, the remains of your latest meal are caught in your throat and you're trying to stay hydrated and stop your stomach from rumbling with crap that you buy from a set of rusty vending machines."

"She's either dedicated or desperate," Mike said.

"Maybe a bit of both. Anyway, I'll talk to you in the morning."

TEN

"What's that you're munching?" I asked. We were zooming on one of Mike's screens as he was monitoring Bluebell's movements with the one adjoining.

"Some kind of trail mix protein bar," he said. "Not my fav, but I ran out of Rice Krispies treats."

"I love those, but they have to be homemade," I said. "I like them soft and gooey."

"Of course," Mike said. "Gotta be fresh. I want to taste the ingredients, not the glue in the cellophane wrapper. OK, here we go. She's heading out, almost surely for the airport. Go have your morning run and I'll be back in touch in an hour or two."

I said OK, but decided instead to check in with the Director first, hoping he'd release me into the field where I could do more than receive reports from Mike Liu. Peggy told me he was just getting out of a dawn meeting. "I'll give him a minute to gather his papers and refill his coffee mug," she said. "Do you want to hold?"

"Sure, thanks," I said and made a quick, second cup in my room.

"Gwen, how are you feeling?" His voice was gravelly.

"Fine, Sir. Taking reports from our tech-savvy man in Salt Lake. I'd like to be doing more."

"Understood," he said. "I've been following your notes on the many travels of Ms. Barry. Some interesting patterns but nothing definitive yet."

"No, Sir, but there's an urgency to her movements. It makes me think she's working under some kind of deadline."

"I thought that too," he said. "I wish we were more lucky with the CCTV positioning. It would be nice if we had something for our lip readers to work on."

"Right, Sir. On the other hand she appears to be very guarded. A woman of few words. There's also been some note passing. Nothing significant, but probably part of her usual protocol, just in case someone is watching or listening in."

"As to the field work…"

"Yes, Sir?"

"Let's play it this way. You stay put until an occasion arises where you think it would be advantageous. Then go ahead. The problem now is that your Bluebell is taking so many meetings that any direct observations could be compromising. So far we've been able to track her without utilizing your considerable skills. On another front…"

"Yes, Sir?"

"Our friend Hassan…no movement of any significance. He's still at home on the upper east side. He went to *Le Bernadin* with a business friend the night before last. They did the tasting menu with wine pairings. That's $530 a pop for each. Not that it matters, but I find it amusing to see what your basic hardened criminals do with their ill-gotten gains. His companion was a woman from Shanghai. Elderly. No romance involved. Probably just bringing each other up to speed on available merchandise and potential purchasers. What would you call her—a middlewoman or middleperson?"

"How about an as-yet unconvicted felon?"

"Works for me," he said. "Anyway, what else can I do for you?"

"I'll let you know and keep you posted, Sir."

"And Gwen…"

"Yes, Sir?"

"Like the good sergeant says, 'be careful out there'."

"Always, Sir."

Three hours later I reconnected with Mike.

"A little more substance this time," he said. "Not a great deal, but some."

"Shoot," I said.

"Well, first, she flew to O'Hare. She already had her ticket for her succeeding flight, so I had to wait to see where. She was walking through the F Concourse when I suddenly lost her. She had taken a hard left turn into the *United* airline club, where she met a well-dressed man who could have been Italian, middle eastern or something similar. It wasn't our previous friend."

"He's in New York; just talked to the Director."

"Well, I found out who this one was. Uses the name Vanzetti."

"As an act of *homage*?"

"Possibly. Paolo Vanzetti. Currency trader. New at the game but apparently very successful. *Vanzetti* is on his birth certificate, but the birth site was on the Amalfi Coast—a summer home for a shadowy figure from Sicily named Palermi. Not clear which is his actual name but the certificate does appear to have been doctored. We do know that the Sicilians like to use points of origin for surnames."

"As in *Corleone*," I said.

"Bingo. Anyway, Vanzetti is young. Twenty-something. His papa sells olive oil, among other things. He must be doing well, since he was able to send young Paolo to Cornell."

"Major?"

"Chemistry, with some later coursework in Pharmacology at their Manhattan med school. He may have started out as a drug dealer."

"Cornell med is on the upper east side. Neighbors of Hassan's."

"And the school has an outpost in Qatar; no idea whether or not that's relevant."

"And he met with Bluebell at the airline club?"

"Yes. I backtracked on their CCTV once he was seen with her. He checked in at the front desk and showed his card. With a full membership (not a one-off for someone in business class, for example) he's allowed two adult guests per visit. If Bluebell's usual itinerary involves the no-tell mo-tel, the club membership would be too rich for her blood. The annual cost is $650 these days. That or 85,000 miles. I doubt that she flies that much…"

"She could use a *United* credit card or something," I said.

"Yes, but it was Paolo flashing the card and after their meeting a second person joined her."

"I wonder if that person intersected with Paolo…"

"Doubtful from the timing. Paolo and Bluebell only met for ten minutes and the second person arrived on the hour, twenty minutes later."

"Conveniently distancing themselves."

"That would be my guess."

"Any indication of the nature of the first meeting?"

"Not really. Paolo did almost all of the talking. Bluebell nodded politely."

"Paolo exerting dominance?"

"Yes, but with a light touch, as if he might want to try to date her after they finished with their initial business."

"How about the second visitor?"

"Northwestern undergrad. Young woman. Paula Vestry. Specializes in 'strategic communications' in their J-school."

"Good place for Journalism."

"Right."

"Background?"

"First class traveler," Mike said. "Born on the north shore in Lake Forest. High rent district. Lake Forest Academy for boarding school. Most people in Chicagoland see Evanston as a move up; for people in Lake Forest it's a move down. Nothing in her academic record to suggest that she has a life outside of class. No sports, for example. No clubs. No debate team. Your basic grind."

"How long did she meet with Bluebell?"

"About thirty minutes. They did two cups of coffee each. No note passing, but there were at least some discernible words spoken."

"That's good," I said.

"Well, don't get your hopes up. The words were *miracle mile*, with some numbers attached."

"Primo downtown address," I said. "Maybe a drop-off or pick-up point. Maybe an event site or an assembly point?"

"Could be anything," Mike said. "Sorry."

"Maybe you can home in, slow down the lips, tease out something else?"

"I can try," Mike said, "but so far I haven't been able to get you anything interesting. Just the occasional *yes* or *sure* or *ok*. The problem is that you generally can only see one side of the conversation. And… well…when the people are guarded…."

"How about Bluebell's next destination?"

"That I do have," Mike said. "Actually she's been en route for about twenty minutes. Heading east."

"Detroit."

"I think I'd prefer Lake Forest."

"Wouldn't we all?" Mike said

ELEVEN

"**I** think I will do that run now," I said.

"Catch a sandwich afterwards and stand by," Mike said.

"I've only been there in person once," Mike said, "but that Detroit airport is humongous. Actually, once was enough for me. They changed our gate three times and I felt like I had been in a heel-and-toe race for most of the afternoon. I finally latched onto the flight crew and told them I'd be following them, just to be sure that I ended up at the same place as our airplane."

"I'm sometimes caught there on connecting flights," I said. "Not my favorite place. Anyway…what have you got for me?"

"In some ways this was incredibly easy, once I identified Bluebell's contact there. It seems that he had written a self-published book about his family. I haven't read it, but there was a listing on *Amazon* that provided access to enough sample pages that I was able to get the gist of it."

"So, an older guy?" I asked.

"Yes. Retired early, it seems, so somewhere in his early-mid sixties."

"That's a switch," I said.

"Right. Anyway, he started out in Cincinnati. Actually a place called Norwood—a separate municipality surrounded by Cincy. The family was actually from London. London, Kentucky, that is--the place decimated by tornadoes in 2025. They were part of the group who came north from Appalachia for work in Norwood's plants or the ones adjacent to it. At one time there was United States Playing Card--the ones with the Kings on little bicycles--American Laundry, Cincinnati Milling Machine, and last but not least, a large Fisher Body plant. That's where our guy's dad worked. They generally made Chevrolets; dad mostly built Camaros. I say *built* with considerable exaggeration. The son—Bluebell's guy—used a lot of euphemisms but it sounds as if the old man basically stood on the assembly line and wiped the white waxy stuff off of the windows."

"So nothing serious like an inspector or production operator or supervisor."

"No, but his son was very proud of him. The story that he's at pains to tell is about the family's rise from poverty and the manner in which our strong manufacturing base enabled so many good things to happen for disadvantaged people."

"And you're going to tell me the author's name..."

"Claude Lawson. His father was Clyde, his brothers Clarence and Charles."

"Sounds like the old joke about the family sharing alliterating names so that they could all use the same piece of initialed luggage," I said.

"Claude does joke about it. He says that when his mother called out for them she went through the list of names until she hit the right one. Claude says that she was like a high school Latin teacher, declining a noun or conjugating a verb."

"Sounds like an educated man," I said.

"Norwood High School graduate," Mike responded, "but back in the day when high school was more serious than it is now. Anyway, he didn't make a career of it. He followed his dad on the assembly line until the plant closed in 1987. He then moved to Detroit, where he held some marginal roles in the UAW while building (most recently) Ford *F-150's*."

"Decent truck," I said, "and very popular. Did he have any serious role there?"

"No," Mike said. "Not from his income records at least. Probably a step up from wiping wax from windows, but he isn't an engineer or designer or executive."

"Talk to me about his union work."

"Marginal, at least in the larger scheme of things. No major roles in negotiations or public communications. More than a go-fer but less than anybody who would go to work wearing a suit."

"Like a shop steward, maybe?"

"Right. A guy elected by his fellow workers but not paid by the union (at least not directly). Different from a union rep, who's hired and paid by the union. A shop steward is supposed to make sure that contracts are being followed and he's expected to talk up the union's benefits without getting into any heavy-duty recruitment or enforcement activities."

"So the one thing we could infer would be that he was respected by his fellow employees."

"Yes," Mike said. "That's fair."

"And what was his interaction with Bluebell like?"

"Well, they went to a diner in a city near the airport called Romulus. Unfortunately, the principal lines of sight on the place's CCTV system focused on the cash register and the front door. I could expand the image and tilt it ever so slightly, but they were sitting in the back corner and things got fuzzy when I tried to get up close and personal. I can give you the general outline…"

"I'll take it."

"They were there for a little over twenty minutes. The waitress's movements gave me the best views of the day; they each had coffee and Claude had a piece of pie. It looked like apple."

"Very All-American," I said.

"Yes, but no slice of cheddar cheese on top or scoop of vanilla ice cream on the side. Just the basics."

"Any table pounding or note passing?"

"No, nothing like that. Claude had a habit of slowly peeling the paper from his 'half & half' cups and incessantly stirring his coffee with his spoon. Pure nervous habit. He'd empty the cream or milk or whitener (whatever that stuff is) and then stir it four or five times. He also did a lot of nodding. This time Bluebell was doing most of the talking and her back was to me so I couldn't do any lip-reading (which would have been nearly impossible anyway, at that distance). At one point Claude did take out his phone and enter some information…"

"Probably contact information or appointment dates," I said.

"Yep. That would be my guess."

"And did she check into a hotel afterwards or return to the airport?"

"The airport. She was ready to get out of Dodge (or at least the place that makes their *Durangos*)."

"And did she show up at a gate for you?"

"As a matter of fact she did. Longer trip this time. And she had the benefit of a direct flight."

"To?"

"Hartford."

"Interesting," I said.

TWELVE

"She's renting a *Kia* from *Budget*," Mike said.

"Staying in her austerity lane," I said.

"Yes. Unfortunately I won't have any updates until my facial rec software snags her at a destination with CCTV."

"Understood. I'll sit tight."

I made use of my mini-conservatory and picked up two reading choices: a crime novel and a Bureau tech manual on human trafficking. I also fortified myself with a protein bar with chocolate drizzle over fused macadamia nuts. I read the first page of the crime novel and decided instead to go with the Bureau manual. What I really needed was a crash course in lip reading, but I didn't want to read on my tablet or phone.

By dinner time I reconnected with Mike. Bluebell was having a late dinner at a *Capital Grille* near Trinity College. Her guest was an undergraduate named Jamie Phillips. Jamie was regaling himself with a small shellfish tower, soup that looked like lobster bisque and a big-and-bloody bone-in ribeye. The only thing modest on the table was a bottle of Rioja, but Jamie was putting it away without any serious help from Bluebell, who was apparently trying to stay sober for their meeting.

"My Lord, he looks like Tucker Carlson," I said. "I know Tucker's a famous Trinity alum, but this looks like a formal uniform—the tattersall shirt, blue blazer, pocket square, along with the pricey tight and wavy coiffure."

"I was thinking the same thing," Mike said, "but Tucker majored in History while Jamie's majoring in Econometrics and quantitative economics."

"The real thing, not what they used to call cookbook economics."

"Right," Mike said. "Minoring in math, of course. You can't do the former without a heavy dose of the latter."

"Good camera angle, Mike."

"Yes, but pure luck. They probably were unable to get a good reservation and had to come in a little later than they wanted and had to sit near the front door. All to our benefit. Finally we have some identifiable speech, even if it's not always in English."

"Really?"

"Yes, but it's not unfamiliar. As soon as he scarfed down some of the goodies from his shellfish platter he posed an important question…"

"Which was?"

"*Ubi est mea?*"

"I suppose an economist would always ask that, but so would an as-yet unindicted co-conspirator."

"I might have expected *Cui bono?* but if you're thinking about your own role in an operation that's not unlike 'Where is mine?'"

"They're talking about money and she's trying to get him to work *pro bono.*"

"So it would seem," Mike said. "A few minutes later he said something similar but a little less refined: *whack for my daddy-o.*"

"From 'Whiskey in the Jar'," I said.

"Right," Mike answered. "The lyrics change all the time and you can infer multiple meanings. *Thin Lizzy's* version contrasts with *The Dubliners'.*"

"I like *Metallica's*," I said.

"To each his own," Mike said, "but the meaning is more or less the same—where's the piece for my daddy? Or where's the shot of whiskey for my daddy?"

"They're negotiating," I said, "or he's trying to start afresh and change the rules of the game."

"Or maybe sorting out the division of the spoils within some larger framework," Mike said.

"Works for me," I answered. "Now the next big question…"

"What are they having for dessert?"

"Right."

"Bluebell's not having anything but black coffee or some kind of strong, hot tea," Mike said. "I can't see her face, but the smart money would assume that she's a little taken aback at the moment and wants to keep a clear head. Her dinner companion has surprised her with an unexpected question. She expected him to salute and accept his marching orders. Instead, he recharged his testosterone supply with a handful of oysters on the half shell."

"Do oysters really have anything to do with testosterone?" I asked.

"Apparently," Mike said, "but I would have no way of knowing since I spend all day looking at computer screens. But back to the question at hand…I figure him for a hefty slice of cheesecake."

"Or flourless chocolate cake," I said.

Eventually Bluebell bedded down for the night at the local *Best Western*. Mike commented that it was an expected choice given the room charges but an odd title since it wasn't the best choice available and it was located in the East. His mind works that way.

In the morning Bluebell rose a little later than usual, loaded up her Kia and headed north to parts unknown. Mt. Holyoke? Smith? Amherst? UMass? Hampshire? The academic cup runneth over in those environs, assuming she was heading to a college and not a meeting with some rich and shady foreigner like Darvish or Vanzetti.

She actually surfaced in Holyoke and had a late breakfast at a place called *Mrs. Mitchell's Kitchen*. She dined alone on tea and muffins with a side order of crisp bacon. Mike opined that she may have gotten in too early to check into her room and that the late-ish breakfast suggested that the next meal would be an early dinner. As it turned out she checked in to the *Baymont Inn* in Chicopee/Springfield, a serious step-up in quality but a long distance from anything posh and (its long suit) much closer to the college than the more budget-friendly places in the area.

This time her dining companion was a bit out of the ordinary.

THIRTEEN

The restaurant was definitely downscale, perhaps some sort of blue collar-chic choice, a surprise given the fact that the yearly cost of Mt. Holyoke for tuition, room and board was above $85K. Jamie Phillips, in his blazer with pocket square, would never have tolerated an evening at a place known for its cheesy fries and onion rings.

Her dining companion was ambiguously female, with short purple hair and an exceptional number of oddly-placed piercings. Mike reported that her name was Theresa Carlson and that her point of origin was a manse on a tree-lined street in Westchester (New York, not Los Angeles).

Her demeanor was much more calm than her appearance would have predicted. Her dinner consisted of soup and tea. "Chowder," Mike said, "with English breakfast tea"; he had a superb angle on their stained oak table and he was enjoying homing, panning and observing details.

Ms. Terry kept her gestures to the barest of minimums and seemed to be concentrating on her chowder as much or more than the words issuing from Bluebell's mouth.

"Her major is Biological Sciences," Mike said, "but she has a hefty minor in Environmental Sciences. I like that. I can imagine her in a speech-a-thon on lefty politics, but it looks like she also walks the walk. Give me somebody who can talk about actual genes and chromosomes and not just gender ideology."

"I'm sure she would appreciate all of your support," I said. "I bet you're also a sucker for that purple hair."

"Not so much," he answered, "and I would settle for a single golden nostril loop—very small and elegant—rather than that array of bullion protruding from her ears and lips."

"Why, Agent Liu…I'm learning all kinds of things about your romantic tastes."

"Unintended," he said, "so back to business. Her father is a hedge fund manager and her mother was also a Mt. Holyoke grad, so there may be a slight bit of rebellion at work along with a modest bow to tradition."

"Everybody wants to march in that laurel parade," I said.

"The what?"

"It's a graduation tradition there; the seniors carry these long laurel wreaths to honor the college's founder and signify that they're transitioning to alumnae status."

"There's a lesson there somewhere," he said. "Everybody loves traditions."

"Well…some more than others."

"How do you know about that stuff?"

"I thought about going to Holyoke, back in the day."

"I have trouble imagining our Terry dutifully carrying the laurel," he said, "but I have to admit that she does look pretty docile sipping her tea."

"They also wear white dresses," I said.

"Vestal virgins," he answered.

"The virgin part is probably a bridge too far these days," I said, "but you never know…."

No notes were taken; no information was passed hand-to-hand. Dinner (such as it was) lasted a little more than 40 minutes and Bluebell returned to the *Baymont* and Terry (probably) to her dormitory.

Bluebell stayed in her motel for another day but drove in to Amherst to have lunch with another undergraduate woman, this one from Hampshire College. They had turkey on plain bagels at *Bruegger's*; this time the other woman was far more animated and edgy, interrupting her sandwich bites to enforce each point. Bluebell seemed to be annoyed by it, but she did her best to retain her composure.

The woman's name was Marion Lemon (obviously no relation to Don). Her home base was the bay area, actually a bit north, halfway to Sacramento, in Vacaville. Her father did some sort of social work at the two prisons there and her mother taught social studies at Vacaville High School. The interesting thing about Marion was that she was majoring in Legal Studies. The Brits do that as an undergraduate field of study but the Americans usually reserve such things for law school. Given the breadth of the curriculum Mike described it as 'Activism 101' (or at least the possibility of exploring a host of subjects with activist dimensions).

His description squared with her demeanor, which was nervous, bordering on agitated. In the course of their lunch Marion passed a piece of wrinkled 8"x10" paper to Bluebell.

"Damn," Mike said, "I wish I had a better angle. It could be a flyer or the first page of her thesis on all that's unholy about America. Whatever it is, she's passionate about it, but Bluebell seems disappointed…as if she wanted something more businesslike and straightforward."

"Agreed," I said.

The next day Lady Allyson was in New Haven. Both Mike and I were surprised that she had bypassed Worcester and Boston, at least for the moment. "It's not really a college town," he said, channeling 'Spinal Tap'.

Her new digs were in the *La Quinta*, which had the dual benefits of a low room charge and an available swimming pool. The pool had a well-positioned CCTV camera. Mike was discussing the quality of her strokes to a degree that edged closely to the beyond-the-clinical, for which I teased him.

"This investigation is finally providing you the opportunity for a life that borders on the emotional," I said.

"Pathetic, isn't it?" he answered.

"No comment," I responded.

In New Haven she and her prospective dining companion(s) finally had the opportunity to indulge in inexpensive Italian food of decent quality. Their choice, however, did not meet with Mike's approval.

"*Villa Lulu*?" he said. "They're going vegan/vegetarian? Eggplant meatballs? What a waste."

"Your toxic masculinity is very much in evidence," I said. "I'm considering reporting you to Marion Lemon."

He laughed, but his laughter quickly turned to astonishment when Bluebell's dining companion came into view.

"A man!?" Mike said.

"That would certainly appear to be the case," I said. "What's more, he appears to be in full 'Skull and Bones' or 'Book and Snake' uniform: simple cotton pants and a tweed jacket that set his parents back at least a grand, barely-ironed bespoke shirt and a Rolex *GMT-Master II* for use on daddy's yacht when the family is sailing between time zones."

"How can you see the watch when I can't?"

"I'm just guessing, Mike. It's part of the required outfit."

"So is that toxic masculinity or upper east side-chic?"

"It's pure Yalie, Michael. Think Poppy Bush. Oilman, bomber pilot, left-handed first baseman and captain for the Yale Blue. Noblesse-obligeville incarnate."

"Tough sell, Gwen. El Presidente, Ambassador to China and major-domo of the CIA out on the town eating vegan?"

"The times are changing, Michael."

"Wait a minute. My faith is restored. Damn internet. I went to the website and Lulu offers meat and seafood galore. Check it out…he's avoiding the wait and ordering two martinis up front—each straight up with an array of speared olives as garnish. I'll bet each is drier than a popcorn fart…uh, sorry about that."

Forty minutes later the main courses followed the appetizer orders of arancini. "My man," Mike said. "Bluebell's doing the crab cakes but Poppy Jr. is about to attack the biggest hanger steak in captivity."

"Perhaps we should be checking out his identity…?"

"Give me a few minutes on that," Mike said.

FOURTEEN

"To the manor born," Mike said. "In spades, but with a few hearts thrown in as well."

"I'm listening…"

"Kenneth Carrington. Almost surely 'Ken'; surely not 'Kenny'."

"Looks more like a 'Sean' to me," I said.

"Wasn't that Barbie's Ken's middle name?"

"Too deep in the vaguely-gay cultural weeds for me," I said.

"I hear you, but it's definitely Kenneth. This will please you, however…"

"Yes?"

"His dad is a Sean, but he goes by 'John'. L.A. lawyer-type, as we say in the Army, but playing down his ethnic side."

"No one with a sweet name like Sean would bill at $2 grand an hour," I said.

"Right."

"What kind of law—intellectual property?"

"No. General corporate. Big contracts, that kind of thing. Could still be intellectual property involved, but the big money passes through the hands of the producers, not the hired help."

"Domiciled in…?"

"San Marino. Oxford Road. Right by the Huntington."

"Ouch," I said. "Bring your gold or platinum *American Express* card."

"I think that would be the black or so-called *Centurion* card," Mike said. "By invitation only."

"Oxford Road is probably an $8-10 million dollar habit," I said.

"The area is old money/protestant. A little smoggier than Beverly Hills or other pieces of the platinum triangle but still very, very upscale. Unfortunately for mom and dad, that means that Kenny is disqualified from any need-based scholarship money."

"Old Eli is going to require around $91K per annum, but in Sean/John's firm a mid-range senior partner is probably not going to find that to be too much of a stretch. Also, there are no other siblings. Mom is bringing in some cash as well. She writes cozy mystery novels in which her protagonist's goldendoodle helps solve the crimes. But under a pseudonym: Janet Carey. Her actual name is Jane."

"Not my taste," I said. "I want hunky, lonely men walking down my mean streets. Tell me more about Kenny."

"How about Harvard Westlake for high school?" Mike asked. "Current tuition just a smidge under $50K."

"Top of the list," I said, "but a hell of a drive. It's (where?) in Coldwater Canyon?"

"Yep, but that's no prob when you've got your own Audi *RS 5*. Prior to that he would doubtless have had his own driver. He could sit in the back seat, doing his homework while the driver slogged along the 110."

"I thought I was in high cotton when my parents sprang for a used *Corolla* for me," I said.

"I walked to school," Mike said, "but school was in the place above our garage and my mom was my teacher, cook and disciplinarian."

"It somehow worked out OK," I said.

"Right. Anyway, young Kenneth is majoring in Econ, like so many in the Ivy league. Good grades. Gentlemen's A- with grade inflation. Next stop: Wall Street."

"Anything else?"

"Well, he's not in the Whiffenpoofs, if that's what you were thinking. He did start up a business when he was a sophomore. Strictly online, no product beyond electronic data. He and a classmate created an app that enabled you to access info on decentralized cryptocurrency. Unfortunately for him the field was moving so fast that he couldn't keep up with it and continue to pursue his day job studying the wonderful world of digital labor markets."

"Why would he be meeting with Bluebell?"

"That's the question, isn't it?" Mike said. "Why are any of them meeting with her? Is she a recruiter? A coordinator? A middleperson? At first I thought she was hooking up with the vaguely disaffected. I haven't seen any Molotov cocktails or pitchforks, just some kids that might fall into broad categories with social concerns. In young Mr. Carrington's case you have what appears to be a completely-dedicated capitalist, seeking to out-earn his mom and dad. And with no apparent animosity or rebellion. He dresses the part; he walks the walk; he's not imitating Lenin, Trotsky or any other of Marx's merry men; this guy acts like a happy leprechaun, but without the leather apron and cocked hat…"

"He's just looking for the pot of gold at the end of the rainbow."

"Exactimento," Mike said.

"Naughty people still need people with his set of skills."

"No question about that," Mike said. "Each and every one is what you call your basic *transferable*."

"When does our lady fair check out of her room at *La Quinta*?"

"Tomorrow morning," Mike said.

"I'll wait for your call," I said.

FIFTEEN

"**G**ood morning, Agent Harrison."

"Good morning, Agent Liu. What's up on the Bluebell front?"

"The lady is en route to the large Apple."

"By train?"

"Yes. She dropped off her rental and headed toward Grand Central. At the moment she's probably trying to decide whether or not to spring for the wilted salad or the cellophane-wrapped sandwich."

"What do they say in 'The Odd Couple'—it's either very old meat or very new cheese?"

Mike laughed before I continued.

"Maybe a two-hour trip?"

"With some change," Mike said.

"So I'll sit tight and wait for your next installment."

"That would be a good idea," he said. "Give me about two hours and a half for her to arrive and get settled."

"Done," I said.

"Well, she's staying at the *Belvedere*. Actually a pretty good choice. Inexpensive…"

"In Hell's Kitchen, right?"

"Yes, but good walking distance from places with more honorific names, like *Radio City Music Hall*."

"Got it," I said, "but a fairly good trek to NYU and Columbia, assuming that she's meeting with someone from one of those schools."

"We'll know more later. She's passing on lunch or at least she hasn't left the *Belvedere* since she arrived. My guess is she's getting horizontal and catching some Z's after her train ride."

"Then I'll sit tight again and wait for your call."

"I'll say this for our Bluebell, she's got good taste."

"How so?" I asked.

"She's at my favorite NYC restaurant, waiting for a dining companion for an early dinner."

"Which is?"

"*Cafe Fiorello.*"

"Love it," I said. "Lincoln Center. Great food."

"I live for the antipasto bar," Mike said. "Wait a sec…"

"Has her guest arrived?"

"Yes, but I think that she's going to be the one who's considered the guest."

"How so?"

"For starters he's not an undergraduate. I make him late 40's or early 50's. Dressed for success. And intimidation."

"Hugo Bossy?"

"No, more like 'speak when you're spoken to, if you want to be able to speak at all.'"

"Any facial rec yet?"

"Not yet, but let them settle in and I'll see what I can do. The cameras are sharp, but the angles are not exactly where I'd like them to be."

"Is Bluebell bowing and scraping?"

"I can show you some stills. Just a sec.…"

"She looks as if she's trying not to be threatened or browbeaten, but the blinks and squirms are noticeable tells. From the way that he's leaning in with his shoulders and elbows I'd say he wants her to come as close to tears as he can manage."

"They're ordering," Mike said. "She's studying the menu, probably trying to give herself a chance to stop looking into his eyes. He hasn't even picked up the menu. When the waitress put it in front of him he looked at it as if it was covered with germs…or worse. He's going to tell her what he wants, regardless of what's officially available."

"Mean-spirited and arrogant move," I said. "I don't care for him at all."

"Neither does Ms. Barry," Mike said, "but she doesn't have any other options than to smile deferentially and try to maintain her composure."

They sat in relative silence for fifteen minutes, while Mr. Charcoal-Gray Suit sipped what was probably 15 year-old Scotch. The waitress then brought their food. Bluebell was having the crab and avocado salad with a cup of tea. All very prim and proper. Her host (or captor) was having a very large, center cut veal chop, something that was actually available on the menu. He was having a bottle of Amarone (Mike was able to zoom in on the label) and when the waitress brought a second glass for Bluebell he brushed it away.

"Is that a good thing or a bad thing?" Mike asked. "He's drinking Hannibal Lecter's favorite wine but not allowing her to have any of it."

"Yes, they changed it to Chianti for the movie. I hate it when Hollywood thinks we're too stupid or uninformed to understand what was in the real script."

"To get back to your question…" Mike said. "He's intimidating her. 'No wine for you.'"

A few minutes later he called the waitress over and ordered what turned out to be a side order of spaghetti. I asked Mike if he ever felt sorry for the young calves that had to be sacrificed to create veal dishes. "I'll bet that our undergrad from Mt. Holyoke would."

"I try not to think about such things," Mike said, "but I'm sure that the man in the gray flannel suit doesn't care."

As Bluebell nibbled at the edges of her food the man attacked his. He may have been sitting across from Lincoln Center but he ate his food like a ravenous cave man who had just dislodged some Neanderthals from his domain.

"Here we go," Mike suddenly interjected. "Incoming."

The man had gotten up to go to the bathroom at the back of the restaurant and Mike got a perfect facial shot as he rose and turned. He sent it to me immediately. "Look familiar?" the attached note read.

"No, nothing beyond the OG sneer," I said.

"Give me a few minutes," Mike answered.

As Bluebell attempted to enjoy a single scoop of gelato the man opted for chocolate mousse with whipped cream. At *Fiorello* it's served from tubs the size of wine coolers, with visible frost on the sides of the container. It's not so much spooned onto the dessert plates as it is ladled out in small mountains.

"I've got the son-of-a-bitch," Mike said. "And he has the temerity to use my name. Mikael Petrov. A made-up name. Generic Russian. Think John Jones or Bill Smith in our world. His father was an enforcer (again, with a nondescript false name) for Evsei Agron back in the 80's."

"The Russian mob in Brighton Beach. 'Little Odessa'," I said.

"The very same. They ran extortion rackets, among other things. Tortured the unwilling with cattle prods."

"And what's he doing now? Or what does he claim to be doing?"

"NYC real estate," Mike answered. "He works out of the top floor of a building he owns on Madison Avenue. Interesting place. It looks like it's capped with a copper tent, with 360 degree views through narrow, horizontal windows. He was interviewed by the *Daily News* a few years ago. His 'office'—the entire top floor—was empty except for a few desks with stacks of paper scattered hither and yon. The 'real estate mogul' nomenclature is euphemistic; 'slum lord' is far closer to the reality. The property he owns is on the darker edges of the Bronx and Queens. His muscle guys collect rents while he spends a lot of his time in a restaurant that he owns and operates in SoHo.

"It's called *Odysseus*—Mediterranean fare. Pricey and very upscale. He must have a friend at the *Daily News*, because they did a second story on the restaurant. The accompanying picture was of an archway that led from the entry hall into the principal dining room. On either side was a Picasso print of a minotaur...."

"Brutal, bestial," I said. "Picasso was obsessed with the notion and the imagery."

"That's where our boy's head is at, I would guess," Mike said. "Not in some place sweet and sentimental."

"Poor Bluebell," I said.

SIXTEEN

After dessert Bluebell took a refresh on the hot water for her tea while Petrov threw down a double espresso. By now he was doing all of the talking and Bluebell was reduced to nodding politely and agreeably. He paid the bill in cash and left the restaurant, leaving her to stew and attempt to recover from their encounter.

"I couldn't see clearly," Mike said, "but it looked as if a car pulled up for him the moment he walked out the door. Definitely not a taxi; possibly an Uber, but it looked a little longer and grander than the usual. Uber does operate a premium service in Manhattan, however...."

"Where does he live?" I asked.

"Central Park West," Mike answered. "Not in a famous building; a freestanding three-story just around the corner from the Park. He actually could have walked home. Unless he was crossing the Park and doing some more work at his office."

"I'd love to know who he's calling on one of his burners," I said.

"As would I," Mike said.

The next morning Bluebell checked out early and took a taxi to LaGuardia. Destination: Boston.

"She could have checked in there while she was still in the general area," I said. "The meeting with Petrov must have been a command performance that interrupted her pattern."

"I think you're right," Mike said.

"Picked her up at Logan," Mike said, "but lost her thereafter. Either she's not checking into a hotel or she's checked into one that doesn't have a decent CCTV setup. I'll get back to you."

Fifteen minutes later we reconnected. "Ms. Bluebell just ordered a skinny latte thingie at a *Starbucks* by the Charles. Her guests (yes, guests, plural) have already arrived. I caught up a few minutes later than I would have preferred, but the pair are at least doing me a favor by facing the camera. Back in a few...."

"Brother and sister team," Mike said. "Yousef and Hanan Baroudi. He's a senior at BU; she's a junior. Both studying Econ."

"Following in AOC's footsteps," I said.

"True," Mike said, "but I won't hold that against them, at least not yet."

"Michael, your politics are showing again…and again."

"Pathetic, I know. Please forgive me."

"Well, you're only stating a fact and expressing an interest in being fair."

"I'll take that," he said. "And what do you think these earnest young students identify as their homeland?"

"Oh, I don't know, Palestine perhaps?"

"Different branch though. They don't live amid the rubble of Gaza. Their dad sells concrete and does very well at it."

"Always a market for that," I said.

"He sells it by the linear mile."

"The bin Ladens were in the construction trade," I said.

"Roger that," Mike said, "but their father—Ibrahim—is not quite in that financial league. He does, however, have the means to occupy a home away from home in the heart of the Marais."

"Paris."

"Yes. Not an uncommon place to hang your keffiyeh if you have the means. Not that he'd wear it when he's dining out under the Michelin stars. Just in case you're wondering, it started out as a piece of clothing for farmers; it protected them from the sun."

"I think I knew that," I said.

"But it doesn't really fit with the family name. *Ghannam*, for example, might mark you as coming from a family of shepherds. *Baroudi?* Not so much."

"What did the Baroudis do?"

"They made gunpowder."

"Now we're getting somewhere," I said.

"Probably not," Mike said, "but it's a nice thought. Well, not *nice* but indicative of potential progress."

"Today they would be making Semtex or C-4. Seriously. A guy who lays concrete has to blast away whatever was lying in its path. How would you describe the conversational dynamics?"

"Hanan is sitting politely and quietly, deferring to her brother. Yousef is sitting ramrod straight, leaning in, exuding skepticism and impatience."

"He doesn't like what Bluebell's selling."

"Hard to say," Mike responded. "More like 'I'll hear you out but I don't have all day.'"

"Clothing?"

"Student chic. My guess is they're not at BU through the grace of need-based scholarships."

"Bro and sis both drinking coffee?"

"Yes, but with croissants all around, though no one is nibbling on them. Bluebell looked at her's longingly but she's waiting for Hanan to eat her's and Hanan is waiting for Yousef to eat his."

"Stalemate," I said.

"Yes, kind of funny when you think about it, but somehow I doubt that there's much humor in whatever it is that they're actually discussing."

"Any possibility of lip reading?"

"I think Bluebell said something like 'Just hear me out' and 'I understand', but there's no larger context to enable me to make sense of it. A lot of times she's holding her cup in front of her mouth when she speaks."

"Damn."

"I second that," Mike said. "Well, they're all standing up; I think the meeting is over. Bluebell just slid her luggage out from under the table. I was right. My guess is that she's heading back to Logan for the next leg of her journey."

"That's damned hard work," I said. "People who never travel might think it's romantic to bop from the Big Apple to Beantown, but those who do it for a living would prefer to log some time in their own beds, with their own routines."

"Unless they're crusaders," Mike said.

"That's true," I said, "but what is Bluebell? Personally I wouldn't enjoy being berated by people like Petrov, even if I believed I was operating on behalf of a good cause, and with people like him...how could the cause be good?"

"I'll let you know as soon as she surfaces again."

I ate the remainder of my room-service club sandwich, washed it down with some nice lemonade-like drink from the mini-bar and stretched out on my hotel bed. An hour later Mike returned.

"Well, I was right. She checked in and went straight to the gate. Not only is she losing any time for a siesta, she's being forced to do it on a tight schedule."

"Where is she going?"

"Our nation's capital."

"Or capitol (-ol)?"

"Maybe both; we'll see."

"I might have thought of taking the train and catching some sleep there," Mike said, "but you're looking at something like 7 hours rather than just under 2. She just checked in at a place called the *Baron Hotel*. El cheapo, even with all the talk in their website about proximity to Georgetown, Embassy Row, Dupont Circle and other hangouts of the glitterati. There's a comedy club and tavern attached. My guess is that she'll pass on the comedy, grab a sandwich and hit the hay. I certainly would."

"Yes, me too," I said. "I figure it will take her at least an hour or two or three to reduce the feeling of motion in her head and back. Presumably she needs to be fresh in the morning."

SEVENTEEN

"*F*unny," M:ke said. "All of the odds are on the likelihood that she's up to no good, but somehow I feel sorry for her."

"Eyes on the prize, Michael," I said. "Remember the crusader category. She's probably channeling her energy in a direction that's somewhere between unsavory and evil."

"I know," he answered. "Anyway, she's having a lie-in this morning, so she's at least getting some needed rest."

"Or trying to," I added.

In the early afternoon she appeared at a restaurant in Georgetown, a block from the University, within sight of the Exorcist steps. Called *The Tombs*, it was the beer and burger joint frequented by the local students. Above it sat the *1789*, a restaurant for those students' wealthy parents.

She arrived a few minutes before her dining companion--a tall young man wearing beige chinos, a white shirt with no tie and a slightly wrinkled blue blazer. He appeared to be in his early twenties, probably a student living on cups of noodles and trying to get by on 5-6 hours of sleep a night. When he appeared he was blinking his eyes in an attempt to become accustomed to the subterranean space beneath the brightly-lit, white siding and raw cement on the adjoining buildings.

Bluebell waved to him; he lifted his arm in a gesture of recognition, and joined her. There were no blow-by kisses or mini-hugs, just a simple handshake.

"He's not putting his napkin on his lap," Mike said.

"Maybe he doesn't get out very often," I said.

"Quite possibly," Mike responded. "His eyes still appear to be dazzled by the sun. I don't like the name of the restaurant; it sounds too much like the old prison in New York."

"I don't think too many people miss it," I said, "certainly not anyone who was incarcerated there. Still, I wouldn't want to see this restaurant in the middle of the night when the single flick of a light switch could arouse the permanent residents."

"Well, I've got enough shots of his face to run some software. While they pore over their menus I'll check him out."

By the time their food arrived Mike was ready to give me a run down on his not-so-distant past.

"They're both going for the crab cakes," Mike said. "Either Bluebell is on an expense account or she's treating herself to something other than the usual grass clippings. Anyway, here's the guy...."

"Ralph Willis from Lansing, Michigan. His dad Carl assembles Chevy *Traverses*; his mom Louise is an oncology nurse. The interesting thing is that Ralph goes by the name of 'Rafe'."

"Very British," I said.

"Yes, especially for the progeny of a blue collar worker. Anyway, he went to the University of Michigan as an undergrad and must have done well enough to secure substantial scholarship assistance from Georgetown Law, something they don't dole out indiscriminately."

"That school is the university's long suit, isn't it; I mean rank-wise."

"Yes. They've leveraged that by installing a long list of joint programs. Rafe is actually doing an M.P.P. with the public policy school on their main campus."

"Oh, that's right…the law school is down on the Hill."

"Right. He's probably taking a class or two on campus today; hence their dining choice."

"Anything shadowy from his past?"

"Nothing remarkable. He was an officer in the College Democrats as an undergraduate and with his degree programs he probably plans to do something in public interest law. I'd say he's too disheveled to run for office, but that may be unfair of me."

"What's the dynamic between them?"

"Calm, collected. He has some tics and he tends to tap the table with his index finger, but he's not in her face and he isn't poking at her. It's more like they're having a polite give-and-take on a complex subject. They're both concentrating and…I suppose you'd say…reasoning together. No smiles. No laughs. No scowls. It's more like they're studying together for a math test."

"Got it," I said. "Anything interesting in his parents' pasts?"

"No. Salt of the earth Midwesterners. From their ages I would guess that they had him a little later in life than usual, but that's increasingly the pattern."

"Certainly among the so-called elites," I said.

"Slippery term for me," Mike said.

"Agreed," I answered. "What are they drinking?"

"I'd guess that she's drinking ginger ale and he's drinking coke or pepsi. It's possible that there's something alcoholic in her glass, but that wouldn't fit her usual pattern."

"And no luggage underneath her table…"

"Not that I can see," Mike said. "All in all I think she looks considerably more relaxed than she did with the Baroudis and much more relaxed than she did with Petrov."

"Probably looking forward to a good night's sleep," I said. "Or maybe she's doing double duty today and meeting someone for dinner."

"You were right," Mike said. "She's back in the *Tombs* but this time with a young woman. She looks very earnest. Short hair, a little jumpy. Leaning forward as if she's not comfortable in her seat. Bluebell must still be full from lunch. She's sipping from a small cup of soup. Could actually be chili. The woman with her is doing the grass clippings but with a piece of salmon on top. No alcoholic drinks. Either simple water or possibly some kind of lemon/lime soda.

"Does the woman look like an undergrad?"

"She does. Give me a couple minutes...."

"Old joke at GU: with so many coming from New Jersey the standard conversation starter is 'what turnpike exit'? In her case she's from New Brunswick."

"And her parents teach at Rutgers."

"Mom does. And...yes...Sociology, with a specialty in the sociology of sexuality."

"Hmmm," I mused.

"From what I can determine, her father is either dead or out of the picture. Mom's recent 'partner' was a DEI administrator at Princeton before his position there was eliminated. He's now at Rutgers but with some dubious 'lecturer' title. Non-tenure track; probably a course or two at a time."

"Department?"

"Learning and Teaching. In the College of Education."

"That sounds dubious too," I said. "Mom is supporting the family."

"No doubt," Mike said. "You haven't asked me the daughter's name."

"I'm thinking something like Rachel," I said.

"Actually 'Rain'," Mike said. "Rain Goldman. Mom's maiden name. Dad's name was Klein."

"Major?"

"CULP in SFS."

"Please translate, Mike."

"Culture and Politics in the School of Foreign Service. It's like the humanities wing, as opposed to things like political economy or international business."

"I get the picture," I said. "Probably wouldn't help all that much if your actual goal was to join the foreign service."

"No, and that exam's pretty hard, from what I can tell," Mike said.

"Dynamic between them?"

"Slightly uncomfortable. No shouting or table pounding, but Bluebell looks as if she wants to kick back and enjoy her dinner, while Rain appears to be the sort who only has one speed."

"And it exceeds most peoples' limits."

"Bingo," Mike said. "It's like she's lecturing on a subject that she considers to be of cosmic importance."

"What did Archie Bunker say?--'I know the tribe'."

"That would be a Roger," Mike answered. "I don't think we're going to see her stop talking and ordering a hot fudge sundae."

EIGHTEEN

The next morning Bluebell slept in and I went for a quick swim, followed by a breakfast of pancakes and sausages. She met a student from the University of Maryland for a late lunch at a place in Silver Spring called *Miss Toya's Creole House*, where they each had seafood mac and cheese with iced tea.

The student's name was Ta'quan Foster. A college junior, he was majoring in Criminology. "Not sure whether he wants to catch the criminals or free them," Mike said.

He and his mother, Louise, lived in Takoma Park with his younger brother Xavier and their older sister, Brianna. Brianna was a nurse, Xavier a high school sophomore.

Their lunch lasted less than an hour. Ta'quan's demeanor was one of impatience. Not aggressive or angry impatience, Mike was quick to add, "but he looks as if he wished he were somewhere else and he never fully settled into his seat comfortably."

Bluebell did most of the talking. "In a house dominated by older women that would be his fallback behavior," Mike said. "It may also be part of the reason for his impatience."

No paperwork exchanged hands and no notes were taken. When she returned to her hotel the on-duty clerk went into a paneled space behind the check-in desk and returned with Bluebell's luggage. "No early to bed for her this evening; she's off to a new destination," Mike said.

That destination turned out to be St. Louis, where her following day consisted of both lunch and dinner meetings. Her dining companions appeared to be polar opposites. The first was a young woman from Harris-Stowe State University (formerly Harris-Stowe Community College). A local resident from East St. Louis, her name was Carol Green. She was majoring in Urban Affairs.

Less impatient than Ta'quan, she seemed to be uncomfortable at *Starbucks*, perhaps because the prices generally exceeded her budget. "She doesn't want to impose," Mike said. "She just got a small cup of tea."

"Is she engaged in the conversation or politely checking the time?" I asked.

"Engaged," Mike said. "Not passionate and intense, but attentive. I would describe her as mildly skeptical."

"Family info?"

"Intact family," Mike said. "Dad works for a moving company; mom is a practical nurse. No siblings."

Dinner was with one Laura Cohn, a sophomore at Wash U. Laura seemed much more comfortable with overpriced dining. They were at a French cubbyhole in Clayton, the Lou's most upscale neighborhood. Bluebell was back on her grass clippings, but with giant prawns; Laura was doing some *Dover Sole* with white wine. "Not *Franzia* from a box," Mike said. "From the cost of the other menu items I'm thinking some serious white Burgundy."

"You're making me hungry, Michael," I said.

"Normal fare for Ms. Cohn," he answered. "Mom and dad live in North Hempstead; he commutes to his office on Park Avenue from whence he does general surgery."

"That part of Long Island…Jay Gatsby country," I said.

"Yep."

"But no *pied `a terre* in Manhattan."

"Nope. They have a nice sunny place up the coast from Mar-a-Lago."

"What's young Laura majoring in—wealth management?"

"Nope. Something called 'Global Studies' with a concentration in International Affairs."

"I wonder what that means," I said.

"Don't know yet. She's doing prep work in languages, at this point. The program sounds a little vague. It could be for people who want to change the world and right all of the planet's wrongs or people who want to do risk analysis in distant lands in an attempt to determine whether or not the high streets could welcome and protect a *Gucci* outlet."

"Sounds very modern," I said, "whatever happened to Classics, History and Philosophy?"

"Too much work; not enough payout," Mike said.

"Sadly," I added.

"Your next question would concern demeanor…"

"Yes," I said.

"Very comfortable. Laura is used to dining out and she's used to dealing with authority figures, if that's what Bluebell actually is."

"Money is a great insulator," I said.

"There's social capital and then there's real capital," Mike said. "In many cases they're closely related. Anyway, there's no note-taking or phone-checking. Laura looks as if she can hold all of life's details in her head."

"What languages is she studying?" I asked.

"French and Mandarin."

"Hmmm, the old language of diplomacy…"

"And its colonies," Mike added.

"And the language of, what? Commerce? Mitigated Marxism? The latest technology used for the oldest purposes?"

"Global business? Armageddon?" Mike added. "Taipei? Singapore?"

"Always the big question," I said.

"They're having dessert," Mike said. "Odd for Bluebell. She's nibbling on some palmiers while Laura is digging in to a nice slice of apple tart."

"Washing it down with…what?"

"Bluebell's doing tea; Laura's doing some dessert wine in a tiny glass. I'm betting on a playful Sauternes."

"I bet you're right. By the way, where is Bluebell staying?"

"Someplace a tad more fancy than usual—the Hilton in Frontenac, just west of Clayton."

"But not the *Ritz-Carlton* near their current restaurant."

"Nope."

"Wonder where she's going next," I said.

"Time will tell," Mike said.

NINETEEN

"So far no movement," Mike said.

"I'll have some breakfast and be back in an hour," I said.

"She threw me a curve ball," Mike said.

"How so?"

"I had the main entrance to the hotel on my center screen, but it's a big complex with multiple points of ingress and egress. I figured she was headed to Lambert Field (and she was, more or less) but I think she slipped out the back and caught an Uber. No idea why she wouldn't take the free ride on the shuttle bus. Maybe she's feeling edgy or suspicious. Anyway…"

"What did you mean by 'more or less', Mike?"

"She went to the airport complex but she didn't get on a plane. She rented a car there."

"Brand?"

"Nissan *Versa*, through *Enterprise*. They're from St. Louis; they must have been having some sort of special deal because it was the cheapest car of the day. I hadn't even heard of a *Versa*."

"A subcompact, somewhat larger than a $50 soap box derby kit. She's really back in poverty mode," I said.

"Yes. Anyway, I've lost her for now. I'm sure she'll turn up somewhere on 70. Whether east or west I can't say. Sit tight.…"

somewhere else, somewhere thousands of miles away. She passed on coffee; Curtis is on his third cup.

"Now he's standing up and reaching for his wallet. He threw several bills on the table, either in anger or disgust, as if he couldn't wait to leave. Bluebell's forcing a smile and I do mean *forcing*. She's arranging the bills in a tight stack…and…heading in the general direction of the ladies' room."

"I'm still wondering about that proximity to Wright-Patt," I said.

"Yes, well there probably wouldn't be any problem for him with regard to gaining access, but he's not going to slither in and muck around on their computers or take notes on their 'eyes only' files. People like him…they want their insulation. He'd have an informant or two on the inside who could take the fall for him if anything untoward turned up in the public record. He would also be spending someone else's money in the process."

"It's what he's done all his life," I said, "spending other peoples' money. He's probably taken so many backhanders in his life that he's dislocated both of his shoulders."

"He was making $174K a year and he's worth over $40 mil," Mike said. "I want a piece of those side hustles."

"Not if it means moving from Lakewood to Leavenworth," I said.

"The sad thing is that his financial path is closer to the norm than it is exceptional. It's like the congresspersons are issued a get-out-of-jail-free card the moment they enter the hallowed halls."

"So where do you think she's headed next?" I asked. "Besides the first place she can get a hot shower and wash away the sleaze?"

"You're asking me to guess," Mike said. "All I can tell you is that the possible end point of I-70 would be Baltimore."

"Once again, I'm beginning to feel sorry for her, despite the company she keeps, or maybe because of the company she's forced to keep."

TWENTY

By the time it was 10:00 p.m. eastern time she still hadn't checked into a hotel or stopped at a restaurant for dinner. Mike had kept me posted, but his updates were all empty reports. He was becoming nervous. I turned in early, but I was equally nervous and couldn't keep my legs still. At 4:30 my cell phone rang. It was the Director.

"Gwen, how soon can you get packed?"

"Fifteen minutes, sir. Something's come down. The Barry woman is dead, isn't she?"

"I'm afraid she is. (He let that sink in for a moment and then continued.) Do you know where Polaris is?"

"Busy shopping area just north of Columbus. Big mall; the complex adjoins I-71, the road to Cleveland."

He paused again and then doubtless remembered that I had gone to college less than an hour from there.

"Right. If you're heading north out of Columbus and you get off of 71 heading west there's a large Hilton that is right next to the east end of the mall. Big parking lot in front; big parking lot in back. The body was found in the back. Hit-and-run. Make that a *putative* hit-and-run. Her body was found next to that toy car she was driving. Definitely not an accident. Whoever drove over her backed up and drove over her a second time."

"Pretty amateurish," I said.

"Yes, but there were no skid marks and little or no forensic evidence left behind. The scant good news is that the Columbus Division of Police covers Polaris. It's the biggest force in Ohio and it has had its share of problems over the years. I do have a contact there who I trust. Fortunately he's been put in charge of the case. He vouches for their medical team, whose initial guess is that someone met her in the lot and then inflicted some blunt force trauma. Their vehicle drove over her to cover up the actual execution but there was already so much blood and fractured skull on the ground that the second go-round was an unnecessary insurance shot. It crushed her neck and part of her shoulder."

"That was certainly quick," I said, musing. "She has an unpleasant lunch and suddenly she's en route to her eternal reward…or damnation."

"True. It's as if she just got started recruiting her team and suddenly she receives the pink slip with the red edges."

"Yes, Sir. If I can speak freely…"

"Always, Gwen."

"I think we have to be honest with ourselves about this. In some ways we're dealing in pure guesswork. I happened to catch her and Darvish having dinner. Suddenly she's in our sights, but we really have no idea when her connections with this syndicate (if that's the right word) actually began. Our awareness began with our first sighting, so it feels like Act 1, Scene 1, to us. Actually it could have started months ago. Or years. Finally the syndicate lost its patience. We don't really know the actual timeline."

"No doubt, Gwen," the Director said. "We really have no idea whether her elimination was precipitous or long overdue. Anyway, I want you on the scene ASAP. As luck would have it, the SecDef was visiting the academy, along with the Chief of Staff for the Air Force and the Secretary of the Air Force. They're returning to Andrews at first light and I've secured a seat for you on their *C-32*. We've shoehorned in an adjusted flight plan so they can drop you off at *John Glenn Columbus*. Peggy will have a car there for you from the Cincinnati office. Gwen…"

"Yes, sir?"

"I wish you could have had a longer rest, but I need you there."

"I wouldn't want to be anywhere else, sir."

A *C-32* is the military version of a *757*. Commonly used for cabinet members and other high pooh-bahs, the military model is divided into four sections. The forward area has a communications center, head, galley and ten business-class seats. The second section is the man (or woman) cave for the principal passenger, with private head, comfy couch and two first-class swivel seats. It also has its own entertainment center, though at first light most occupants would probably want an extra hour or two of sleep. The third section is a conference and staff facility with eight business-class seats. The aft portion has a separate galley, two heads and thirty-two business-class seats.

When I got to the tarmac I was greeted by a bright-eyed young major named Dawson who told me that the SecDef wanted me to join him in his private section of the plane. He also took my suitcase ahead, so I didn't have to wrestle with it getting on board. I was pleased, surprised, and a little embarrassed. The men and women with eagles and stars on their shoulders smiled and nodded at me and no one seemed bent out of joint by the fact that I had been issued a go-to-the-front-of-the-line ticket.

The SecDef was lean and chiseled; he reminded me of a younger version of the actor Scott Glenn, who played Alan Shepard in *The Right Stuff*. A former Army officer, he was dressed in a dark suit with a starched white shirt and muted maroon tie. I thanked him for making space for me on the plane.

"I wanted to meet you," he said. "Walter and I have done business in the past. We were once in a godforsaken combat zone under heavy machine gun and mortar fire and his tanks supported my infantry battalion. Saved our bacon that day, that night and the next morning. When the dust settled and we gathered together under our canvas roof he slipped out a bottle of *Johnnie Walker Black* and a bag of ice cubes. He wouldn't tell me how or where he got the ice cubes but he poured us each four fingers of liquid gold and told me that it was not designed to settle our nerves but rather to lift our spirits in victory. Who talks like that besides him? Anyway, he tells me that you're his best tracker and I wanted to meet you up close and personal."

"Great honor, sir," I said.

"I should also be honest and tell you that the soirée at the academy was a simple grip-and-grin after a routine visit. Your assignment was far closer to real action and that's where I prefer to be."

"I hope I can be of help," I said. "It's not entirely clear how my case bears on national security, but it's very suspicious around the edges."

"I talked to Walter while we were en route to the plane," he said. "He gave me a few of the details. Young woman meeting with suspicious people. Probably a little over her head. Then it all goes belly-up. Tale as old as time? The idealist crashes into the wall of reality and finds out that her sand box mates were playing for keeps?"

"Could well be, sir," I said.

"Too many feelings, too little rational thought? I'm not disparaging women; I'm talking about something generational. When I was at WooPoo the key courses were in math. You had to stand tall, put your answers on the board and defend them to your classmates. If the answers were beyond them you had to defend them to your P. It was all of a piece—the math, the precision, the rationality, the exercise of leadership (however abstract), the building of self-confidence that had to be anchored in facts rather than shifting sand…now, who knows? How do you *feel* about that, Cadet Jones? *Feel?* Back in the day that question was never asked. I'll tell you what I *feel*: the problem goes to the top. In those days the Supe had two stars; now they have three. Grade inflation all around…"

"I understand that you're trying to remedy some of that, sir," I said.

"Easier to turn a battleship around than a college," he said, "but we're trying. Gwen…can I call you that?"

"Of course, sir."

"Help us find out what that woman was doing and why she died in the process."

"I will, Sir."

TWENTY-ONE

When we got to Columbus, Major Dawson passed my luggage to an FBI special agent, who handed me a key fob for a nondescript *RAV4 LE* and an envelope. The envelope contained a picture of a middle-aged CDP Detective named McConnell.

I rallied with him in the Hilton parking lot after making my way to the entrance on Lyra Drive, the link street to the hotel as well as the east end of the mall. Even this side street was crowded, but nothing like Polaris Parkway, which reminded me of 123 at Tysons Corner on Black Friday.

Detective Sergeant (Frank) McConnell was close to retirement age but still thin and firm. He told me that he had served for two and a half years as the 'General's' driver, usually in a *Stryker* or *M113A3* when the Director was in command of the 2nd Armored Division. In garrison he drove him around in his sedan or *F-150*. "He changed my life," McConnell said. "I was a raw kid from the Missouri bootheel who enlisted because I wanted other choices in life than growing peanuts, soybeans, rice and cotton. General Gradison persuaded me to sign up for courses from the University of Maryland and I eventually ended up as a Detective Sergeant in the Buckeye state."

"The Director seems to have known everyone and helped all of them in some way," I said.

"He asked me to extend you every courtesy and share everything I could with you."

"I appreciate that," I said. "I see that the body's been removed."

"Right. We're still combing over the asphalt, looking for anything that could be of help. We've already checked the Hilton's CCTV. The only camera in the rear of the hotel was over the main entrance there, and as you can see, the murder took place in the far east corner."

"Almost as if they knew we'd be checking and were staying out of range and out of frame."

"Exactly," he said. Most everyone parks in the front and you don't get spillover unless the facility is full or in use for a wedding or major conference function. Last night the occupancy was just over 30%. You might expect someone parking at the west corner so that they could walk over to the mall and eat at someplace like *The Cheesecake Factory*, but these days most everyone drives over and parks as close to the restaurants or other destinations as they can. They only exercise at an actual gym."

"And the CCTV inside?"

"Nada," he said. "We checked the bar and the reception desk, the restaurant and the rest rooms, but...again...nothing. A murderer or murderers would be pretty stupid to expose themselves like that..."

"But pretty smart to know where she was heading for the night and how to rally with her in a deserted area without raising any suspicions. It's also odd for her to be bedding down in the most expensive place on the Parkway. She usually goes for the low end."

"On a tight budget," he said.

"Yes, or maybe a fixed per diem such that she could turn the fungible cash into a salary top-off."

"Good point," he said. "Her car was rented at the St. Louis airport, but you probably already knew that."

"Yes, we did. We also know that she has been meeting with various individuals over the last week and a half or so, but I haven't been given clearance to discuss the specifics because of possible security implications."

"Understood," he said, "but we do know that she met with Congressman Anderson at the Springfield *Big Boy*. One of our counterparts there picked up the license plate of her rental at a nearby intersection and we checked out the camera footage from the most likely locations in the area. You know, he really is a piece of work…."

"Glad-hander, macher, gonif. I've heard him described as the lead Conductor of the Gravy Train," I said. "How about you?"

"We've been instructed to consider him radioactive," McConnell said.

"In the sense of…?"

"Don't touch him. Don't mention him. Don't go near him. Don't even think about going near him."

"Because everyone is in fear of him because of the strings attached to his sleazy largesse."

"Exactly. And that injunction is still operative, even though he's in semi-retirement. Just because he's no longer in the House he still exerts tremendous power. He knows everyone. He knows the burial sites of all the bodies. He knows what kind of knowledge to bring to bear in order to influence other people."

"And he hasn't positioned himself in this manner because of his overweening patriotism."

"No. The winners of the contracts that he's engineered are all pals, buddies, lackeys…and in the most egregious cases, actual relatives, but the money is still coming to Ohio. What did Lyndon say, something to the effect that he never trusted anyone until he had his hand up their pantsleg? Everything he's doled out has ultimately come with a price and the price is that you're in his debt, forever."

"Somehow I doubt that he has that kind of sway over the Bureau," I said.

"Certainly not over the General. If he tried to bribe or embarrass him the General would break him into small pieces and feed him to the sewer carp."

"I agree," I said. "Of course, the AG or someone higher might be vulnerable and could try to remove the Director, but that would be a very difficult task."

"I've never seen a man with such integrity and I've seen him under fire. Literally."

"So have I," I said, "and when he's challenged or threatened he turns the steel eye on his adversaries, the one that promises retribution that is best left undescribed."

"That's why he's a good person to work for."

"The best."

"Unfortunately, the people around me are still guarded about Anderson. If the hammer comes down on him it will have to be from FBI Headquarters. In the meantime, I'm your man behind the scenes."

TWENTY-TWO

"Here," McConnell said, handing me a manila envelope. "The pre-liminary medical report. I'll call you later with any information we might turn on the actual crime scene. There's also a flash drive in there with a copy of the conversation between Anderson and the victim at the *Big Boy*. There's no sound, but you may be able to have a Bureau lip reader take a look. There's also a copy of the rental agreement for the car and pictures of the contents of her wallet. You'll get all of the originals when we formally hand over the case, but I thought you might want to start working with them now."

"Thanks. Much obliged," I said. "I'll talk to you first thing in the morning."

"How about breakfast? There's a *First Watch* on the other side of 71. We could do mid-morning…give you some time to check with your people and give me some time to check with mine."

"11:00?"

"Done," he said.

Peggy had set me up with a nice room at the Hilton. Before I ordered a sandwich and coffee I hit the mini-bar for two minis of bourbon. I poured one, straight, over some ice cubes and checked in with Mike. I told him about my contact at the CDP and about the materials he had passed on.

"Pity," he said. "We've already got everything except for the generic stuff from her wallet. Unfortunately, there was only one camera at the

Big Boy, but I've already been working on the conversation. As I told you earlier, she was intimidated by the old pol and was spending most of her time nodding obediently and sitting in silent subservience."

"Nice alliteration," I said.

"My forte," he answered. "I was able to come up with one thing. I'll spare you the technical details, but he was sitting with his back to the camera and there was an occasional reflection in the window beyond. It all depended on pedestrian traffic and the variations in light that it produced, but I did manage to catch one word. He said it twice and each time he poked his finger at the bridge of her nose."

"And what was it that he said?"

"Only one word was discernible. He said *chaos*."

"*Chaos?*"

"*Chaos*. And he was definitely angry when he said it."

"How angry?"

"I would say that at the very least he was insistent enough to come out of his glad-hand posture and lose some of his composure in the process."

"What do you think—he was complaining that her work was muddled and disorganized?"

"That would be my guess," Mike said. "He was mansplaining. He wanted logic and order, systematic planning and execution, not bubbleheaded bouncing off of the walls."

"Sounds plausible," I said. "Perhaps that's why they (*whoever* that is or includes) decided to remove her from the team."

"Harsh," Mike said. "A baseball bat to the temple is nasty but a *Michelin* driving over your eyes is an even less pleasant way to depart."

"Yes, I haven't completely read their medical team's report, but that's been their story line from the get-go."

"Just a thought…I probably wouldn't mention the *chaos* bit to the locals."

"No, I'm mostly all gratitude in my demeanor, but very guarded in what I reveal. It's our case and I don't want anyone else mucking around in the details, especially with all of the contacts that Anderson has across the state."

When I got to the *First Watch* McConnell was already there, organizing the napkins, ice water glasses, silverware and menus. Old military habits die hard.

"Let's order and then we can talk," he said, "not that I have anything of great significance to pass on."

First Watch is never my first choice for breakfast because their pancakes are strictly multigrain and I don't like people telling me (or inferring to me) what I should or shouldn't eat. Instead I went traditional with some oatmeal, toast and a double order of bacon. The sergeant chose some breakfast tacos.

"As I said, I don't have much for you. Our uniforms combed through the parking lot as carefully as they could, but all they found were some slivers of red plastic, presumably from one or more cracked turn signals or taillights. The pieces were so small that there was no way of identifying the vehicle or vehicles from which they came.

"We also worked our way through the footage from the local CCTV and traffic cameras, but there's always serious traffic on the Parkway, even in the middle of the night. No one was speeding away or exhibiting any other type of suspicious behavior. We also checked the license plates in the front of the lot, in case our perps were playing coy with us, but each of the plates corresponded with the names of the registrants at the hotel. Our guess is that the vic was asked to meet with someone in the back of the lot; it turned out to be an ambush rather than a meeting and the perp or perps were professional enough to take her out without drawing any serious attention to themselves. In other words, a dead end. At least for now."

"I agree," I said. "I would like to know about any recent movements by the congressman in your particular neck of the woods. For that matter…any recent movements at all. Who else has he been meeting with, for example."

"Like I said before, I have to tread lightly on that front, so I'll have to see if I can learn anything on my own without talking to anyone else in the office."

"I understand. There's no way of knowing who might already be compromised." (I didn't mention the fact that Mike Liu was already tracing Anderson's movements, along with those of Darvish, Vanzetti and Petrov.)

"I'll turn over a few rocks and see if Anderson slithers out," McConnell said. "It may take awhile, but I'll keep you posted as things develop."

After we finished our breakfasts and a third cup of coffee each, we said our goodbyes. I returned to the Hilton and reconnected with Mike.

TWENTY-THREE

"Just one new development," he said. "You remember the meet with Vanzetti in O'Hare…"

"Right."

"He actually lives in Manhattan."

"Interesting, but not terribly surprising, is it? He deals in money and that's our country's financial capital."

"No," Mike said, "but I'm always a little guarded when I see that people are linked geographically as well as…well, we're not yet sure how they're linked…but they're not part of a VFW bowling team or fellow members of the local Moose Lodge."

"I couldn't disagree there," I said. "Do we have an address for Vanzetti?"

"Give me a few," Mike said. "I picked him up on the city income tax rolls; my guess is that the home is owned by some shell corporation."

"It's not surprising that people with serious money have Manhattan addresses," I said.

"I know. I may be making mountains out of molehills but it's the only connecting point that we have, except, of course, for the meetings with Bluebell."

"I agree," I said. "Maybe the syndicate (if that's what it is) is a collection of funders of Allyson's efforts. Anderson could be their manager. He needed investors; he went where the money was, and always is—in the hands of the criminal class."

"Give me a few," Mike said. "I'll dig deeper."

"Do me a solid and keep an eye on all of the members of the gang of four, not just Vanzetti, and keep a particularly sharp eye on Anderson."

"Already doing that," Mike said. "I noticed that Ms. Barry is no longer *Bluebell;* you're grieving over her."

"I wouldn't say 'grieving' because I don't like the company she kept, but she's now a bona fide victim and that somehow moves her in the direction of the side with the light."

"I agree," he said.

"Stay in touch," I answered.

The next morning the Director asked the Sacramento SAC to send one of his senior special agents to meet with Allyson's parents. His name was Louis Newman. I knew Lou, but we were not old and established friends. He worked white-collar crime and our paths rarely crossed. I did know the SAC, however, and I trusted his judgment.

The Director sent in a local so that if we were under surveillance—remote and/or direct—my involvement could be concealed. We didn't want any bad guys to know the extent of our current investigation and the fact that their potential involvement with Allyson was already on our radar screen (or four radar screens, in the case of Mike Liu).

The Sacramento field office is actually in Roseville, a northeastern suburb, 14 miles from Del Paso Heights. Lou arrived at 9:00 a.m. He was wearing a wire that transmitted to the Director, to me and to Mike. The fact that the Director was involved directly was an indication of how seriously he took the case. I suspected that he was particularly interested in the involvement of Curtis Anderson. When a former member of congress is potentially involved in a homicide the D.C. media begin to throb like a 6.5 quake along the San Andreas.

"Good morning," Lou said. "I know how you feel and I dearly wish we could be meeting under happier circumstances. My name is Special Agent Louis Newman, from the Sacramento field office of the FBI. I know that you've already heard the terrible news about Allyson and I wanted to meet with you and share what little we know."

Allyson's father, Ted, shook his hand, said 'I'm sorry…' and burst into tears. Her mother Marianne shook his hand and invited him into their living room. "Can I get you some coffee?" she asked.

"Only if it's already made," he said.

There was then an extended silence as she went into the kitchen to prepare a tray. "I'll let you fix it the way you prefer," she said, and we all heard the sound of clinking spoons.

"You know our question," Marianne said. "Was this an accident or something far worse?"

"We've classified it as suspicious," Lou said. "It occurred in the middle of the night when an accident would be far less probable, particularly in a largely deserted parking lot. We think that someone might have asked her to meet with him or her there. Is there anything that you could tell us about her work or personal relationships that could be of help?"

"Allyson was a political consultant," Marianne said, "so she came into contact with a great number of people. There was no romantic relationship that we were aware of. She had a tiny place in New York and rented an equally small place in a part of Washington called Cathedral Heights. We visited there once. She lived in a tiny studio apartment. It's very expensive there, you know, but you want to be close to the people you could be meeting with."

"I understand," Lou said. "I trained at Quantico and I have to visit the FBI headquarters occasionally, but I still try to avoid the District whenever possible. The traffic is awful. Part of the problem is the designation of historic highways that can't be expanded; that exacerbates the problem. Forgive me, we're not here to talk about District traffic. Have you been in contact with Allyson recently?"

"I think she was in Colorado the last time we spoke with her."

"That was…when?"

"I'm not sure, perhaps two weeks ago. Ted…"

When she called to him there was no perceptible answer.

"He's taking it very hard," Marianne said. "Of course, I am as well, but they were very close."

"Can you tell me anything about her current work?" Lou asked.

"Well, her title was kind of a catch-all. She was still very young. It's not as if she turned up as an expert on one of the cable news channels. She would sometimes help with everyday things: polling, organizing operations for special and national elections…she would sometimes do advertising and press releases…she was a very good writer; I don't know if you knew that or not. She had good people skills. People liked her; they would open up to her. She was a wonderful young woman…"

As she paused we could all hear the sniffling.

Suddenly her father's voice: "I can't imagine who could possibly want to hurt her. She never did any harm. If she had a fault…"

"Yes?" Lou said.

"It's…it was…that she always tried to see the best in people. Some might say that she was a little naïve. She was too optimistic, too trusting. That may be why she was so easy to hurt."

TWENTY-FOUR

The Director thanked Lou for his help; Mike signed off, deferring to me so that the Director and I could debrief.

"What do you think, Gwen?"

"The parents may have been close to their daughter emotionally, but they had little or no idea what she was actually doing. Very sad, actually. I think her father's comment was particularly telling. She was over her head, not fully cognizant of who she was actually dealing with, and the lengths to which they would go. She paid a heavy price for it."

"Agreed," the Director said. "Especially the congressman. The four musketeers could all be nasty, but from his age and past experience I would expect the congressman to see the others as little more than staff and go-fers, even Darvish. It's in his nature by now."

"Murder's a big step though, even for him," I said.

"Indeed," he answered, "but he spent the better part of his life destroying reputations and threatening reprisals for any disobedience, real or perceived." He paused before continuing. "I guess the fact that she had an apartment in the District is new information, but it's hardly surprising and probably not significant."

"Let me try something, Sir. I'm seeing a major…well…let's call it a *mismatch*."

"Go on…"

"Allyson Barry misunderstood her role from the start. She thought she was meeting with people to arrange a garden party and her handlers thought she had been hired to arrange a revolution. That may be a little too strong…"

"No, I know exactly what you mean. None of her conversations with the students and others seemed particularly animated, as if they were expecting something more intense, something imminent and perhaps something far more serious. Instead, she was acting as if she was conducting a preliminary screening for…what…a later, more important job interview?"

"How about this…" I said. "When she was meeting with the congressman he was insistent in his use of the word *chaos*. Mike and I thought that she was being criticized for being disorganized or muddled. Maybe it was something altogether different…maybe she was supposed to be *creating* chaos, perhaps even on a large scale…"

"Interesting," the Director said. "Continue to keep that possibility in mind. I will as well. I'm interested in the fact (which could be nothing more than coincidence) that three of your people are all located in Manhattan. Anderson is not, but he was always close by and knew where the banking headquarters (and dark money) were. I want you to go to New York and huddle with the Assistant Director and his people, see what they know about these characters. The AD is *acting* now, but the appointment is likely to become permanent. Have you met him yet? I know you were here last February when we had the general confab."

"We were mostly on distant sides of the room, but I'm looking forward to something more personal…and possibly operational."

"You'll like him," the Director said. "One other thing…"

"Yes, Sir?"

"I want you to give some thought to Ms. Barry's *list*. Who were these people (mostly students) she was meeting with? Were they individuals with common elements in their pasts? Was she recruiting them for an operation? For an organization? Who constructed the list?"

"I'll talk to Mike," I said. "He's probably already looking for the connecting strands in the spider web."

I got in on a late flight in a little plane and met with the AD first thing the following morning. "Welcome to New York," he said, but I had to turn 90 degrees in order to see him. He was hanging from a fixed pull-up bar apparatus in an alcove to the right of his desk.

"Ralph Dexter," he said. "Call me 'Dex'; everyone does."

He said these words without catching a breath, even though he continued to do pull-ups. As he rose in the air I could see that he had two prosthetic feet and calves that were fitted below his knees."

"Go ahead and have a look," he said. "I'm used to it. Every first-timer in the office wants to look, but tries not to be obvious about it. Middle East. IED. I never lie and say I no longer notice them, but I do my best to stay fit. As you know, we have high physical standards and I want my SACs and Special Agents to feel as if I'm doing my part.

"I stayed too long at the fair," he said. "After Hudson High you owe the Army 5 years, but I thought I'd stick around and do the full course. Fortunately, the Bureau was generous in taking me on after the camel riders took me off the battlefield…"

After the last of several dozen pull-ups he approached me and extended his left hand. "Surprise," he said. I then noticed the flesh-colored prosthetic right hand. "I'm afraid that wasn't my day."

I shook it firmly.

"At this point I usually say something about how I eventually landed on my feet, career-wise, but that's become an old and now-tired joke. I noticed that you yourself have recently caught some bullets but were obviously able to dodge the reaper."

"I have," I said. "The Director just pulled me off of some resulting R&R to chase some bad guys who live in your town. At least that's what I believe I'm doing. It's a murky case."

"Pull up a chair," he said. "You'll want your coffee black and thick, the kind that will float a horseshoe."

"Yes, sir."

As I said that, he raised his eyebrows and tilted his head to the side like a curious terrier.

"Yes, Dex."

"There's also some croissants from some place in *Chelsea Market*. Reputed to be the best in town." They were sitting on the corner of his desk on a china plate covered with a linen cloth. He removed it with his right hand.

"Now you're supposed to say 'dextrous'," he said.

I smiled as he retrieved some steaming mugs from the credenza behind his desk. He also handed me a small plate with a paper napkin for the croissants.

"You're Native American, right?"

"I am."

"The Director's prime tracker."

"I wish that name were not so firmly attached," I said.

"Great plains-type. Lakota."

"Close enough for government work," I said.

"Bad-asses and mothereffers," he said.

"We have been known to be," I answered, smiling.

"Had one in my Company at WooPoo," he said. "The only one who could outrun me, both long distance and in short sprints. Full bird now. Seldom happens that early. Strictly prime.

"You could relate, however. He took some serious shrapnel to his left shoulder on a sand dune in the middle east. He was laid up for months and kept asking the medics when he would get his picket fence back. Couldn't wait to get back in his tank and kick up some serious dirt."

(The picket fence is the set of 1's that you want in your PULHES physical profile, an acronym which refers to body parts.)

"Anyway," he continued. "You're here to talk about some of my ne'er-do-well neighbors—Darvish, Vanzetti and Petrov."

TWENTY-FIVE

"The names are all phonies," he said. "That would make anyone suspicious."

"You've had time to check them out."

"We've been looking through their windows and underneath their tables for quite some time," he said. "Vanzetti is actually the newest arrival. He bought up four units in a building in Hell's Kitchen, knocked out some walls and created a full floor of rooms, with lead partitions, crevices and hidey holes. The neighborhood's become a foodie Mecca and Paolo enjoys find dining, along with a host of other creature comforts. Darvish peddles military secrets; Petrov peddles fentanyl and Paolo deals in foreign currencies. He buys low, sells high, wrecks the economies of small countries and uses the proceeds to drink first-growth red Bordeaux and watch waiters shave slices of white truffles into his soup."

"Pity you can't scoop them all up and drop them in a secure federal hole somewhere."

"A great pity," he said. "Much of what we know has been obtained through unconventional means and each of them is scrupulously careful to insulate themselves from our people."

"Do you ever see them working together?"

"They don't dine out at *Nobu* and scarf sushi together. They're much too careful for that. You see some overlap around the edges: club memberships, common charities that they use for street cred among the glitterati, slips at the same marinas…but they operate independently, and while all of their activities are sleazy and ultimately criminal they know how to skate around the CCTV cameras and elude direct action. Vanzetti often operates abroad, as does Darvish, and Petrov will do things like supply precursor chemicals, but you'll never see him directing people across the border with bags of product that look like kids' candy and contain enough material to kill millions."

"Could you get me a list of the occasions or institutions in which there has been that overlap?" I asked.

"On the thumb drive in the dark pouch on the side table," he said. "Figured you'd want it."

"Many thanks. And are they all under constant surveillance?"

"To the extent that we can do that. They spend a lot of their time out of the city. They often fly private out of smaller airports. Sometimes they'll even take the Amtrak. They've been seen in state-of-the-art limos, Carey cars and even Ubers or common taxis. They suspect they're being watched so they do their best to remain elusive. We do have cameras on their homes here in town. When we see them on the move and can detect their destinations we contact other field offices, but, as you can well understand, Manhattan is filled with suspicious characters and a lot of our time is consumed with investigating cyber crime, public corruption, other white-collar crime, and so on."

"And potential WMD events of various types."

"A biggie for us," he said.

"Can I check through the materials you've provided and get back to you?" I asked.

"Absolutely," he said.

TWENTY-SIX

I checked into the Hyatt *Grand*, which would normally be out of my price range, but the hotel provided a very friendly rate for the government, including a service that recorded the rack rate on our public bill and masked the fact that the private list of guests might include serious officials from our intelligence and law-enforcement agencies. Peggy had made the arrangements; all that I needed to do was present myself at the concierge's desk, give a code name and receive my room key without showing any identification or credit information.

I checked in with the Director's office. He was in a meeting at the WH. I thanked Peggy for her help, asked her to convey my appreciation to the Director for arranging a meeting with the AD and told him that I would be studying the materials that he had shared with me.

The fact that the Hyatt was so centrally located made it far easier to navigate the city and check out the domiciles of the individuals under investigation. She told me that the Director would be available first thing in the morning and that I could call him between 6:00 and 8:00 a.m.

After settling in I put on a nondescript outfit and proceeded to check out Darvish's home on East 64th Street. He had good neighbors. Just down the street was the recently reopened *Plaza Athénée*, the late Queen of England's choice of hotels when she visited New York. Two blocks south was the Mellon Foundation, with a tidy endowment of around $8B. I wondered if Darvish had found a way of getting his hooks into a piece of that action. They generally supported the arts, humanities and 'culture', but the latter could cover a multitude of sins and would naturally attract the attention of gonifs and outright criminals, even if they were told that the gates to the vault were formally closed to them.

Mike had already notified me that Darvish was in Honolulu for a golf tournament that attracted middle eastern potentates. I imagined him in a walnut-paneled 19th hole, peddling his wares to one or more of them while they sipped aged scotch from crystal glasses.

His home was a stone-front, stunning townhouse with *Zillow's, Realtor.com's* and related guesstimates placing it just below the stratosphere of local pricing. I found a dark corner of the street, placed a portable camera in an inconspicuous crevice and found a nearby coffee bar from which to observe. I was on my third cup when a figure emerged from the lower-level entryway beneath the front door. A swarthy man in a dark suit with an obvious shoulder-holster bulge was speaking to someone on a cell phone while looking east and west along the street. After a few seconds a dark *Suburban* came slowly down the street and double parked. The figure from the basement approached the SUV and passed a large envelope to the driver, who passed a tiny envelope in return.

I caught enough images to help Mike identify each of them, but neither said anything, so there would be no possibility of lip reading. They obviously knew one another and were comfortable exchanging cash for contraband (or so I assumed). The swarthy, armed man then returned to the basement entryway. Conclusion: Darvish was working out of his home, employing at least one thuggish individual. The product he was purchasing was probably a thumb drive and its contents would be unavailable to a warrant-less beat cop because they would be immediately transferred to the big guy via a state-of-the-art electronic system. They could even be in Darvish's hands already and the original thumb drive floating in a bowl of acid. Timing and speed are everything, especially for those who work in the shadows.

My next stop was Vanzetti's domicile near West 57th and 11th Avenue. The building was tall enough to afford a nice view of the Hudson. I followed my camera and coffee routine but was unable to see any human activity beyond the delivery of a set of pizzas. The apartments in the building would be pricey. The NYC 'mansion tax' is $10K on the first million of value and the percentage goes up on a progressive scale. This is just a tiny add-on to the other costs, payable when the property is transferred. A million dollars at that address might get you 1,000 square feet of space. Bottom line: if you can afford to live there you can afford to order in some food that would be significantly more interesting than pizza in a cardboard box. In this case there were several boxes. Conclusion: this was lunch for the hired help, probably in a distant wing of Vanzetti's place. He too was 'working from home' as it were and for all I knew he could actually be in Pago Pago. (He hadn't yet hit any of Mike's radar screens.)

The good news was that Mike got back to me on the guy at Darvish's townhome as well as the delivery man. The bad news was that neither was in the system. "You throw a *Wham-o Superball* in Rug Alley at the Casbah and it'll bounce off a dozen guys who look like that," he said.

"Your favorite expression," I said.

"Unfortunately it's often the most appropriate one," he answered.

My final stop was at Petrov's recently-discovered SoHo loft, a secondary hidey hole just above Canal Street in lower Manhattan identified for us by the New York field office. The rest of the building was owned by a shell corporation, with the exception of an art gallery on the sidewalk level. I wondered if Petrov would have the stones to operate a drug lab in this old commercial space, but thought it unlikely because the risks of suspicious smells were too great. I thought of Capone's brewery in the 'cooker in the sky' episode of 'The Untouchables.' Better and safer to operate multiple money laundering operations there. Again, however, I was struck by the ways in which all three of these individuals worked from home (or homes). Each was in his own silo and each mixed business with whatever it was that they considered pleasure. Anderson was a ringer, with no Manhattan address, but each of them had met with Allyson Barry, whose services were deemed to be no longer necessary. Why were they drawn to NYC (beyond the usual reasons—fun, games and vast sources of cash) while Anderson stayed in Ohio, Washington, and California? Perhaps the obvious answer was that he preferred the California coastal weather to that of coastal Lake Erie or the gritty shores of the Hudson River.

Just then a message came in from Mike.

TWENTY-SEVEN

"Business completed in Hawaii," he said. "Both Darvish and his contact were exchanging information from tablets. Presumably one was transferring information and the other was transferring money."

"Any i.d. on the contact?"

"Yes, as a matter of fact. His name is Anwar Fadel. Syrian freelancer. Close to being something like a middle eastern Darvish. A middleman. A go-between. Shady but clean enough to be able to travel on an Egyptian passport. Probably bought and paid for. Governments would use him as an insulator. He's been known to work for the Iranians, the Houthis, Hamas and Hezbollah."

"All pretty much the same thing."

"True, but he's managed to stay sufficiently above the fray by making some philanthropic contributions in Jordan, Saudi and the UAE."

"Always the way," I said. "Hand you pennies with one hand and stab you in the back with the other."

"*Greasing the skids*, my father would have said. "Keeps the splinters down and the product flowing. So what's up with you?"

I brought him up to date on my real estate tour.

"The key may be Anderson," Mike said, "even though he's out of the Manhattan loop."

"Maybe all roads ultimately lead to Washington," I said.

"Always possible. That's always been the land of milk and honey for the congressman."

"Sutton robbed banks because that's where the money was," I said. "There's a whole hell of a lot more money on the banks of the Potomac."

"Indeed," Mike answered, "but the last administration has shut off a lot of those spigots."

"Mercifully," I said. "If Anderson is what you call your basic 'system navigator' there's been much less of a system to navigate."

"But he's still involved and as far as we can tell he's the last person to see Allyson alive. That has to count for something."

"True that," I said. "Where is he now?"

"In his home in McLean."

"I'm going there," I said.

Actually I was scheduled for a morning talk with the Director, so I contacted Peggy and told her I was coming to town. She scheduled a dawn meeting at his new DC office and I grabbed a deli sandwich, some kosher dills and a piece of cheesecake, picked up my luggage at the Hyatt and headed to Penn Station.

In DC I checked into the Holiday Inn within walking distance of the new Bureau offices adjoining the DOJ. The hotel was a nice facility with a rooftop pool and a first-level bar and grill. The soup of the day was Manhattan clam chowder, a rarely-seen version. I went the full seafood route and coupled the soup with some crab cake sliders, washing it all down with some passable chardonnay. I decided against any coffee because I wanted to sleep well and be ready for my morning meeting.

When I returned to my room, took a shower and checked my email I saw a note from Mike, which bounced me to a secure site. His longish note informed me that Paula Vestry, the Northwestern J-school student, had been detained in Daley Plaza at a human rights demonstration. The activists had threatened to do damage to the Picasso sculpture, which Pablo had said was inspired by the head of his Afghan hound, Kabul.

The theme of the demonstration was 'human rights over dog statues'.

"Not terribly persuasive," Mike wrote, "but the statue is enormously important culturally and any threat to it would automatically draw media attention--always their ultimate goal."

The statue was the scene of a Yippie press conference just before the 1968 democrat convention and was mentioned or shot in multiple noteworthy films.

"The interesting thing," Mike continued, "is the fact that Vanzetti (with whom the Barry woman met in O'Hare) was nowhere in sight, but Curtis Anderson was interviewed on WBBM, the CBS affiliate. He expressed concern and anger, exclaiming like an 18thc actor, with fulsome gestures. He had been part of the original funding for the project, serving as a congressional liaison with several foundations which were putting up the cash for its creation and installation."

Mike had conveniently attached the film clip, which ran as part of a late-night alert.

"Who would know of Anderson's involvement?" Mike wrote. "Who would contact an Ohio congressman in his home in Cleveland and make sure he was decked out in a smart suit and tie?"

I connected with Mike and we talked briefly about the situation.

"Why was Paula Vestry detained?" I asked

"She was on the scene, putatively covering it as a freelance journalist. When one of Chicago's best asked her to step back from a barrier she poked him in the chest, called him some crude and vulgar names and suddenly found herself with her left cheek wedged firmly against the pavement and her hands in cuffs."

"Trying to establish her street bona fides?"

"Could be. I haven't seen any pronouncements from the J-school. They could be supportive or disapproving…"

"Depending on possible effects on their endowment and admission statistics?"

"Exactimento." (Mike's default response.)

"I'm meeting with the Director first thing tomorrow morning; I'll keep you posted."

"I'll be here," he said.

I walked to the Director's DC office early the next morning. Peggy was making coffee. I thanked her for all of her help and she gave me an affectionate pat on the shoulder. "He's already here," she said. "He must have come in very early but I know he didn't sleep here because his clothes are daisy-fresh and the laundered, backup shirts in his cupboard haven't been touched."

We greeted each other. He knew I would want coffee and Peggy was at that point in their relationship that she could read his thoughts 90 percent of the time, so she brought in a tray without milk or sweetener two minutes after I had entered the office. "There are also some almond croissants," she said.

"Maybe in a few minutes, thanks, Peggy. Gwen?"

"I could do one but let me savor some of your coffee first."

Peggy left ; we talked briefly about the contretemps in Chicago and the Director got right to the point. "Not a great surprise that Vestry was acting out on the streets, but what do you make of Anderson's availability for an interview? Most reasonable people would find it highly suspicious, even though he had early connections with the project. Who didn't?"

"Prior planning/proper performance," I said. "And there was a lot of both. He knew about the event in advance and had one of his lackeys line up an interview."

"You're probably right," he said. "So they've dumped the Barry woman and gone ahead with some part of their as yet unexplained operation (or operations)."

"Unfortunately," I said. "Unfortunate that they've gone ahead and unfortunate that we don't know why."

"One interesting thing…" the Director said.

"Sir…?"

"Their signage was highly professional and each of the demonstrators was wearing a matched tee-shirt and color-coded mask. That's not something you can order up in ten minutes. And it's not inexpensive, even if they have contractors within their organization. These were clearly made to order, not something thrown together at the last minute. There's an image of the statue on both the shirts and the placards, along with the date of the event."

"I'm sure that Anderson is distancing himself from the demonstration. Otherwise, why step forward? And why go to the trouble of pulling some strings at CBS to make sure that he got the screen time?"

"Agreed," the Director said. "It could have turned ugly. The statue is 50 feet tall and weighs over 160 tons, so any real assault on it would have involved explosives, explosives which, needless to say, would propel significant shrapnel in all directions. No one found any on the scene but it wouldn't take much C-4 or Semtex to bring it down and the material could be brought in on a messenger's bicycle or carried in a bystander's brief bag. Some of the demonstrators were carrying spray cans of paint and small buckets of it…again, all color-coded. That, of course, could all be part of a diversionary action."

"Or the whole event could have been diversionary, a test for Paula Vestry."

"Explain…"

"Let's say that they were upset with Allyson Barry for not being sufficiently aggressive. The people with whom she met were usually listening attentively but they weren't raising their fists in anger and saying, 'let's storm the battlements.' Allyson's handler or, much more likely, handlers, wanted some serious action, so one or more of them approached Paula and told her that she should make herself available for the event and be prepared to act with sufficient urgency to convince them that she was committed to the cause."

"Or to tell her that if she didn't demonstrate the desired level of commitment that she, her family, friends, professors, et al. would risk the fate accorded Ms. Barry."

"Yes, Sir. Perhaps the carrots were discarded and the sticks were brought out in their place. I wonder if someone failed to do due diligence on the Barry 'appointment'. They thought they had a winner who could whip the local actors and actresses into shape. Instead, they found a kinder, gentler, more idealistic team builder. Now they're going for *harsh* and beginning by threatening a major cultural landmark. We'll keep an eye out for any indication of her possible replacement."

TWENTY-EIGHT

As he let that sink in, the Director hit a button on his desk and without further prompting Peggy brought in a plate of the almond croissants.

"These are the best," he said.

I tasted one and agreed. Then I took up the conversation again. "This may be a reach, Sir," I said, "but let me try to think out loud on this…"

He took a bite of his croissant, tipped the end toward me in a gesture that said 'continue'.

"The demonstration seems almost too…generic. It has to do with human rights. That's a pretty big and vague cause. If I'm demonstrating in Chicago over human rights I'm going to be holding up a placard that deplores the nightly murders on the south side or the pathetic quality of the local public schools. If I look over the list of people with whom Allyson Barry met I can imagine a whole host of potential players in potential demonstrations—protests over the middle east, Gaza and the Palestinians, the usual LGBTQIA+ concerns, gender issues, eco-warrior actions, pro-DEI movements, anti-nukes, union organizing, pro-immigration actions or the ever-popular pro-abortion rallies. Anything opposing the current administration would be a hardy perennial and there is always a special form of animus reserved for particular members of the president's cabinet and inner circle. They've been tugging at the Chicago mayor's beard for years."

"And yet," the Director said, "nothing of real note actually transpired.

resources instead of the jungle fighter with a sharpened machete and punji sticks. Now we have to look for her replacement. And Gwen…"

"Yes, Sir…?"

"Take some of those croissants with you; I don't want to be tempted to eat all of them myself."

"Will do," I said, smiling.

"One last thing. I don't want your presence here to attract any unnecessary attention. If this impending operation is truly a big one we can probably assume that they're watching us in the same way that we're watching them. I've got a full electronic set-up in a place above my garage. The garage is on a pipe stem behind my house and there are two units above it. My security detail uses half of it and the head of the detail is one of my old tank company commanders. I'd trust him with my life and you should as well. There's also a nondescript *Camry* that you can use. It's in the end bay; the keys are in the glove box."

"I'll get right to work, Sir."

"Fueled by those croissants."

TWENTY-NINE

The Director's description of his electronic hidey-hole was considerably understated. The garage had four wide bays and it was approximately 40 feet deep, with heavy oak cabinetry on the sides and a number of steel compartments at the rear. His armory?

The head of his security detail was a man named Charles Bondi. He asked me to call him Charley, though he persisted in calling me Special Agent Harrison. He reminded me of one of my surgeons during my recent recuperation. Always smiling, he would lift his freshly-washed hands and say 'hands of a woman, heart of a lion'. Charley was more of a 'hands like sledge hammers, neck of an offensive lineman' type of guy.

He showed me the *Camry*. "That's at your disposal. We try to keep some dust and grime on it so that it doesn't attract any unnecessary attention, but the inside is clean. There's also a false back inside the glove box that's held in place by small magnets. If you pull on any of its edges you'll find a Sig *P365 micro-compact* with 3 flush-fit 10-round magazines."

"I've always had a soft spot in my heart for Sigs," I said.

"So have we all," Charley answered.

The tech center (as Charley called it) was actually a two-bedroom apartment, the second bedroom containing the multiple-screen computer setup with printer, landline, charging ports and all of what Mike would consider the comforts of home. The kitchenette was all *KitchenAid*, the refrigerator stocked with the Director's favorite potables and the pantry filled with his guilty pleasure snacks, from cherry *pop-tarts* to *Cheetos* and pretzel slims from *Trader Joe's*.

"Help yourself to anything you want," Charley said. (I hadn't heard him slip open the door.) "We all tease the general about his preference for *Pepsi*; he tells us he would opt for *Diet Dr Pepper* if we weren't all such wiseasses. We then respond with some comment about his secret love for *Mr. Pibb*."

I could see that Charley was the gregarious type who was forced to spend too much time alone. "I think they call *Mr. Pibb* something like *Pibb Xtra* now," I said. "A guy in my class at Quantico used to drink it and we questioned his taste for (accenting the second syllable) *pan`therpiss*."

Charley laughed.

"I figure you for a PBR guy," I said.

"The pride of Milwaukee," he answered, "but now based in San Antonio of all places."

"'All change is of itself an evil,' Dr. Johnson used to say."

"He was right," Charley said. "Anyway, I should let you get to work."

"Fun talking to you," I responded. He couldn't see that I had felt the twitch of my cell phone a minute earlier and I was anxious to see what my inevitable correspondent—Mike Liu—had turned.

"I've been checking on PV. Interesting stuff around the edges, but unfortunately nothing very specific. Up until the time of the demonstration at Daley Plaza she was communicating via burner phone. No specific information, of course, but repeated calls from the same source."

"Anderson?"

"That would be my guess. Possibly Vanzetti because of the earlier Chicago connection, but Anderson seems to be the heaviest hand here."

"I wonder if the cops who stopped her retrieved the phone."

"Doubtful, but I can't say definitively. I say *doubtful* because I was able to access a press interview with the lead officer on the case and he said that she was not carrying anything that would aid in PV's identification.

He could have been lying, of course, but I was also able to hack into some CCTV cameras in her neighborhood and there were no flashing light bars or, for that matter, any exceptional volume of traffic. She shares a rental with some other students in Evanston and everything in the neighborhood was quiet."

"Anything else?"

"Yes, but again nothing specific. Earlier in the day she drove toward the city from the north shore, but there were no traffic cams or private CCTV cams that I could use and she was suddenly lost in the ether."

"A final meeting before the event?"

"Possibly."

"How about Anderson?"

"Just beginning my deep dive, but I haven't been able to detect any recent presence in Chicagoland."

"Damned long drive from Cleveland…what?…6 hours if you're heading through town and up to Evanston?"

"Probably," Mike said. "He could have flown private, of course, but that always leaves more of a potential paper trail than a nondescript car with darkened windows, sharing rte. 90 with 30,000 other vehicles."

"When and where was he last sighted?"

"Two days earlier he did a fundraiser with Michael Symon at the *West Side Market*."

"Beneficiary?"

"A local sports center for poor kids."

"Plenty of time to get to Chicago," I said.

"Right, but this gonif knows everyone, from the sunny lakeshore homes to the dark alleys of the inner city. He could always hire somebody to rendezvous with Paula Vestry and either pump her up or fill her with the fear of God."

"True, unfortunately. Was Paula Vestry ever actually arrested?"

"Yes and no. Mom and Dad had a lawyer there so fast that the local cops call him the *Flash*. Actual name: Louis Gold. He sprang her before the ink on her fingers could begin to dry."

"Thought they'd use digital systems these days," I said.

"Figure of speech," Mike said.

I could envision his smile. I then told him about my new base of operations above the Director's garage and he promised to do a full workup on Anderson's various pomps and works.

We signed off and I got myself squared away in the Director's apartment. I usually live out of a suitcase, literally, but I figured I would be there long enough to make it possible to actually remove my items, stack them, hang them, fold them, and, in general, live like a civilized person.

Charley had shown me the washer/dryer combination in a cupboard between the two units and I found their presence reassuring. "We never really go to the mattresses," he said, "but it's nice to be able to do a quick wash-up if necessary."

I also familiarized myself with the Director's tech setup so that I could do more with Mike than communicate via phone and tablet or laptop. In each room of the apartment there was a made-in-China battery-operated clock indicating a British train or tube stop, from Paddington to Victoria to Charing Cross. I wondered if that was designed to carry some symbolic significance. By now it was 4:30 and I decided to eat early so that I could put in a full day tomorrow.

I drove into McLean to the *Giant* store on Chain Bridge Road (everything in McLean is on some segment, strip or version of Chain Bridge Road) and picked up some butter, muffins, K-cups of coffee and *Bonne Maman* strawberry preserves for breakfast and then thought about my dinner options. That wasn't easy, since the choices change constantly and one of my old favs, *Café Oggi*, was now closed. A former Irish pub with a CIA clientele, it had been replaced by the best of the McLean trattorias. It had always accommodated me with made-to-order pasta in vodka sauce or anything else which struck my momentary fancy.

One mainstay, however, was still in place after 40+ years: Café Tatti, a French bistro. I started with a glass of white Burgundy and agonized over the menu, vacillating between the bouillabaisse and boeuf bourguignon. Mike Liu would have been pleased at the alliteration, but my mind was on the white wine I was enjoying and decided to continue the march by pairing it with the bouillabaisse. Eventually I was forced to confront some impossible dessert choices but decided instead to go with a glass of limoncello. The fact that there was a tiny crack in the decanter assured me that the stuff was homemade. The price was right but the glasses were small, so I indulged myself and ordered a second.

THIRTY

I was up early and hoping to go for a run, but decided not to risk the exposure. Charley Bondi's morning replacement was a man named McCaffrey, who showed me a mini-gym at the rear of the garage. "The door is always unlocked," he said. "Feel free…"

I tested my almost-healed shoulder with some wall weights, spent some time on a stationary bike and completed my *run* on a treadmill set at a 7% incline. By then I was in need of a slow cool down, a shower and an honest day's work. I noticed that the pain in my shoulder was receding in a noticeable way.

Mike had a preliminary report on our wayward congressman. "He's always been associated with Cleveland, but he got his start in Cincinnati, doing his undergraduate work at what the locals call 'UC' and following a major in political science with the expected sojourn in law school. He actually worked his way through each at a local mainstay called *The Wheel* café. It was right in the heart of downtown, on Walnut Street—a legendary place with nasty bathrooms, sawdust on the floor and burgers, brats, sauerkraut, et al. on the menu. When you entered the military in Cincinnati you received a voucher to eat there before shipping out to your duty station."

"A place to develop your street bona fides in southern Ohio," I said.

"Exactly, but he also did some caddying when he was younger. He worked at a CC called Losantiville, which was the original name of the city—a nonce word made up from several languages that began with the city's position by the Licking River. Losantiville used to be exclusively Jewish but now its membership is broader and more varied. When Anderson caddied there it was all surgeons and manufacturers with names ending in -berg and -stein. He always speaks of that experience fondly."

"Developing his street cred among the liberal, professional and donor class," I said. "I hope that doesn't sound as if I'm stereotyping, but let's be honest. We're looking at the social and political scene from *his* perspective."

"Yes. He always had his political associations in the back of his mind, probably hoping to spend time north and south and eventually run for the senate, but that never happened."

"He could make just as much money in a House seat."

"You got it. Anyway, he moved north to Columbus in his late 20's. Puttered around in state government for awhile before relocating permanently to Cleveland, where he quickly embedded himself in local politics. He worked in the office of economic development which, even today, touts its skills in 'creative financing'. That would prove to be his primary achievement—securing the means (no matter how shady) to give the people nice things. When he successfully ran for congress he continued the practice but took it to a much higher level, always reserving a nice piece for himself in the miscellaneous funding processes."

"Was he ever questioned about his actual wealth in relation to his modest congressional salary?"

"Very rarely," Mike said. "He had a kind of diplomatic immunity because of his ability to deliver pork to his constituents, but he usually dodged the question by commenting on his family's wealth which came via hard work, dedication and, hence, their full realization of the American dream. The fact that his dad owned a small candy, news and tobacco store was a noticeable impediment to his story line, but there were also opaque references to money on his mother's side. Her father was associated with a famous furrier but those who took the time (and had the testicular fortitude) to probe more deeply realized that he was more of a tailor than a titan of industry."

"Ever arrested?" I asked.

"Not even a traffic violation," Mike said. "Clean nose, even if his pockets were lined with filthy lucre."

"And a hell of a lot of it," I added.

"*Beaucoup*."

"Religion?"

"Putatively Roman Catholic, but the only explicit evidence of it was his ability to find some serious funding for a renovation of their cathedral on the grounds of its historicity. A picture in *The Plain Dealer* shows him with a line of monsignors, all smiling as if they've just tapped into the prized oak barrel of brandy."

"The friars in the basement, hoisting their flagons on high. I think I've seen that image," I said. "How about his love life?"

"Married to Louise Ferney, going on 55 years. No stories of extramural hijinks. Four kids, all born early in the marriage. Mostly scattered to the four winds and living largely nondescript lives. A son in Tampa who manages a car dealership, daughter in Seattle who teaches high school social studies and a son in Alabama who describes himself as a 'simple country lawyer'. The fourth—Wayne—works as his office go-fer. Louise stays firmly in the background. Hasn't changed her hairdo in decades; dresses in nice suits with gawdy lapel pins and hats with feathers. Throwback city."

"How does he spend his time? Let me rephrase that: how is the press led to believe that he spends his time?"

"Dullsville incarnate, at least from my point of view. An endless round of luncheons, Rotary Club addresses, ribbon cuttings, face-time appearances…the gamut of grip-and-grins."

"Remember, Mike, you're a recluse."

"Guilty," he said.

"I was kidding," I said. "That need for attention…it's some kind of disease or affliction that only affects people with a hole in the center of their souls."

"Being recluses?"

"No, needing to be seen at endless ceremonies where you play a fatuous role and listen to the audience's applause."

"I was kidding too," he said.

I sent him some emojis. "So…nothing new on his potential relationship with Paula Vestry?"

"No, but also nothing new on her relationship with Vanzetti or anyone else in the gang of four."

"Stay in touch," I said.

"Always," he answered.

THIRTY-ONE

I popped in a fresh K-cup and made myself a cup of coffee. 'Espresso style' it read, but I went for a midsized cup. I didn't want to repeat Mike's work, so I did some mini-research on currency trading, trying to figure out how Vanzetti actually made his money. I quickly reached my level of competence in attempting to penetrate the foreign exchange forest. The biggest takeaways were that this is a much larger operation than stock trading, but much smaller in its choices. It is not for the faint of heart or the inexperienced. It is an ancient practice but its present form dates to the 1970's. The most interesting (but not surprising) aspect of the currency markets is that they are moved by many of the same things as the stock market, e.g., interest rates, but one of the noteworthy determinants of value is related to geopolitical tensions. If you can induce the latter you can generate change that can result in profit-taking. As I said, it wasn't a surprise, but it was one of those kinds of things that you needed to be reminded of, early and often.

I also did some checking of the drug market, particularly the fentanyl market, as the new administration's border policies had clearly affected the supply. The weapons market always seems to be positioned for significant profits, but the reduction in geopolitical tensions would adversely affect demand. I suddenly realized that I was sounding like a sophomore in the second week of Econ 101, but I reasoned that that was ok, particularly in light of the fact that, as Chaucer knew, *radix malorum est cupiditas*. The root of evil, is, ultimately, the desire for serious coin. We can talk about sex and jealousy and the seven deadlies; we can *cherchez la femme* and all that, but when the chips are down you want to have more of the red/white/blue ones than the white. And you want them in high stacks.

After my brief coffee break and tutorial on currency trading I sent a secure email to the Director, asking his permission to approach the Chicago SAC in order to see if I could get some additional information on the Daley Plaza demonstration. He returned a positive answer immediately with the comment 'good idea'. While I didn't expect it to be of direct use I noted that the SAC had spent some time in the Cincinnati PD back in the day. He wouldn't have overlapped with Anderson there, but he might have heard something that could be of use. As it turned out he had something even better.

I asked him if I could be wired in to any interview/interrogation of one of the demonstration's participants. "Most of them just spout ideological nonsense," he said, "but I can help you far more directly. We have a CI who's a regular astroturf demonstrator. I would want to keep that individual's identity secret, if that's ok, but you could speak directly with him/her. We would distort both of your voices, but that's not because we don't trust you. It's because it will loosen his/her tongue if he/she feels that his/her anonymity is sacrosanct."

"Totally understood," I said, "and very much appreciated."

"The person is coming in in late morning. We'll tell him/her that you're based in D.C. and are looking for something like color commentary on the event, as well as the standard specifics that could be shared."

"Perfect," I said. "And no visuals, I assume."

"No, those head bags with eye slits or blurred images are usually more annoying than helpful. It'll be a simple phone call, but over a secure line."

"I'll look forward to it," I said.

"We'll shoot for 11:30," he answered. "If the person comes in a little earlier we'll just fill him/her with coffee, so you can actually plan on that time. If it's a little later we'll express some regret that could induce a little guilt and loosen his/her tongue further. Either way you'll get regular updates from my assistant."

"Much obliged," I said.

The person actually arrived at 11:23 and had time to hit the head as well as the coffee urn. When the voice came through, the person sounded like a cross between Val Kilmer's southern gentleman accent in *Tombstone* and an ivy league-educated Donald Duck. I wondered what I sounded like. Fortunately, the SAC's assistant told me that I would receive a full recording of the conversation after we signed off.

I began by asking about the person's background in the CI role.

"Actually I'm an aging relative of someone in local law enforcement. I told the FBI people that I wanted to do whatever I could to be of help. So…your basic volunteer. I know…in the Army they warn you against volunteering for anything, but I had some time on my hands and I knew the locals well enough to be assured that my anonymity would always be protected."

"How about the overall organization?" I asked.

"It's usually pretty loosey-goosey and you never get specific information on the funders or their larger purposes. You get a call a day or two in advance with the details of the operation and the fee structure. Once in awhile the caller's voice is familiar, but often it's a rotational thing, with bright-eyed and bushy-tailed youngsters calling one day and tired bureaucrats the next."

"Do the fees vary greatly?" I asked.

"Not too much. It's never munificent but it's enough to make it worth the while of someone who wasn't planning to do anything that day anyway. I'd say it's seldom less than $75 and seldom more than $100. They also cover expenses. You come to a pre-announced point and you're bussed to the site. If there's more than four or five hours involved you'll usually get some sandwiches and soda, along with the preprinted signage, masks, shirts, and so on."

"Can I ask you something that's always concerned me?"

"Sure. I'll answer it if I can."

"What do they do about bathrooms? You see these crowds…they're often people with aging bladders…"

"I wondered that also. There's usually a toilet on the bus and they try to hold events at sites that contain public restrooms. Failing that, they'll usually have port-a-potties somewhere off camera. For example, if we're off on the highway somewhere, obstructing traffic, they'll have a facility in some nearby woods for the women. For the men it's more just catch-as-catch-can. It *is* an important issue, given the age and gender demographics, but the organizers are chiefly concerned with camera angles and sound systems. They're seeking maximum exposure on the local and, if possible, national news."

"How about the Daley Plaza event? Take me through that, if you will."

"Most everyone came from the north shore. In this case we met in a corner of the parking lot at the *Old Orchard* mall in Skokie. We were greeted by a young woman who said that she was a journalist and that she would be covering the event. She told us that we looked great and that the demonstration would be very important and that it would do a lot of good in raising the consciousness of everyone ('the thousands') who would see us. We were then given twenty minutes to use the restroom facilities at the mall or simply to 'stretch our legs'. There was a toilet on the bus but it was more 'for the desperate'. A lot of people aren't able to maintain their balance and they don't like the sloshing, green water, etc. etc."

"And the shirts and placards?"

"The shirts were distributed as we got on the bus, almost all in extra-large sizes so that they could be slipped over whatever we were already wearing. The placards were in the luggage bins beneath the bus. As we got on the bus we were paid in cash ($80) by a man who was actually armed.

(They used to do that in the Army back in the day, when wages were paid in cash. The distributors carried .45's in case someone attempted to rob them.) I thought that was odd. Usually the atmosphere is all peace, love and joy. Anyway, once we were on the bus the young journalist rehearsed us in several chants that we would use as we marched. One thing you have to remember is that some of these people would frighten Che Guevara while others are simply looking for some pocket change or something to do on a slow evening. You know how in big cities they will pay people (or at least give them free tickets) for concerts and shows? They simply want to fill the seats so that the performer or production company won't be embarrassed. Fortunately for them, there are people who will do that for them. Anyway, some of the demonstrators or protestors are like that, not at all like the true believers or the passionate haters. That's one of the reasons for the chants—to focus energy and make it look as if there's commonality of purpose…"

"So was the bus ride in like a pep rally or something similar?"

"Yes, exactly. They wanted to get the blood pumping. This time they had a couple of people telling personal stories about how their loved ones had been screwed over by the system, etc. etc. The purpose was to induce anger. 'I want to see your glasses steam over and your voices ring down like thunder,' one person said. You know, for me…it's really hard…"

"Because you've heard that song before…"

"Because I know it's all such bullcrap."

"And potentially dangerous."

"That especially," the disembodied voice said.

"And the young journalist was eventually arrested…"

"Yes, so I heard. I didn't get a good view of it because we were marching in an elongated circle and I was at the far end, facing away. When we got back on the bus someone described her as a heroine. At least they didn't say that she had 'stuck it to the man'. Some of these people are unaware that they sound more like George on *Seinfeld* than Trotsky."

The more this person talked the more I liked him/her.

When we were finished the SAC told me that they would send me the unedited tape of the event as well as the recording of our conversation. I thanked him profusely and waited for the files to drop.

THIRTY-TWO

Before I listened to the recording or examined the video I bounced a copy of the latter to Mike and asked him to scan it with his facial rec software. Then I broke out a bag of the Director's favorite nibbles and listened to the not-so-mellifluous sound of my own voice. I sounded like a mix of Lee Marvin and Yosemite Sam. Definitely masculine. I wondered if the male voice at the other end masked a female presence, but with the various Army references I figured the CI to be a late middle-aged former military man. I couldn't be sure of that because I understood the references myself and I was of the female persuasion.

I listened to the interchange from start to finish. Twice. Hence my surprise when Mike contacted me and mentioned the fact that Paula Vestry spent much of the several-hour demonstration time standing on the edge of the march, distributing flyers. There was no particular reason why the CI should mention it; flyers didn't have the cachet of chants and vulgar placards and they would seldom draw the attention that the more strident actions always did.

"That's only part of the story," Mike said. "You didn't see all of the images and clips that the looky-loos had on their phones. Only the Chicago Bureau had that and you told me that you hadn't reviewed it yet. Anyway, the material wouldn't have been particularly useful without the application of the facial rec software. That's where the story gets interesting…"

"How so?" I asked.

"I've got an edited clip that should have just hit your in-box."

"OK," I said. "I just heard the ding."

"Open it and slowly advance it to the 17-minute spot."

"Done. OK, I see what you've got. Somebody is standing in the shadows, filming Ms. Vestry. Checking out her performance, presumably, or perhaps the level of its intensity."

"That's part of it," Mike said. "You would want your flyer distributor to be excited about the task, not just handing something off because she's tired of holding a 5-pound ream of paper."

"Right. She seems pretty happy with her task. She engages the recipients in conversation if they balk at accepting the paper and she stabs at it from time to time to reinforce the weighty message that it purports to be conveying."

"So she gets a…what…B+ for her work?"

"A-. Remember we're in the days of grade inflation."

"Right," he said, laughing.

"But that's not the point…"

"No, there's one more thing and it's a large one."

"The identity of the person in the shadows catching her in the act of trying to look engaged."

"Indeed."

"And you'll identify her for me."

"I will. Her name is one Carrie Muller."

"Doesn't ring any bells."

"It wouldn't," Mike said. "She's kept her maiden name. Ms. Muller is Curtis Anderson's daughter-in-law."

"Whoa, son," I said.

"His son would be easily identified, so he (or the two of them) talked her into showing up at the scene and checking out Paula's performance."

"Very good work," I said.

"Dumb luck," he answered. "She turned up at a society wedding that earned a spot in the *Plain Dealer*. She was standing next to hubby; the beautiful people in the picture were identified in the space beneath the photo; the facial rec software sprung into action and Robert, as they say, is your uncle."

"Still damned good work," I said. "That could mean that the whole family is dirty," I said.

"Especially this son, who could star as the premier exemplar on *The Weakest Link*. No visible means of support of course, but his name is often attached to his father's campaigns and philanthropic enterprises, seldom as more than a slightly animate piece of furniture or a spear carrier with a glued-on smile."

"He has no actual skill set and hence no fall-back position."

"Not beyond the role of evil servant, at least not anything that I could find in the public record."

"And the wife is available for events that require maximum anonymity."

"Yep."

"I'm going to go out for a drive," I said. "It's a long shot, but the old boy lives in the neighborhood. Perhaps he's in town and perhaps he has a visitor or two parked in the driveway."

"Anderson *is* in town, as a matter of fact. I'll send you the address."

"That's interesting," I said, when the number, street and zip came up on my screen. "He and the Director are practically neighbors."

"You've got to appreciate the irony," Mike said. "The conductor of the gravy train is right off of Georgetown Pike, by Langley High School."

"Which puts him, more or less, in the backyard of the Company."

"Maybe he feels safe there," Mike said. "He believes that the CIA only operates outside of the United States."

I couldn't stop from laughing at that.

Anderson's home was on one of the tributaries of Turkey Run Road. Nice digs. Center hall, red brick colonial with semi-circular red brick steps. Virginia incarnate. Checked it on the real estate sites. Five beds, eight baths, 8,000+ square feet; guesstimated price tag: $6.65 mil. Not too far out of line for the neighborhood. I knew a guy in the Bureau, senior type. He was able to get in the general environs of the area, back when the high school district for his home was Langley. He wanted that school for the academics, but his son also wanted to play on their tennis team. Dad should have done his due diligence. The kids on that team all had courts on their property and something like 80% of them had private coaches. Langley is one of those actual public places that the ivy admissions directors will deign to visit after they pop by Groton, Harvard-Westlake and Phillips Andover.

Unfortunately, Anderson's driveway was angled away from the street and I had to park hundreds of yards away and make my way through some backyards to get a clear view. Fortunately, those backyards were filled with dogwoods, magnolias and Virginia pines. I put on a baseball cap and carried a clipboard, just in case someone thought I was anything but a busybody from a local agency.

There were two cars in the driveway, parked in front of a four-bay garage. One was a new *Mercedes* sedan with an Ohio license plate. The second was a decade-old *KIA*, also with an Ohio plate. Each was marked Cuyahoga County. Sonny boy was in town (or perhaps his wife was there, flying solo).

Mike later confirmed that one Carrie Muller had flown on *Southwest* from Reagan National to Chicago Midway two days before the demonstration. I wondered if she was paranoid about being there in time for the event (wanting to fly direct and fearing possible cancellations) or that she had a meeting with Paula before the event.

The plot had thickened, or at least the direct involvement of Curtis Anderson had been reconfirmed. I asked Mike to do a deep dive on Ms. Muller and her husband and then called the Director.

THIRTY-THREE

"Very interesting," the Director said. "I can't say that I'm surprised. I knew his tentacles were long and undiscriminating, but I didn't think he would be so crass as to implicate his own daughter-in-law."

"Maybe she's the one implicating him," I said. "She may have married his son to get closer to that kind of action."

"A naughty girl. Remind me of the son's name."

"Wayne," I said. "Mike's checking on both him and his betrothed."

"And there's no evidence of Darvish, Vanzetti or Petrov's presence at the protest event…"

"No, Sir. Nor in the city of Chicago and its environs, at least not in the last two weeks."

"Then we'll continue to focus on Anderson and the members of his family," he said. "You know, Gwen, I never liked him. I never liked his greed or his arrogance and I especially disliked his hypocrisy—the false smile and the glad hand. Except for the bank account there's no there there. He's a lamprey, a parasite.…"

(I had never heard the Director describe someone so determinedly.)

"The general moral stature of the republic would rise visibly if he departed," I said.

"I'd settle for a permanent home consisting of vertical steel bars," he said.

"I'll try to make that happen," I said, "assuming I can assemble the proper evidence."

"Of course." he responded.

Mike was ready with his preliminary report two hours later. "We'll start with the two crazy kids," he said. "I'll then get back to my work on Anderson himself."

"Great," I said. "Whenever anyone new enters the picture I want the deep background."

"In this case it may actually be the shallow background, at least for little Wayne."

"Whatever you've got I'll take," I said.

"OK, the two love birds met in Providence back in the day. Wayne was a History major at Providence College. I don't think he absorbed very much about the past because he always seems doomed to repeat it, at least the part about the need to actually accomplish something if you want to have any visible effect on it."

"And Ms. Carrie?"

"She studied poly sci at Brown. They label it political science and government."

"Brown: the Ivy League fallback."

"More or less, still," Mike said. "Not a cakewalk by any means, but still below Cornell."

"I wonder how far down the list you'd have to go to find Providence College."

"I'm not up for that trip," Mike said. "Anyway, they met at some social function. Maybe they called it a *mixer* then?"

"That was just after the Renaissance, I think, Mike."

"You're probably right. The sad thing is that Wayne was forced to drop out after his junior year and transferred to the University of Rhode Island."

"Money issues maybe?"

"No, I think it was what was once called *deportment*. He was arrested for public drunkenness."

"But Carrie stood by him…"

"Probably more because of the opportunities he represented via his father than any personal love or loyalty."

"What happened next?"

"Well," he said, "like any good poly sci major she went off to law school; Wayne worked for his father."

"Nepotism: the mother's milk of Washington."

"You got it."

"Where did she go…Georgetown? GW?"

"American University."

"Ouch…and after all that investment in Brown's tuition."

"I want to say that she chose AU because of their areas of study, even though the overlaps with GU are obvious. The things which appeared to have caught her eye were Advocacy, Environmental Law, Gender and the Law and Human Rights Law. GU does those also, but it looks as if AU had some firebrand faculty in those areas. The Georgetown faculty attempt to appear more decorous; they may idolize Lenin but they also like to dress in tuxes, sip white Burgundy and listen to Vivaldi. (Or so I've been told.) Anyway, after she graduated she went to work for a white-shoe firm that was known for its activism and its humongous volume of pro bono work."

"Possibly paid for with Government backhanders."

"Roger that."

"Which one?"

"Covington and Burling, which was quite a coup. Apparently she wanted to stay in the area with Wayne, but even though they have a masthead of gazillion associates it's considered a highly-desirable landing place."

"And she's now a partner there?"

"Driving a KIA?"

"That's *her* car?"

"That's what the registration says. Actually she left after a couple years and went to some smaller firms that specialized in personnel conflicts, hirings and firings and so on. Most recently she has worked for various government agencies that focus on a left-leaning agenda. Can I say that?"

"You can to me," I said. "And she moonlights for old man Anderson…"

"Yep."

"I'm not sure if that's legal or not."

"Maybe she thinks it's pro bono," Mike said.

"Where does the happy couple live?"

"Silver Spring. A tiny cottage that could use a coat of fresh paint."

"Probably not worth more than \$700K," I said. "Lots of temples there and lots of mosques. Known for its religious diversity."

"I'm not sure how religious these two are," Mike said. "I figure them for an active membership in the First Church of Karl Marx."

"Wow, very judgmental today," I said.

"Just trying to keep it real," Mike said. "Actually, Uncle Karl's daddy was a lawyer, but his son didn't have a lot of good things to say about the tribe."

"Somebody had to protect the bourgeoisie's control over everything," I said.

"Well, I can't disagree with that," Mike said. "You know that I have always considered myself to be a card-carrying member of the proletariat. All I have to offer is my labor and I have no desire to control the means of production because I don't want to have to fill out all of those forms."

"I'm with you there, big guy," I said. "So if Carrie works in DC and lives in Maryland, can we arrest her for registering her car in Ohio?"

"Very good question," he answered, "but probably not our highest priority at the moment, not if she's helping (in one way or another) to organize demonstrations, protests and other actions that disrupt the peace. Actually, she may find that Ohio registration convenient because it makes her look like a tourist in Washington and deflects any possible attention from her activities there."

"Possibly, but maybe a little too arcane…"

"You're right," he said. "Sometimes you can dive so deep that you could end up emerging in China."

"They could actually be one of her clients," I said.

"Noted," he answered. "But in the meantime I think I'll shift my focus to the old man. His boy Wayne's activities appear to be principally focused on making sure the coffee is hot for daddy's meetings and that the bloodsuckers who attend them are always greeted with a smiling face and a willingness to please."

"I await your intel," I said.

THIRTY-FOUR

That evening I returned to *Café Tatti* and ordered the boeuf bourguignon. For some reason or other I couldn't get it out of my head, probably because I wanted to wash it down with some red Bordeaux. When I entered, the waiter asked me if I wanted my usual table. *Mon dieu*; I was becoming a local institution. I passed on the soup/cheese course but succumbed to the profiteroles for dessert, drove back to my home away from home above the Director's garage and thought about our operation. I even added a cup of chamomile tea to help me sleep.

The box of teabags said that it was not recommended for people with allergies and people who were pregnant. Fortunately, neither applied to me. I studied hard in my biology classes and as a result I was well aware of the fact that in order to become pregnant you actually had to have some minimal human contact with another party. I was also savvy enough to realize that talking via phone or computer with someone 2,000 miles away plus change did not qualify in that particular regard. I was afraid that I was becoming as single-minded as people like Carrie Muller-Anderson but then I took a final sip of my tea, drifted off to sleep and reserved my consideration of the case for the morning.

With our time difference I gave Mike some time to sleep in while I made myself some breakfast and coffee. The Director's apartment was cozy and efficient and I appreciated the use of the car but I still wished that I could go for a morning run and release some of my action-deprived endorphins. Since that was not to be, I finished a muffin, replenished my coffee and got on the Director's computer.

I didn't have Mike's array of software but I could do a lot of basic searches and I started with Anderson's son, Wayne. Given the nature and proclivities of his father and his spouse I checked police records but found nothing of any substance. The only new event of a vaguely criminal nature that I saw in the files was a moving violation that was now 8 years old. The local press had picked it up because of his famous parentage. He was driving across a flat, open area in which he had 360 degrees of visibility. No one was near the intersection he was approaching and he rolled through a STOP sign. A cruiser emerged from behind a stand of trees and ticketed him.

The story was probably run because it had some minimal human interest and because everyone (regardless of their views on law and order) hates speed traps. He also appeared in a single story concerning his father's promotion of a night basketball program in which he appeared— in shorts and gym shoes—playing with a set of black and Latino kids. From all that I could find and see the guy really was (my math teacher would have said) a denizen of the null set. He had once gotten drunk in college (heaven forfend!), rolled through a STOP sign and principally spent his life attached to his father, working in capacities that required little more than an 8th grade education. The only strange thing in the record was the fact that Providence College had bounced him from their ranks when he had consumed too much cheap beer, thus incurring the loss of his future tuition fees. Perhaps they wanted to virtue signal their moral purity in the face of his father's prominence.

Carrie's career was a bit more substantive, even though it appeared to have ended, more or less, in the same place—doing the bidding of the old man. I was about to look further when there was a knock at my door. It was Charley Bondi.

"Heading out for some groceries," he said. "Can I get you anything?"

"Maybe McCaffrey's first name," I said. "I don't know what to call him."

"Just call him Mac," Charley said. "It's something like 'Leonard' or 'Leo' and he hates it."

"I can understand that," I said. "Actually I could use some more coffee." I told him the brand.

"Didn't you see the Director's secret stash?"

"No, I didn't."

"It's in the bottom drawer of the chest of drawers."

"If it's private I don't want to raid it," I said.

"I understand. Actually I'm also going to pick up some donuts. Can I tempt you?"

"Tempt away," I said. "Cake donuts dipped in chocolate; jelly-filled, powdered jobbies with strawberry jelly (or raspberry in a pinch) and anything that looks like a cinnamon roll. Two of each."

"You got it," he said. "Back in an hour or so."

I returned to the computer just as Mike's first message of the day came in. The subject line read: 'further stuff on the old man'.

"First off, he had 22 terms in the House. I don't know if that's a local record, but it's a long time to sit on hearings, hurry to the floor for votes and supervise staff who are mostly interested in building lines for their resumés. One noteworthy thing is that he was responsible for absolutely no legislation whatsoever…none…nada. Let me correct that. There's an item or two of local interest—fisheries and wildlife stuff—but nothing of substance, either regionally or nationally. Now, on committee work… that's a whole 'nuther story. With his longevity came seniority and with seniority came plum seats and chairmanships. In his case that's simple and straightforward…"

"Ways and Means and Appropriations," I said aloud.

"Appropriations and Ways and Means, in that order," Mike said. "Follow the money and you'll find old Curtis. He loves to spend; he loves to insert items of the porcine nature and he loves to, shall we say, 'maneuver'."

"The words *macher* and *gonif* have long come to mind," I said.

"In other words," Mike continued, "he stays so close to the line between legal and illegal that he obliterates it with his shadow. So far I've only seen a single instance in which he obviously crossed it, but the moment he was caught in the act of being himself he apologized and divested himself of the spiritual (and probably material) profits. It was a case in which an appropriation went to an NGO on whose board he sat. He beat his breast publicly, contributed his unspecified share of the ill-gotten gains to a children's hospital and went back to his normal day job of funneling money to contractors who could provide kickbacks from the shadows, far away from the public record. Since the contractors were doing projects for his constituents everyone turned their heads in the other direction, including the local media.

"He was also very careful about his public appearances. He was always there for the cutting of ribbons and the digging of the first shovel full of dirt, but he didn't grandstand or make his pivotal role clear. His consistent persona was one of a humble servant who was 'simply very honored and grateful that he could be of some help or service'. When the mayor, governor, or city manager whose personal wallet or little empire was the beneficiary of his largesse stretched out his arms, he smiled broadly, hugged them profusely, and then blushed, as if he was saying 'oh what a good boy am I'."

Mike followed with a host of examples, some with attached film clips. Whenever Wayne was standing at his side Mike noted the fact. He also noted that Ms. Carrie was never at his side, with one exception: his videotaped reaction to a protest at Oberlin College in which he attempted to be both measured and statesmanlike. Carrie was identified as a lawyer for one of the victims of the protest, whose car was overturned and set afire. "Oberlin is about 400 miles from Carrie's domicile in Silver Spring," Mike noted. "Pretty large operational orbit, in my opinion. Too oderiforous for my antennae. Sorry about the mixed metaphor."

"This is one slippery son-of-a-bitch," I thought, as Charley delivered my donuts. "Got you the fixins for your sugar high," he said.

"I'll need them" I said. "Many thanks."

THIRTY-FIVE

I went for the cinnamon roll first. How could I not? Then I thanked Mike for his notes. I confirmed with him our initial impression that Wayne was essentially a nonentity, asked him to continue the deep dive on his father and his father's daughter-in-law and told him that I was going to check in with the Director and see if he had any ideas.

"Some guesses though no ideas *per se*…but I think I could be of help to you."

"How so, Sir?" I asked.

"Let me make some calls. I think we can obtain access to some materials that might interest you and help us get closer to the bottom of this, or at least the bottom of some of it."

He called back in fifteen minutes. "Tomorrow is Wednesday, correct?"

"Yes, Sir."

"Come on into my new office tomorrow morning at 7:00 and I'll brief you. And tell me, Gwen, what size shoe do you wear?"

"Usually between an 8½ and a 9, depending on the manufacturer, Sir."

He paused to write that down.

"Wear clothing that will go with black flats."

"Will do, Sir," I said, wondering what in the world he was talking about and why. I had learned never to question him, because he was unfailingly clever and accurate in his judgments. On the other hand…?

That night I ate at *Rocco's*, a simple drive-up restaurant in McLean, a red/ white (vinyl) tablecloth place, where I had some rigatoni, meatballs and house Chianti. I had given up trying to suss out the Director's instructions with regard to tomorrow's footwear and chose to keep my head clear by limiting the wine to two smallish glasses. The pasta included a side salad and garlic bread, so I passed on the spumoni, even though it had tempted me.

Always wary of the local traffic (even at morning nautical twilight) I was at the new HQ at 6:40. Peggy was already there, setting up the coffee machine and putting some fresh milk in the Director's refrigerated cabinet. There was a shoe box on her desk. I wanted to question her about it, but chose to hold my curiosity in check. The Director arrived at 6:50.

"Coffee's ready if you want to start early," Peggy said.

"Sounds good, thanks," he answered and waved me into his office.

"I know the shoe business is driving you crazy," he said, "but it'll all be obvious. The cache of information to which you will have access is highly classified (though much of it will probably be drivel) and you're not allowed to take notes. If you reach inside the left shoe you'll find a little slide thingie under the instep. When you slide it to one side (I can't remember which, but it'll be obvious to you) the insole is released and you'll have access to a pad of paper and two pencils—the tiny kind that you use to keep score when you're playing golf. The second one is there for backup in case there's a problem with the first one."

"All to use in order to take forbidden notes."

"Right," he said. "We're the Federal Bureau of Investigation and should have access to these sorts of things, so we do what we can. My conscience is intact; this is all just bureaucratic maneuvering. The room will have more cameras than a TV sitcom set, but there's a unisex bathroom adjoining, which, in a civilized bow to modesty, is camera-free. Since I know that you have an impressive memory..."

"I remember the important intel, pop into the head, and take some quick note, as needed."

"Exactly."

"Can you tell me about the location of the cache, Sir?"

"It's in the Executive Office Building."

"Next door to the White House," I said, holding my expression.

"Yes, that one," he said, smiling.

"And the nature of the documents there, Sir?"

"All of the raw data and specifics of the DOGE investigations."

"The unit was always known for its transparency."

"Much more than most," he said, "but you know how these things go. There are always some materials that are eyes-only."

"And you're thinking that some of the names that have arisen in our investigation might surface in the DOGE files."

"Always a possibility," he said. "I'm thinking especially about potential linkages. These characters have a way of distancing themselves from one another in public, but they have Ms. Barry (and now her demise) in common. I'm wondering about who they really are, what they're really up to and…how we can put a definitive end to it."

"How soon can I get in there?" I asked.

The Director looked at his watch. "In about 40 minutes."

"Time to change my shoes," I said, smiling.

"You'll go to the fourth floor. If anyone asks, you'll tell them that you're going to the Indian Treaty Room. No one knows why they call it that, by the way. When you get there you'll be greeted by a woman named Casey. She actually works for the National Security Council. Very no-nonsense, but highly competent. She'll direct you to the materials."

"I should be going…"

"I have a car for you. You won't have to negotiate the parking at the White House. Peggy…" he said, over the intercom.

"The car's ready when you are," she said.

When I arrived at 1600 Pennsylvania Avenue a uniformed Army sergeant looked at the coded license plate number, approached me with a clipboard and asked my name.

"Gwen Harrison," I said.

"Come with me, please," he answered.

When I got to the Indian Treaty Room he told me that we were in the original Navy department wing, which housed a library and reception room. "President Eisenhower used it for press conferences." He looked as if he wanted to continue his spiel when he saw Ms. Casey approach us. He then clicked his heels as part of his about-face and departed quietly.

"Everyone wants to be a tour guide," she said. "Patricia Casey…"

I shook her extended hand. "Gwen Harrison…"

"Please follow me," she said, and led me to a small office just off of the main room. "Everything is labeled and self-explanatory," she said. "You'll have no difficulty locating the materials; the only challenge is their rather significant volume. I'm sure that the Director has told you that you're not permitted to carry anything in or out beyond the materials in your purse, which has already been inspected…"

"Yes," I said, withholding any 'ma'am' in order to protect my bureaucratic turf.

"And you're not permitted to take any notes…"

"Understood."

"You may stay as long as you like; if you wish to return tomorrow or some time in the future, call me at this number." She handed me a 3x5 card with a phone number and extension on it. No name or title, just her initials.

"Thanks, I appreciate that," I said.

"You'll also want something for lunch. We do sandwiches on Wednesday, probably ham and swiss on rye with some chips and a pickle on the side."

"Sounds fine," I said. "Again, much appreciated." I was wondering why the Director asked me if today was Wednesday. Perhaps he knew something about their protocols and was reinforcing the date for some as-yet unknown reason.

"Drink?"

"I'm fine," I said.

"I meant with lunch. There's a coffee and tea setup in the room."

"Any diet soda," I said.

"Unlike most restaurants we do both Coke *and* Pepsi," she said. It was the only mildly funny and human thing that she had yet said.

"Pepsi," I said. "Sugar and caffeine-free if possible."

"We can do that. Now…you'll want to get started. You'll see that there's also a restroom adjoining the document room."

"I appreciate that," I said. She then offered me the thinnest of smiles and walked away without any fond goodbyes or 'happy huntings'.

When I entered the room and assessed the situation I realized that my jaw had dropped to a degree that would have been noticeable (and perhaps pleasing) to Ms. Casey.

THIRTY-SIX

The library/document room was little more than 10'x10' and contained a single table and chair. The latter was simple and functional but, fortunately, well-padded. The table was surrounded by oak cabinets with narrow drawers. Above each drawer was a printed card, encased in plastic and identifying a federal department or agency whose records were contained therein. I opened the drawer for the Bureau of Land Management (very important to some, perhaps to many, but chosen purely at random) and found a set of partitions each of which contained a flash drive. The flash drive partitions also included brief descriptors (e.g. Contracts, 2015-2025). Each drive was a different size, ranging from a few megabytes to several terabytes of information.

None of the material was passworded, but when I randomly checked several drives each contained a gray banner specifying that none of the material contained therein could be printed or transferred. The material was presented in an utterly dull governmental format with no emojis, color (except in a few graphs) or background imagery. The information, however, was electric and the very good news was that each drive could be easily searched. Given the fact that I was dealing with something like 400-500 federal departments and agencies it was helpful to be able to type in a name like *Curtis Anderson* and see whether or not there was anything in the documents there that might be worth pursuing.

I began my scans after deciding that I should move from least likely to most likely. For example, the American Battle Monuments Commission came well before the ATF. I wanted to make sure that I had given a glance—even a cursory one—to all of the possibles that sat before me. There was also the matter of the heavy odds that our gang of four were not entirely stupid and that they might well utilize something less likely than something more obvious. There was money to be had in most all of the nooks and crannies of the government's offices and agencies and money would be their primary interest.

That they might find the U.S. Government to be a useful source for funds was undeniable. The Sutton principle of robbing banks because that's where the money is was always a good starting point and the enormities recently uncovered by DOGE were still fresh in the public's collective memory. Who would have ever thought that the National Science Foundation might actually pony up some $300K to promote diversity, equity and inclusion among bird watchers?

My one nasty little challenge was the fact that all of the drives were in alphabetical order. It made perfect sense, given the alternatives, but within each fascicle there were agencies of significant importance and others that would strike the reasonable individual as more or less trivial. For example, there were 21 units under 'P', including the Pacific Command and the Presidio Trust. The problem was that if I were going to go from least important to most important I would need to record which agencies I had set aside for deep dives versus those which I had breezed through rather quickly. Should I trust myself to remember which ones had already been inspected and which ones had been reserved for later? The one thing I could not do was get out my handy dandy mini-tablet from my SAS shoe and take notes while the cameras were busily recording my actions.

What saved me was DOGE's anal-retentive consistency. Each drive was positioned in the same direction within its little wooden holding cell and there was enough room in each slot to reposition them. I quickly concocted a rotation system, with one position denoting that the full drive had been inspected, while another position reminded me that the drive was (I said to myself) *virginal*. This is one of the ways that one gets through arduous tasks.

There was still another hurdle that I would have to negotiate: the cunning and subtlety of those seeking to attach their lips to the row of porcine teats that constituted the public trough (two can play at that mixed metaphor game, Michael).

For example, a sophisticated development or 'advancement' operation will have a wily drone on staff whose job it is to actually read through the federal budget. Perhaps it is a university and that university wants to erect a new building which will house faculty who study the grammars of obscure medieval languages. (Actually, that is a poor example; no one studies such things anymore except at a tiny handful of European institutions.) The point is that in my example there is a vast gulf between the uses of the building and the sources of its funding.

Our wizened individual, poring over the federal budget in a dark cubicle, determines a number of things. The governmental greenies are always looking at efficient HVAC systems and solar panel installations. The military are concerned with issues that fall under the broad umbrella of material sciences. What sorts of buildings are particularly vulnerable to certain forms of munitions? Which are not? The chief members of the Army officer corps were originally engineers. How does one construct bridges most efficiently? What are the materials involved? What are the mathematics involved? What weights will this or that material carry?

If our budget analyst in his distant cubicle only needs pennies, the National Endowment for the Humanities or Arts might have had an interest in certain aesthetic issues concerning the construction of his campus' new building. If he needs more he can promise more. ("We'll put solar panels on the roof or some Kevlar concoction on the siding if you'll buy the rest of the building.") The bottom line is that the federal government is potentially interested in anything and everything and our university in search of greenbacks for a bricks-and-mortar project could represent itself as ready and anxious to construct a 'demonstration project' that will help answer the questions of an agency which has no putative relation whatsoever to the university's individual goals.

In other words, the logical connection between the individuals seeking a seat at the public trough and the food therein may be nonexistent. It's more an 'I'm willing to do this in return for that' kind of thing and this is where both the cunning development office and the greedy office of Congressman Anderson overlap. Curtis 'gets behind' the university's search for prime bacon and then offers a list of potential contractors from his home district who can be counted on to present bids that will contain backhanders for Uncle Curtis, often via a foundation or other organization that will employ his pals or relatives, who will then kick back to the big guy. The greasing of these skids also often includes first-class flights and other emoluments which put smiles on faces, tasty food in hungry tummies and thick, soft cushions under fat asses. In short, this is how the system works and why our friends at DOGE filled the oak drawers with flash drives containing the epic accounts of the system navigators' exploits. Unfortunately for me the story was seldom told in linear fashion. A six year-old might understand all of the underlying principles but the actual dramatis personae and the convoluted plots were something else altogether.

Lunch was served promptly at 12:30, but I felt that I was just getting started. By 4:00 I felt like Lewis and Clark crossing the Rocky Mountains, hoping to somehow, some day, some way find a flat and fertile plain again. At 6:00 I decided to call it a day. When I was able to retrieve my phone I called the extension number of Ms. Casey (whose nickname for me had become 'Patty'), expecting her to be gone for the day. She was still at her desk; she asked me if she could expect me in the morning; I said yes; she said, "I thought so" and I walked out of the building and into the remaining sunlight, anxious to find something appetizing, but first and foremost something very alcoholic. I ultimately found my way to a place in McLean called *The Italian Oven*, where I first ordered a bottle of Amarone before even considering my choice of food.

That turned out to be a cup of Pasta e Fagioli and an order of Veal Marsala. I still felt a bit wired and finished off the last of the six glasses in my bottle of Amarone. Usually I would worry that that might make me sleepy, but after a day staring at a computer screen and trying to keep all of my personal flash drive position codes straight I knew that I could still pass any physical dexterity tests that a local cop might want to administer.

I left a message for Peggy, informing the Director that I was wending my way through DOGE's system but had not yet struck anything of value. 'I'll be there first thing in the a.m.' I said and slid between the sheets, not yet considering that tomorrow might be quite different from today.

THIRTY-SEVEN

9:00 a.m. sounds like a late-arrival time for work, but with Washington traffic, parking, et al. it comes on all too quickly. Patty Casey had changed her outfit from gray to grayer and generously told me the Thursday lunch selection: "Turkey club with a fresh fruit cup." I thanked her politely and entered the document room.

Before I settled in I opened several drawers and found that the drives had not been touched; my primitive but essential coding system remained intact. Bravo, Patty. I did notice that the coffee maker had been plugged in and the water was now fully heated. Bravo again.

While I recognized the need for security I still felt half-dressed without my iPhone and laptop. As I took my first sip of coffee I wondered how many duplicate sets of the drives had been created. One for Defense, one for Justice, one for State, one for the personal use of the President's inner circle? I also wondered how many were set up on computers with massive memory, computers with software that permitted the user to download and print and perhaps even annotate. I was restricted to use the setup prepared for the peons, but that setup still advanced my investigation considerably, as I would soon learn.

By noon I was working on Fannie Mae and the Farm Credit Association, with the FAA, FBI, Federal Bureau of Prisons and FCC looming on the horizon. None of my suspects would be using Fannie Mae for mortgages, but they still might have found a way to rip off the system. They could, for example, offer a portfolio of bad mortgages at inflated prices to Ms. Fannie. I considered that a long shot since the only person with any significant economic chops was Vanzetti and his preference would be for the destruction of a country or two's currencies rather than selling bad paper on cheap properties near a stagnant creek in Dog's Breath, Arkansas.

When the lunch trolley geared up for its midday run I took a quick bathroom break and thought about the afternoon's work schedule. No news (yet) was still news and I looked forward to eventually finding the pony beneath the manure pile (assuming that the poor thing was down there, struggling for air).

By 3:00 I knew that I would be back at work again in the morning. That pony was beginning to recede into the distance but I hadn't yet given up hope that it might eventually be located and ridden into the sunset. If anything, my limited optimism seemed to be increasing, in part because I was feeling more comfortable working the system. I had also gained confidence in DOGE's work product. The data sets were massive but the sense of completeness that they exuded was encouraging.

That evening I broke my pattern and checked out *The Capital Grille* at Tysons. I wanted some seafood. More particularly I wanted some Maryland blue crabs, complete with the little wooden mallets and the butcher paper spread across the picnic table, but I settled for some chowder and lobster/crab cakes, capping the dueling appetizers with some flourless chocolate espresso cake. It didn't make me sweat beneath my eyes (my original intention) and it was made with decaffeinated coffee but it was pleasant enough, even though the full array was a major budget-stretcher. I had counterbalanced the cost by passing on wine, a move facilitated by Mac McCaffrey's informing me that the Director permitted his guests to help themselves to his liqueur stash; I chose a playful little cognac served in a suitable snifter but restricted my intake to two pours. I slept like a teething 1940's baby whose gums had been slathered in paregoric.

The next morning I arose early, checked the slide thingie in my SAS shoe (this was becoming a regular habit) and presented myself to Patty just as the hour hand locked on the 9 and the minute hand crossed the 12.

"We used to do fish sandwiches on Friday," she said, "perhaps because of the chefs' Catholicism, but now we do Reubens. If you wish we can make you a simple grilled cheese."

"I'll take the Reuben," I said, "the real deal if possible."

"Both the corned beef and the turkey are good," she said, "but I'll put you down for corned beef, swiss cheese, kraut, thousand island and rye toast, if that's ok. We used to grill the sandwiches but the result was too greasy."

"Toasted would be my preference," I said, resisting the ongoing temptation to ask whether or not there was anything else on her mind but food, but realizing that this represented her permitted attempts at human interaction. She wasn't allowed to talk to interlopers about anything else.

By 3:00 I was thinking about dinner (the food talk was contagious) and by 4:00 I needed an extra jolt of coffee to make it through the afternoon. Then, at 4:40, the pony emerged from deep cover, came galloping over the horizon and presented its face to my hand in hopes of a nice nuzzle.

THIRTY-EIGHT

In 20/20 retrospect I should have begun there: the USAID. Its mission was as follows: The U.S. Agency for International Development (USAID) is the principal U.S. agency to extend assistance to countries recovering from disaster, trying to escape poverty, and engaging in democratic reforms (the obvious problem being the intended meanings of *disaster* and *democratic*).

The NGO which had received its grant was entitled *The Initiative for Peace in Gaza*. Once again, the trick was to decode the meaning of *Peace*. A word that would potentially attract the support of all was endlessly slippery, as were the terms on which the movement toward that state of affairs would depend.

The information attached to the appropriation and the organization receiving it was more minimalist than a stick figure drawn by a not-very-precocious 4 year-old. That was, clearly, the point. We're not talking about the simple exchange of cash for an ice cream cone; we're talking about Money Laundering and Misappropriation 101. There was, however, a single name attached to the board of the NGO: Paolo Palermi, Vanzetti's actual name. The fact hit me like a jolt of electricity across my vitals.

While the list of the board members ended in 'et al.' there was an attached addendum which included two other names. The first was Hassan Azimi; the second was Mikael Kuznetzov. I couldn't be sure if that was Petrov's real name, but the Azimi name was legit and the given name of Mikael squared with the practice of using current first names with authentic surnames.

The question now was what was the interest of the gang of three in the war between Israel and Hamas? Darvish might have been interested in arms sales but currency trading and drug smuggling were at the very least tangential to the war effort.

As the clock continued to tick I could feel my blood pressure and pulse increase and accelerate. Unfortunately my curiosity would have to wait until Monday before it could be even partially satisfied. Nevertheless, I was making real progress. The curious thing was that with each successful step I could sense an elevation in my heart rate and a reduction in the pain from my shoulder wound.

Friday night dinner services in northern Virginia would look like rush hour at Penn Station, so I picked up some sandwich materials, beer and chips at the *Giant* store and returned to the Director's garage apartment. I kept an eye out for the lights in his driveway; he arrived at 8:45. Long day for most, but much more common for him. I texted him and asked if he wanted an update that represented actual progress. He had eaten at his desk and told me to swing by at 9:00. I had already contacted Mike Liu and asked him to start gathering any information that he could on an NGO called *The Initiative for Peace in Gaza.*

"Sounds like a phony front if ever there was one," he said.

"This may well be the ultimate example," I answered.

"I'm assuming that some of our band of nasties may be involved," he said.

"They sit on its board; at least two do; hard to tell with the Russian's already-phony name. The other two are using their birth names."

"How about our friendly neighborhood congressman?"

"Nothing explicit that I could find," I said. "The problem is that I saw the listing late in the day and just got home. There were a few minutes left for me back in the stash room, but the computer there has no browser and is rigged to prohibit downloading one (as well as, for that matter, an email setup)."

"So you could read eyes-only material but otherwise felt as if you were operating an *Atari 8-bit*."

"Yep, something like that, but with no *Pong* software."

He laughed, happy to be more in his world than in mine.

"I'll lift some rocks and see if anything interesting slithers out," he said.

"Much obliged."

When I walked over to the rear door of the main house the Director had hung up his raincoat and 'gotten out of his wet clothes and into a dry martini.' I smiled approvingly when he offered me one.

"One of my favorite lines," he said, "after 'Say When' and 'Fill your hand you son-of-a-bitch'."

"I've always liked Don Corleone's 'I'm a superstitious man' threat," I said.

"So many great lines, so little time," he answered. "So tell me…what have you turned?"

"The story's still incomplete," I said. "I saw the reference but it was very late in the day; Mike's looking for more details, as we speak. It's an NGO funded by the USAID called *The Initiative for Peace in Gaza*."

"And their secondary motto is, 'if you're interested in purchasing the Bay Bridge we can offer you a very attractive discount'."

"Yes, it reeks of the rankest pile of bullcrap, but the palpable lies are all eclipsed by the membership of its board—Darvish, Vanzetti, and Petrov, but using their birth names rather than their current aka's."

"How about Anderson?"

"Nothing yet, but my gut tells me that if there's money to be made he'll be close to the teller's window."

"I've always liked your instincts," he said. "Maybe Mike will be able to turn something. There's a big problem, of course…"

"Yes," I responded, "the NGO's are black holes. The money goes in and then disappears through chains of offices, contractors, subsidiaries, distant cousins, other black holes, white dwarfs and, in particular, organizations whose goals run directly counter to the announced purposes of the original organization."

"Possibly the murkiest pit that DOGE plumbed."

"Mike would admire the alliteration, Sir."

"And how about doing him one better on a mixed metaphor: roaches check in…but they don't check out."

"Nice," I said. "The makeup of the board is interesting, even telling and probably highly significant, but *cui bono*?"

"Great question, Gwen. I can imagine Darvish being interested in selling all manner of contraband at all manner of prices, but I'm not sure where Vanzetti and Petrov would come into this. You see some Jordanian dinars on the West Bank but the Israeli new shekel is the most common currency in the Palestinian territories. I don't think Vanzetti would want to monkey with the Israeli economy, especially not if it entailed a later encounter with the Mossad. They'd crush him like one of those denizens of the Roach Motel."

"True, and we all know about narco-terrorism, but Petrov's principal channels for fentanyl and precursor products are China and Mexico, with longstanding Canadian routes and India as an emerging player. It could be a subsidiary enterprise or set of subsidiary enterprises, with Darvish calling up some of his fellow villains and asking them if they want to make some quick bucks at the expense of the American taxpayer."

"Good point," the Director said, "maybe they came in as investors for Darvish, who usually deals in high tech information but now needs to modify his operation and sell some plastic explosives and small arms."

"And definitely some anti-tank weapons," I added.

"Surely," he said.

"Drones?"

"Probably. Possibly surface-to-air missiles. Their cups runneth over. Fortunately they can't do much about the bunker busters that we provide for the Israelis."

"That's why they position their hostages where they do for as long as they can."

"True, unfortunately."

"I hope we can also implicate Anderson," I said. "Somehow the whole system seems incomplete without him."

"Let me know what Mike can discover."

"The moment I know…" I said.

THIRTY-NINE

Mike's call came in at 8:00 a.m. With the difference in time zones he had probably been working through the night.

"Gotcha a two-fer," he said. "Anderson double boofed."

"Great," I said. "Ready for the translation on the latter…"

"First," Uncle Curtis was giving a talk to some peaceniks at Cleveland State and he forgot himself for a moment and began preening over the fact that he had given his support to an initiative designed to bring peace to Gaza."

"A nice aha moment. Well done, Kemo Sabe."

"But he boofed twice," Mike said. "I found a full masthead for the NGO in the public record. Guess who was the managing director."

"Carrie freaking Muller."

"Actually C. freaking Muller."

"Kudos to the man with links to the Han Dynasty, a period of great success and prosperity, if memory serves."

"All applause will be remembered, recorded and appreciated."

"And the next question is…?"

"Was she there of her own accord, demonstrating her own shady proclivities…?"

"Or was she there as daddy-in-law's eyes and ears, keeping an eye on *his* investment?"

"The dates fit," Mike said. "She and Wayne were husband and wife at the time. For five years actually."

"Wedded bliss funded by international criminality or fueled

by misguided enthusiasm for international criminality masked as international do-goodism?"

"Or both?" Mike asked.

"That car's dirty, Cloudy," I said.

"Beg pardon?"

"Jimmy Doyle in *The French Connection.* The Director and I have been trading favorite movie lines."

"I remember now. They weren't going to give up until they found the drugs."

"Right."

"I liked the scene where the Frenchman's having a multi-course gourmet meal and Popeye's standing in the doorway, eating a slice of pizza and trying to stay warm. Speaks to the same degree of tenacity, but visually. Was it Hitch who said that you should be able to watch a great movie with no sound track and still know everything that's going on?"

"Probably," I said. "Unfortunately, I don't know exactly what's going on with the so-called Gaza peacemakers."

"You fill in the Director," Mike said, "and I'll go back to work."

"Let me have a long think," the Director said. "I'll rake some leaves, stack some broken limbs and thaw out some steaks. Come over around 7:00."

"Smells like rain, Sir," I said.

"I'll have some dry martinis ready," he answered.

"*Bombay Sapphire* ok?" he asked.

"Always my favorite," I responded.

"Up or rocks?"

"Whatever you're having," I said. "I'm an equal opportunity martini drinker."

"I opened the vermouth bottle and swung my palm over the top to get some faint mist in the area," the Director said. "Dry enough for you?"

"Now that you've already done that I'll have to soldier on," I said, as he smiled broadly.

"Ribeyes already defrosted; no going back."

"No need to, Sir."

"Medium rare?"

"Is there any other way?"

"The Boston SAC sends me potatoes from Aroostook County, Maine. They're oiled, wrapped and already on the grill. I know we should have something green; I sliced an avocado and filled the hollow pit with Italian dressing. That should provide us enough sustenance…that… along with this." He held up a bottle of *Chateau Palmer*.

"Didn't know we had a field office in Margaux," I said.

"Actually, that's a subject of some complexity. I actually receive a yearly allotment. Some think I should report it as a questionable gift. Not sure why. What can I actually do for the French? Wait…forget I said that. It's a legacy kind of thing. You know that I was Abe Abrams' aide at one time. Abe was Georgie's favorite tank commander; Georgie was an aide to Black Jack back in the day, etc. etc. The French have been generous in acknowledging their thanks and I'm the only one left in the chain. To the superannuated go the spoils…"

"If I may ask…"

"Two dozen bottles every year on July 4; delivered in a lovely little set of boxes with an image of the winery burned into the side."

"Cool," I said, "or make that…*cellar temperature*."

"We can have some sips while we wait for the beef to sear and sizzle."

"Back on your alliteration run, Sir."

"Can't help myself, I'm afraid. Michael's the master but I see it as an unavoidable challenge. So let's talk Curtis Anderson."

"Our initial question was whether or not his daughter-in-law is part of the so-called *Initiative* on her own steam or there as a spy for her father-in-law."

"A true believer or an evil servant? Could be both, of course," the Director said.

"Right. I think I mentioned in passing that the dates all align. She was married to Wayne long before the NGO was established and the group had made their application to USAID. Anderson almost surely put in a good word or two but he would have also stayed in the shadows as the process ran its course."

"Sure. Those appropriations were sometimes made in good faith and they sometimes did some actual good, but the entire setup was a license to steal. You slap an honorable title on your organization and then once the money has changed hands you funnel it through a set of dark channels and back alleys, after which it ends up in sleazoid organization coffers, gonifs' pockets, and God knows where else. Years later along comes an organization like DOGE and we discover that the taxpayers in struggling families in rural America have been footing the bill for munitions that ended up in the hands of terrorists killing those taxpayers' sons and daughters."

"And we're told that that was a tiny exception in an agency that has always done a world of good."

"That's the fact. I don't want us to sound like a couple of featured speakers at an RNC convention, but the facts are the facts and USAID once had $40 Billion to distribute, enough to do some good but more than enough to do some serious damage."

"We've been asking how Vanzetti and Petrov could benefit from this activity," I said, "but that may be the wrong question. Once in the hands of the NGO they could simply steal it."

"Put it in their general revenue funds," the Director said. "There was no need to have a specific project in mind; once their's they could do whatever they wanted with it."

"Bank robbery 101," I said.

"So long as the application looked plausible. They tell USAID that they want to deliver food, medicine and childrens' plush toys to the injured victims and then take the money to rent boats to supply ordnance, airplanes to ship fentanyl or use the capital to buy currencies in bulk."

"So what are they up to now?" I asked. "The bank's locked its doors in their face."

"That may be the key matter," the Director said, "not the question about what they're up to. They're probably up to all their usual practices; that's what they know best. The key matter is how they're getting their funding. People like this…they want to spend other peoples' money for their activities."

"Well, I don't think they're getting any of it from the college kids, blue-hairs and aging hippies at their miscellaneous protests and demonstrations."

"No, that's an opportunity cost," the Director said. "Buses, sandwiches, placards, permits, tee shirts, amplification systems, day wages for the marchers…"

"And how is that collective investment related to their promotion of their criminal operations?"

"I have a thought on that," the Director said.

FORTY

"I'm all ears," I said, as I ground some salt and fresh pepper over the butter and sour cream that were settling into the cuts in my baked potato.

"How's the steak?"

"Perfect," I said, "but not *perfect* in the sense that the *Palmer* is perfect."

"I doubt that the French will ever re-classify. As you surely know, Margaux was the only first growth in that area and Palmer was a third growth. Some say it should be a second growth now, but then there are those who say that there are no great wines, just great bottles of wine. It's all a little too chichi for me. I like what I like and I like *Palmer*."

"So say we all," I responded. "You were talking about why the gang of three or four were using the Barry woman to interview students, et al. To what purpose? We probably can say that they weren't pleased with her work and took her off the board before she could spill her guts to the feds, but what was the actual game that they were playing?"

"I think we may have misread Anderson's word when he was pounding the table and jabbing the air in her general direction with his index finger."

"*Chaos*?"

"Yes, *chaos*. We thought he was criticizing her operation or efforts. She was a soft-hearted bubblehead who lacked the eye of the tiger."

"He *wanted* chaos and she wasn't delivering it."

"Give the young lady another glass of that fermented grape juice."

"Milton imagined it as a person with a silent consort, Old Night. It's also a kind of area, a state before the Creation. Satan passes through it as he struggles to set himself up as God's adversary. Your basic allegorical figure."

"A bit above my pay grade," the Director said. "I'd put it more simply. The gang of four (yes, I'm comfortable with that number) wants to turn our country into shit through constant turmoil, turmoil that will draw attention from their activities which had been masked, in part, by the fact that their funding came via circuitous routes. They wanted to be able to make mischief while focusing everyone's attention on their noble motives. These days they're still selling guns to terrorists, ruining economies and poisoning teenagers, but in this case they think we'll all be less likely to notice because we're becoming obsessed with the screamers upsetting our sleep and the masked boys and girls in black throwing truckloads of Molotov cocktails into the hearts of our cities."

"And Allyson Barry was either not up to the task or thought she had signed on to persuade the uncommitted through the use of sweet reason."

"A real possibility," the Director said. "And a major miscalculation on their part. When they killed her they showed their hand."

"Not to trivialize the evil, but the long and the short of it is that their clear and present goal is little more than a studied attempt to control the news cycle," I said.

"The news cycle is not unimportant," the Director said, "particularly in a world where the bulk of the voters are staring at screens and accepting what they find there as some actual and ultimate form of reality. They're trying to control public consciousness. To put it in the military vernacular (and you'll forgive my saying this) they're grabbing the country by the testicles and pulling hard in the hope that the hearts and minds will follow."

"And our task is to strike them across the wrists with something that largely consists of hardened steel."

"Add some spikes and a nice leather grip and I'm there," the Director said.

After the dinner and some coffee the Director offered me dessert. "The name is a little off-putting. It's a favorite in St. Louis: ooey gooey butter cake."

"Don't tell me, Sir. The SAC from the field office sends it to you regularly."

"Guilty as charged," he said.

"How about if I take some with me for breakfast?"

"Done," he said. "Back in the day we might now have turned to cigars, but I know you won't turn down some of my best Armagnac."

"Another gift from the grateful French people?" I asked.

"No, I get it at Bassin's."

By now we were both smiling.

"I don't heat it or anything," he said. Too decadent."

"Agreed," I said.

As we started in on a second glass the Director's face became more serious. "You don't believe we're overthinking this, do you Gwen?"

"How so, Sir?"

"Creating protests, directing demonstrations, marches, sit-in's, whatever...all to mask some ongoing criminal enterprises?"

"I think it's a matter of scale," I said.

"Go on..."

"A handful of snot-nosed kids with some spray cans of fluorescent paint...some angry old ladies taking leave of their cats on a Thursday afternoon and gathering together for a good chant...no, that's more comic opera. The conservatives turn it into film clips for their next political campaign. As often as not they make people...well, not laugh so much as to feel superior: 'Don't they have jobs? No, of course not. They're angling for handouts from the government or short-term, mindless employment paid for by George Soros. Note the purple hair and the nose piercings, the granny gowns and the tie-dyed scarves, the girly men along for the ride...' The clips rotate endlessly through the Fox cycle. I think the gang of four would have to set their sights much higher. They'd have to take these things to a different level, something that will prompt a more all-encompassing response…make everything else stand still, frozen in space…"

"Something like Covid," he said.

"Yes, exactly, something that could be the stuff of fear and outcry. Something that moved everything off of the front page (if people still read newspapers). Something that could lead to obsession, something that crowded out everything else in your brain so that you take 'routine' criminality as little more than background noise…"

"Country-wide demonstrations and protests could do that," the Director said. "It could be a form of pandemic, if not the real thing."

"It would also have to be worth the investment," I said. "A few years ago they could count on cash from USAID to finance operations or serve as startup funds. They don't have access to that money anymore…"

"We're assuming that they're using their own money for this activity. If they are they're probably planning to expand their operations significantly. The bigger the smoke screen you create, the larger the operation you're attempting to mask."

"There's another possibility," I said. "They could have a major-league sugar daddy who's investing in the protest operations in order to secure a large piece of the resulting criminal profits."

"I can imagine our sleazoid congressman brokering something like that. He wets his beak the easy way—by introducing people to one another over lunch or drinks at his private club, never really having to get his hands dirty with wet work. Although there is that matter of Ms. Barry's death…"

"Another thought…" I said, "the balance in these protest activities falls in several possible directions. You have the idlers who have nothing else to do. You have the angry ideologues who are against everything. You even have the true believers who think they're hastening the arrival of a utopia in which they will finally be exonerated and worshiped appropriately. You have the ultra-cynics and anarchists…the people who are simply frustrated and angry and want everyone else to be so as well. You have the pols who see this as an opportunity to advance their own careers…purely and simply…no matter what the cost to their personal constituents and other taxpayers' dead children."

"And if you're looking for funding, the easiest way might just be to find someone who is angry with the country. Dare I say, someone who simply hates it and has the means to act on that hatred."

"Very true," I said, "but often with some kind of backstory or personal element. The hatred comes from personal shame or some grotesque form of envy…even in someone with the financial means to do pretty much anything he or she desires to do, the kind of person who—despite his or her financial success--can never find contentment. Johnny Ringo with the hole in his soul, but with the resources of Midas."

"*Chaos* is a variant of anarchy," the Director said. "It disrupts the lives of the more…contented…the people who are the object of his or her envy."

"Satan was into envy," I said.

"Very spiritual and religious," the Director said, "and I think I can do you one better. Jesus asked what it would profit you if you gained the whole world but lost your soul in the process. It's the question we pose to the angry revolutionaries, the question that they never answer. We may be finding ourselves in the middle of that world, even as we speak. The criminality, the banal forms of evil…all small potatoes if we're dealing with a shadowy source with far more at stake."

"Like a Bond villain, but in the real world," I said, "someone who wants to take over everything and bend it to his will. His first step is to flood the street with angry screamers who can undermine the faith of those we think of as happy…or at least at peace."

"In which case the criminals are little more than useful idiots. The head villain tires of them, pushes a button and their chair at the S.P.E.C.T.R.E. table explodes and collapses into the floor. They think they're using him and his money while the actual situation is the precise reverse. The money is incidental; the megalomania born of rage is the real be-all and end-all and they're pawns who are easily sacrificed."

"Even if that's the Armagnac talking, I like the message," I said. "Let me take your religious point and recast it a bit..."

The Director topped off both of our glasses, swirled the liquid in his and sat back in his chair.

"Think of Jesus in the desert," I said. "The devil comes to tempt him in three stages. He suggests that Jesus turn the surrounding stones into bread and end his hunger. Jesus passes. He suggests that Jesus throw Himself down from some great height and be saved by a group of angels. Jesus passes again. Satan reaches for his hole card. He offers Him dominion over all of the world. There's only one catch..."

"In for a dime, in for a dollar," the Director said. "You can control the world but in order to do so you have to worship Satan."

"Allyson passed when she saw the direction in which this was all heading."

"And they crushed her beneath a car tire," the Director said.

"Maybe that's where we start," I said. "We find out (and prove) who actually killed her. Then we find out who the real Satan is."

"Assuming that Anderson is our proximate suspect (and that we can convince him that we have the evidence to convict him) we can turn him against the other three. That would give us four paths back to whoever is ultimately behind this, assuming that our *éminence grise* scenario is accurate."

I sipped the remainder of my Armagnac and asked the Director if I could have some plastic wrap for my ooey gooey butter cake.

As I walked toward his back door he said, "And let's not overlook the possibility that the great Satan might actually be a country. Occam's razor; simplest explanation."

"That's what they call *us*," I said, "the great Satan."

"It's called *projecting*," he said. "Let's keep it in mind."

FORTY-ONE

The St. Louis dessert was excellent, especially when cast against the taste of strong coffee. I wondered how it retained its freshness and moistness, from initial packaging and final delivery with an intermittent 800 miles of travel time.

Mike had a number of ideas, all suggesting the use of toxic chemicals, so I steered him away from the subject and told him that our next step was to attempt to find connections between Curtis Anderson and the death of Allyson Barry.

"With sufficient evidence you could sweat him and see if he'd give up some of his partners (or his final boss)."

"Exactly," I said, "but we don't want to let him off the hook completely. Obviously all four had contact with the victim and all could be involved in her murder, but while we would try to work each against the other we would still want all to go down for the crime."

"Always good to remember that we have capital punishment at the federal level, even if we don't use it very often," Mike said.

"Right," I answered. "In this case we would also want to find out who's pulling the strings behind the gang of four. We're thinking that it has to be someone (or some country?) with significant means. These characters can no longer rip off the taxpayers through USAID grants to NGO's, but they're still mounting a large operation, one that would require megabucks. They could be self-funding, but that's not their usual style. These are the kind of people who like to spend other peoples' money first, as well as the kind of people who like to insulate themselves through the use of street soldiers and useful idiots. They want to feast on the fruits of other peoples' labor and they are always at pains to make sure that they can escape undetected, or at least unindictable.

"They'll throw crumbs to the little people to buy some street cred as penny-ante philanthropists and they'll buy the influence peddled by politicians or put bent cops on their pads, but these are not guys who clean up crime scenes with jugs of bleach. They're above all of that."

"But they (or some of them, or at least one of them) will have people who do the wet work for them and you want me to start with Anderson because he was the last person we know of who interacted with the victim."

"And in a particularly aggressive manner," I added. "He may also have the most to lose because he's not in the position of the others, where their crimes are recognized as such and are under constant investigation. They're well-practiced in the hiring of white-shoe law firms to keep investigators at bay. Self-protection is a major cost for them in doing business. Anderson, on the other hand…"

"He counts on his personal status," Mike said, "and on his connections within the system--grateful constituents, grateful communities, grateful cities, grateful states…"

"Yes. He sees himself as above it all. There is no way in hell that he could ever be prosecuted…or so he believes."

"I'll poke around and try to discover the identity of his lampreys," Mike said, "particularly the ones with whom he does not wish to be publicly associated."

"Exactly, but I'm not sure where you start," I said. "The shavetail go-fers and tertiary-level phone answerers will all be long gone. They've moved onward and upward within the bureaucracy or toddled off to Yale law school. They're weasels, not gorillas. I also doubt that his daughter-in-law would be available for serious fieldwork. She might be an out-and-out criminal, but it's a long step from felonious behavior to driving the wheel of a car back and forth over a young woman's head."

"I'd start with his security detail," Mike said.

"That's why you've got the big computer screens," I said, "but your basic congressman doesn't usually have a security detail."

"Technically not," Mike said, "but he'll have the Capitol Police around him when he's in town and it's possible that he could have some state-and-local types when he's back home. They could be assigned some security in the case of things like personal threats or times of crisis. I would assume that a character like Anderson--one with so many markers to call in and with so much longevity--would know how to work the system, especially when he's within the boundaries of his own congressional district."

"He never served in the military," I said, "or in any form of law enforcement, so his path would not have crossed with anyone who could be considered armed and dangerous. Or at least none that we know of at the moment."

"He might have intervened with the Ohio governor or even with the White House to secure a pardon for some ne'er-do-well who could then be tapped to barter his services in return for the favor," Mike said.

"Good idea," I responded, "and his congressional district of Cuyahoga County includes all of Cleveland. There are Crips there, Latin Kings, and all manner of local gangs. It's more than likely that he's done business with some of them and could call in a marker. The problem is that the method of execution of Allyson Barry was more technocratic. The gangs are more into guns and knives than car tires."

"True," Mike said. "Give me a couple hours and I'll see what I can find…"

FORTY-TWO

He took three. By then I had made a run to the *Giant* store and replenished my food supplies. I texted the Director with a brief message to the effect that Mike and I were investigating Anderson's associates who might be capable of Allyson Barry's murder. As always, he volunteered his help, 'should we need it'.

Mike began by telling me that he had good news and bad news. "The good news," he said, "is that Anderson had a Cleveland PD officer on permanent assignment to him, a rough-around-the-edges former marine with an OTH (other than honorable) discharge. Usually this would be a serious impediment to post-service employment, but if Anderson had smoothed the way for him in the Cleveland PD the Cleveland PD might have responded by employing him and then assigning him to Anderson in a kind of 'you broke it, you bought it' action. The guy's name was Carl Snyder and the past tense is the bad news. Snyder died in 2013."

"Damn," I said.

"But there's other good news," Mike said. "Snyder was sick with multiple myeloma for years. He wasn't fully incapacitated but he was under constant medical care that involved long hospital stays. When he contracted the disease they hadn't made the current strides in treatment that they have at their disposal now. He was, however, well enough to mentor a successor."

"Who is still with us, I hope."

"Very much so," Mike responded.

"And you're about to reveal his identity…"

"Of course. His name is Virgil Snyder, Carl's younger brother."

"And does he appear to be capable of murder?"

"He appears to be capable of just about anything. No military background; more of a wannabe. Someone told him once that marines are taught to begin a hand-to-hand battle by pulling off their enemy's ears. The purpose is to 'get their attention' but also to distract them from whatever their plan had been in their attack on you."

"Cute."

"The problem is that Virg actually did it. He was working as Anderson's bodyguard when he was paying a visit to hostile union territory. When a protestor approached Curtis, Virg sprung into action and went for the guy's left ear. When the guy began screaming and flailing Virg went for his ribs, trying to kick 70-yard field goals. The story circulated as an internet meme but Curtis was able to have it suppressed in the local and national legacy media, including the 6:00 and 11:00 news. The interesting thing was that Virgil was able to keep his job. Apparently Curtis thanked him publicly for his dedication to duty and reamed him out privately for his grotesque overreaction."

"I wonder what kind of car or truck he drives," I said, "and whether or not there's any bone or blood left in the tire treads."

"He drives a Ford F-150 when he's not driving Anderson's car," Mike said.

"Got an address?"

"It's in the text I'm sending you."

"Let's hope the truck isn't locked in a garage," I said. "I'll ask the Director if he'll send someone from the Cleveland field office to check it out. Anything else on this character?"

"No local rap sheet beyond some traffic violations. He went to a local high school, did some community college, worked on government-contracted road crews (probably gigs that resulted from his brother's connection with Anderson)."

"Construction crews or cleanup crews?" I asked.

"He picked up dead animals," Mike said.

"Why am I not surprised?"

"He's used to getting his hands dirty," Mike said.

"Roger that," I responded.

After my interchange with the Director a special agent from the Cleveland field office put on a city services uniform and drove to Snyder's home. The driveway was empty, the garage door closed. There was, however, some good news. A short time later, Snyder was picked up on a CCTV camera, driving Anderson to a local ribbon-cutting in one of Anderson's *Mercedes*. It was a community health facility whose funding Anderson had facilitated. The field office directed the local special agent back to Anderson's house, where he found Snyder's F-150 inexplicably parked in the driveway. Equipped with a clipboard and a bored expression the special agent walked up and down the street, inserting natural gas line flags. When he got to Snyder's truck he slipped down quickly and dislodged gunk from the tire treads. His hopes fell, however, when he smelled the bleach that had covered the left front tire, the wheel well and the bumper and undercarriage.

"He must have bathed his truck in it," the Director told the SAC.

"Good news and bad news, Sir," the SAC responded. "There's probably no remaining evidence involving blood, bone, tissue, etc., but there's definitely evidence of a cover up. When's the last time you saw someone dip his truck in Clorox?"

The Director communicated the result of the search to me, reinforcing the conclusion of the guy who had attempted to take the samples. "It's like the scene in that James Bond movie, where Bond is walking through the wooded area with the voodoo signs warning him to stay out. He knows the signs are phony but he also knows that he's going in the right direction."

"Mike's looking for more evidence," I said. "I know we can't take any of this to court but I'd love to see this lowlife on the stand, trying to explain the reason for the bleach bath."

"I hit an animal on the highway; thought it might be rabid," the Director said, in a higher-pitched voice. "Given his line of work he's probably an experienced liar. He could always come up with some excuse, but it might still raise a jury's collective eyebrows."

"That's true, Sir," I admitted.

"Either way, Anderson would probably be a golfing partner of the judge, a drinking partner of the bailiff, a contributor to the DA's campaigns and a friend of half of the members of the jury."

"True, Sir; that's what we're up against," I said.

"It's still damned good work," he said. "Michael can focus his attention on Anderson and his minion rather than his explicitly-criminal syndicate partners. While I have you on the line…"

"Yes, Sir?"

"A couple of our field offices have CI's in the local political communities. The word is that we can expect some major demonstrations and protests, One has already been scheduled for tomorrow afternoon."

"Location?"

"Right here in old DC," he said.

"Anything more specific?"

"Air and Space."

"Interesting," I said. "Not much of a political target, but a major tourist site."

"Want to observe first hand?"

"I would love to," I said. "I'll try to dress for the part."

"Gwen…"

"Yes, Sir…?"

"Stay on the periphery. This could be ugly."

"Understood," I said. "And thanks."

Once again, the pain in my shoulder diminished as I thought about participating in an actual operation.

The target (if that is the appropriate word) was a complicated one. Because of its popularity the Museum was a continuing work-in-progress with multiple new galleries recently opened and a number of additional ones under construction. It had the protestors' prime desiderata: it attracted a lot of people. Those people had to make arrangements via timed-entry passes. If their experience was frustrated or disrupted they would be angry. If they were there in serious numbers they could be confused and frightened. There could be medical emergencies, significant injuries and possibly even deaths. The full gamut of experiences was possible, from a memorable outing in the sun to a horror show of violence and gore.

I was wearing plain jeans, a dark sweat shirt and a baseball cap with a Washington Nationals logo, picked up from a souvenir stand on the opposite side of the Mall. I had also brought along a recently-purchased DSLR from *Best Buy*, gravitating toward an inexpensive *Panasonic* rather than a *Nikon* or uber-expensive *Canon*. I was doing my best to look like a tourist rather than a snoopy poop from one of the intelligence agencies. Fanny packs had made a comeback so I could wear one in lieu of carrying a purse. The camera hung from mid-sized leather straps across my chest. I also sampled a food truck hot dog and carried the required *Starbucks* venti cup.

The National Mall is large—approximately 2 miles from the Capitol to the Lincoln Memorial; the width varies from approximately 600+ feet to 1,500+ feet. Bottom line: a little over 300 acres. This is all helpful, since there is ample space in which to disappear, ample sites to photograph, and ample activities to provide distractions, from serious individuals visiting the Vietnam Memorial to young, shirtless government workers tossing baseballs and frisbees and a panoply of tourists trying to wend their way through pedestrian traffic while also attempting to corral small children and leashed dogs, the latter always pulling in opposite directions from the kids.

I was comfortable with the fact that I was able to maintain

my anonymity but also take high quality photographs in the event that activities required them, which, as it turned out, they most definitely did.

FORTY-THREE

First came the chants. They were designed for this particular occasion, with lots of rhymes and alliteration. The general theme was that we should forget about exploring space and instead look for suitable housing sites for the poor on terra firma. There were particularly snarky asides with regard to the newly-created Space Force. I thought about associations with Cheyenne Mountain, the Air Force Academy and Wright-Patt. Were there any possible connections there?

The chants were followed by the spray paint. The Museum itself is something of a fortress (with the exception of the walls of glass panels) but the defacing of the pink Tennessee marble would make an ugly and noticeable statement. At the first sighting of paint cans the area was swarming with police. The DC Metro police were joined by the Park Police as well as the Office of Protection Services from the Smithsonian. Protestors were promptly thrown on the ground and subdued with heavy-duty flex cuffs. I was surprised to see the degree of vigor in the police actions; these were no-nonsense takedowns and if some cheeks hit the pavement with particular force it was unlikely that any apologies would follow.

If anything brought cash to the city (beyond the White House itself) it was the Air and Space Museum and this golden egg-producing goose was receiving the full protection of local law enforcement. This gave the visitors from the south and midwest who were observing the action a particular frisson of pleasure. Some of the tourists (who had been moved to the grass on the Mall) looked as if they would have enjoyed participating in the action.

Then things got serious, as a flash of fire struck and spread from the base of the Museum's main entrance on Independence Avenue. While there were multiple phalanxes of police, there were far fewer firefighters. Station 11 on H Street was only a mile away, but that trip could easily be extended by DC traffic, particularly during a moment of crisis.

While there was no great damage done to the building proper, a number of police officers who had attempted to put out the flames were injured seriously, which precipitated increased violence in the capture of individuals suspected of throwing the Molotov cocktails. These sorts of protests tend to begin with formulaic actions—the drawing of lines, the lodging of taunts, the utilization of bullhorns, the swinging of placards and the establishment of police positions, but the moment a firebomb is thrown all bets are off and a pitched battle ensues.

I was taking as many pictures as I could, without looking like a cub reporter, and I was struck by the fact that no one among the protesters seemed to be surprised by the escalation. This had been planned and it appeared to have been planned in detail. If individuals were hurt or even killed there would be no regrets. Fortunately, there were no gunshots heard, but the ranks of the protesters were filled with lean young men in black suits and balaclavas. There may have been a cat lady or two with weird-colored hair and multiple piercings but if there were I didn't see any of them. This had the scent of the paramilitary and accounted, in part, for the equal and opposite reactions by the local police.

The chanting continued as the more active protesters were arrested and the police were called all manner of vulgar and obscene names. I continued to take pictures, hoping that I would be able to secure some images of organizers and managers in the background. When there were breaks in the action I sent images to Mike, asking him to scan the shots, looking for any familiar faces.

When the protesters had been dispersed and the police and firefighters were replaced by cleaning crews, scrubbing off the scorch marks as best they could, I was surprised by the fact that the preponderance of the tourists remained on the Mall, waiting to see if there were any further actions that could be recorded on their cell phones. The police continued to tell them to 'move back' but the tourists continued to reclaim their positions, moving a bit but then returning in waves. Curiosity trumps safety.

The firebombing was serious business. As I made my way through the crowds I listened for individual reactions, all of which were decidedly negative. If the purpose of the protest was to win support from third parties it was a complete and utter failure. On the other hand, if its purpose was to draw attention and distract focus it was a demonstrable success.

"Distraction, Gwen," the Director said. "Capturing the news cycle. And think of the target. Think of the kids in the hinterlands anticipating their spring trip to DC. Think of the families wanting to see those space capsules and astronaut suits, Wright Brothers' stuff and lunar landing photos. You think about visiting the White House and the first thing that comes to mind is waiting in line, but the Air and Space…pure fun. Then you think about being engulfed in flames, your babies being burned or maimed, the highlight of your trip ruined beyond repair.

"This has rational impact," he continued. "You think of one of our distant military outposts attacked by terrorists and you become angry and concerned. You want an appropriate and definitive response, but something like this…in the homeland…this makes it all very, very personal."

"They may be evil bastards," I said, "but they're not stupid."

"And they're not timid," he answered. Ms. Barry may have been motivated by some form of misguided idealism. Not these characters. They've stepped up their game. This is about money and power and dominance, damn the costs (human or financial)."

"You said that the Bureau's CI's had identified other possible sites, Sir…"

"Nothing this specific, Gwen, but it was to be something serious. The general site was the eastern seaboard, but we don't yet have a precise location."

"So…possibly New York?"

"Always a favorite target," he said. "Everyone there is now on high alert. There's something else…"

"Yes, Sir?"

"As you know, there's no place to park a bus around the Museum, but the police have been checking the parking lots around L'Enfant Plaza…"

"Yes, Sir?"

"They found boxes with bottles and wicks and jerry cans of gasoline in the trunk of a stolen car."

"Serious planning," I said. "The amateurs are on the sidelines or just being plugged in as spear carriers and robo-protesters."

"So it would seem," the Director said.

"Just a sec, Sir. I'm getting a text from Michael, who's been examining my pictures for familiar faces…"

FORTY-FOUR

"See the attached," Mike said. "Images 142, 157 and 159. One of your old friends."

I had to manipulate the images in order to home in on the specific faces.

"In the deep background," Mike said. "Largely in profile."

"Rafe Willis," I said. "As I live and breathe. The guy from Georgetown in the joint program. Law and Public Policy?"

"The very same," Mike said.

"No clipboard but he's working that large cell phone pretty intently."

"Not the brightest bulb in the chandelier," Mike said. "If you're on the internet you're hackable. Far better to do the paper and pencil thing."

"Unless he's an innocent bystander. What are the odds on that?"

"Standing in the midst of things? One in several million," Mike said. "It's true that he's not dressed like a ninja warrior and he's not throwing any firebombs or yelling any slogans, but he's there, on the scene, receiving and sending information."

"Like the J-school student in downtown Chicago," I said. "What's your best guess—they're trying out to be Bluebell's replacement or they're station chiefs of some kind?"

"The latter," Mike said, "because you haven't seen everything I've been able to turn."

"The floor is yours," I said.

"This was the tough one," Mike said. "Images 173-176."

"Woman. Civilian clothes but her face shaded by the bill of her baseball cap and her chin and lower lip covered by a scarf. Blurry image. Enough for your facial rec software? Oh, wait…of course. That's Anderson's daughter-in-law."

"Facial rec can be iffy," Mike said, "but body type is hard to alter, especially when you wear form-fitting clothes rather than a tent from the House of Omar."

"No bullhorn, no firebomb, no flailing arms," I said.

"She's grading Willis," Mike said.

"Possibly," I said. "Certainly she's reporting back to daddy-in-law."

"She's in it up to her eyeballs," Mike said. "Watch your inbox."

A set of images appeared.

"Parking ramp," I said.

"L'Enfant East Parking Garage," Mike said. "Beaucoup cameras. She thought she was in some sort of safe space once she left the Mall and Air and Space. Dumbass. Look at the last picture."

"Long shot," I said. "Fuzzy. You really had to magnify it."

"Yes, indeed," he answered. "Look closely."

"She's slipping off her hat and scarf and putting them in the trunk. That's suspicious enough; it acknowledges that she was wearing a form of disguise."

"Un-huh. Look in the trunk."

"Scooched under the back seat on the driver's side. Flat box."

"Now look at the other side; it's mostly masked by the rear fender."

"The top of a jerry can," I said. "At least it could be."

"Upstanding citizens don't drive around with the makings for Molotov cocktails," he said, "and no one now would use a jerry can to carry water in the middle of a modern city."

"Her lawyer would plead that the gasoline can was to carry fuel for her lawn mower," I said.

"Of course he would," Mike said, "but we're not in court now; we're still doing the preliminary investigation."

"That car is dirty, Clowny," I said.

"You took the words right out of my mouth," he said.

"So you think old Carrie is the new Allyson?" I asked.

"That's where the smart money would be," he answered.

I brought the Director up to speed and we talked about next steps. He was particularly concerned with the escalation.

"They're ready to hurt civilians," he said, "not *risk* hurting civilians but actually doing so. Back in the days of Vietnam the half-hearted demonstrators would sometimes tell you that they were on the scene because it was a good place to meet girls. Those days are gone. These people are going for a big statement and they don't have any concern for the possible consequences."

"Where next, Sir? You thought somewhere in the east, possibly New York…"

"Too late for St. Patrick's Day, thankfully. You line the streets of New York, the marching bands masking sounds and all the noise and color and activity drawing attention away from the shadows…things could get very ugly very quickly. I'm not sure they're ready for mass murder, but a few Claymore mines along a parade route…700 steel ball bearings propelled by a pound and a half of C-4…dangerous up to 250 meters…3 pounds apiece…slip 'em in your backpack…"

"They seem to be interested in cultural damage as well as political protest," I said. "Air and Space is an institution, in a way. So is Daley Plaza."

"We don't have to confine ourselves to New York," the Director said. "The anniversary of the Battle of Concord is coming up. Odd year however; they've already had their 250th. That would still be a premium target if you wanted to exhibit a hatred for the country. Also, you've got your marching bands, your reenactors and a vulnerable, signature site."

"Emerson's 'shot heard round the world' brought to life again, big time," I said.

"You think you want to fight a war for your freedom…we'll show you how easily we can take all of that away from you," he said.

"Let's hope you're right, Sir. The off year minimizes the impact and the target becomes less interesting to them. It does seem that our original estimates were correct. You fill the Air and Space Museum with flames and murder the visitors from middle America and suddenly a few more bags of fentanyl are of little concern. Ditto the arms sales and the currency manipulations."

"Like Dr. Johnson said about the way in which the prospect of being hanged concentrates the mind," the Director said. "There's something special about certain forms of violence. When you're thinking about the beheading of one of Henry VIII's wives on Tower Hill or a crowd at Tyburn two centuries later waiting for the condemned to kick his legs in the air as he strangles himself on the slack rope or the renters of telescopes as the heads of rebels are put on spikes above Temple Bar you forget completely about the pickpockets and prostitutes along the Strand. Standard criminality recedes into the background and the lesser bad guys enjoy greater opportunities for expanded operations."

"You're basically controlling the focus and the emotions of the people in the city."

"Who metastasize into a mob," he added, "one motivated by shock, awe, anger and fear."

"And depending on the dimensions of the expanded operations the opportunity costs become justified," I said. "Still, we're talking big money."

"A vast amount of money, especially if the demonstrators are real pros and not just bubbleheads looking for something to occupy themselves with on a Thursday afternoon. The weaponry would be easy, however. You wouldn't have to buy special bottles whose manufacturer could be traced and you could fabricate wicks from any number of possible materials. As you and Mike discussed, jerry cans for lawn mower fuel are omnipresent. Claymore mines, however, would be a big leap, though Darvish could doubtless supply them. The principal investment (so far) would be in the personnel, their means of transport, clothing, placards and so on."

"The conveyance of the actual message would be very pricey," I said. "The hatred of America pronouncement would require a noteworthy location, probably one that would involve logistical challenges and obvious threats from law enforcement."

"Go on, Gwen."

"I'm just thinking out loud…perhaps the hatred of America subtext is actually the real text. The demonstration has to be dramatic and it has to be of use to the personal criminal activities of the gang of four, but the price tag of something larger could be covered by someone with very deep pockets. This is not the gang of four upping the ante; this is someone in league with the gang of four with larger ambitions, someone for whom the gang of four could provide insulation…distance…protection."

"An attack on the country itself," the Director said, "or at least an initial action in a propaganda war of some sort, a statement being made by a foreign adversary or a personal pronouncement by some individual hater."

"A very rich hater," I added.

"Unfortunately we have many of them," the Director said. "What you're suggesting is that we're operating on a system of connected levels: the street soldiers and useful idiots, organized by local true believers like Willis, directed by Carrie Muller, for the benefit of the gang of four, but with some as yet-unidentified Mastermind standing above it all…"

"Relishing the coming wet work," I added.

FORTY-FIVE

We decided to focus our attention on Curtis Anderson's daughter-in-law. We knew that she was connected directly to those above and below her in the chain of command.

"First, I have to apologize," Mike said. "I told you that Ms. Carrie was working for government agencies. Most recently she worked in the Civil Rights Division of the DOJ, but that was for a brief period of time. If I had to guess I'd say that she was probably let go because her methods were a little too aggressive for the current administration's taste, not that they're loathe to enforce civil rights legislation but they don't want to see blood on the barricades. She left her post there about six months ago. She's not on *LinkedIn* or *Facebook* or other such platforms, but a recent picture of her standing next to Wayne's daddy identified her as an attorney in private practice."

"To be fair," I added, "(and in her case it's a stretch for me to be fair), the time spent in office by many federal lawyers is very, very brief. At one of my alumnae do's I met up with a former Kenyon classmate who worked at the Federal Trade Commission. The person there with the greatest longevity had been there 18 months."

"I understand," Mike said. "They come to DC, log some time, pencil in a line on their c.v.'s and then head to the big rock candy mountain in the private sector. DC costs too much and pays too little…"

"Unless, of course, you're in Congressman Anderson's world where you move from a relatively modest salary to a net worth in the millions."

"I was still curious about that Kia," Mike said. "If she were a pure idealist or a pure anything I could understand it, but if she's willing to do bad things for bad people I would expect something in the way of a profit motive. So, I checked and I found a second registration. It now appears that the Kia is Wayne's to drive. Ms. Carrie actually drives a Lexus *NX 300*. New model. All the bells and whistles."

"Hybrid?" I asked.

"No, and it requires premium gas. It seems that her hypocrisy only extends so far."

"Slap in the face to Wayne."

"Reminds him to stay in his lane. As it were," Mike said.

"Carrie's the daughter Curtis never had."

"So it would seem," Mike responded. "By the way, I checked on her college experience. She was in a local chapter of the College Democrats."

"Pretty generic," I said. "That's linked with the DNC; it's not the Young Trotskyites or something markedly radical."

"True," Mike said. "You check the cubicles and small offices at Covington and Burling and you'd find such membership to be *de rigueur*."

"*Mais oui*," I said. "Anything on any rap sheets?"

"Nothing of note. She was once ticketed for speeding on the New Jersey Turnpike."

"That's *de rigueur*," I said. "You want to dodge the trash strewn by the Cosa Nostra garbage trucks."

"I love it when you stereotype," Mike said.

"So she generally keeps her nose clean, at least in public."

"She tries to," Mike said, "but every now and again she slips up. The night before the event at Air and Space…"

"Yes?"

"She and Rafe broke bread together… at the *Parkway Deli* in Silver Spring."

"Circumstantial evidence," I said. "Often the best kind."

"And the next morning…"

"Planning the bus route into the District?"

"Among other things. They used a local rental service, based in the District but one that serves the entire area. I didn't see the vehicles but I was able to access the contract. The pickup was in College Park, at the University of Maryland. Lots of bus rentals there. Inconspicuous. Also lots of young people. The big vehicles hadn't arrived yet, but the CCTV cameras were in place. Carrie and Rafe were standing by a mini bus, not a motor coach. I looked up the images on the rental service's site and their buses have classy logos and shiny paint jobs. The mini bus was far more modest. Unmarked. Dusty. Probably ten years old, at least…"

"For the black suits, ski masks, placards, bottles and jerry cans," I said, "with the stolen cars as backups in case the mini bus stalls out."

"That would be my guess," Mike said. "None of those things were in sight, of course, but again it's circumstantial evidence that fits the larger picture."

"Any idea where Wayne's better half is today?"

"Would you believe she was at Dulles airport?"

"I would. Where is she headed?"

"San Francisco via Chicago."

"That's interesting," I said. "Why the intermediate stop?"

"Don't know. She's flying *United*, so she could have flown direct. I assumed she was meeting someone in O'Hare, but she hasn't landed yet. She's actually circling over Chicagoland as we speak."

"Let me know if you can follow her through O'Hare."

"Will do. Get yourself some coffee."

I did. Since there had already been an event in downtown Chicago I assumed that her ultimate destination was the most likely action point and that she would be rallying with the woman from Santa Cruz—Noor Ali—whose brother had been deported.

Mike checked back with me in thirty-five minutes. "She's got a relatively tight connection to make, so she practically ran through the concourses to meet up with her boss."

"Anderson?"

"How did you know?" he asked.

"Just a guess. That was once Vanzetti's stomping ground but I figure we've moved on from his level to that of her father-in-law. Anderson would like the anonymity. I suspect that they were not meeting at one of the *United* clubs."

"No. He'd be more easily recognized there. They met at a bar with minimal food offerings. I'd describe it as a watering hole. She had tea; the old man had something amber-colored in an old fashioned glass."

"It's 5:00 somewhere," I said. "What about their demeanor?"

"She's only been there for a few minutes. We're practically talking in real time. I'd say that their postures and mannerisms were…*conspiratorial*. They're huddled closely, holding their expressions. Nothing has changed hands. He did pat her on the back of the wrist, affectionately perhaps but also just a tad too firmly."

"Good job at Air and Space, but next time I want to see some charred flesh…"

"Exactly," Mike said. "Wait a sec, they're just finishing up. She's hurrying away and he's on his cell phone."

"Planning something for the city on the bay."

"Probably not anything very good," Mike said.

FORTY-SIX

I briefed the Director who promptly briefed the San Francisco SAC. We were already considering the myriad, ugly possibilities for an attack on the city. The bridges were natural sites, both for obstruction and destruction. There were physical landmarks such as the Coit Tower on Telegraph Hill and the Transamerica Pyramid. An attack on Union Square could take out one or more hotels and impact the homeless who gather there. *Gump's* is a short walk away and a gathering place for tourists as well as upscale local shoppers. Nob Hill attracts the rich and famous, particularly to its signature hotels, the *Fairmont* and *Mark Hopkins*. In addition to the hustle and bustle of business and late-night drinking, it's also a site that attracts Asian practitioners of *tai chi* and *qi gong* and conveys a sense of peace and calm that could be seriously disrupted by a firebomb or other incendiary device. Fisherman's Wharf and Ghirardelli Square are both tourist mainstays and natural sites for demonstrations and protests.

The possibilities seemed endless. An Opera House event would draw the attention of the elites and the cognoscenti and an exploding cable car would make the tourists scatter like crows. The Presidio is redolent with historical associations (how many know that Gorbachev wanted to set up shop there?) and an attack on the Haight would devastate one segment of the local culture, an attack on Pacific Heights their rich fellow citizens. Just as the city represents the full spectrum of the American social, sexual and aesthetic experience, its partial destruction would resonate across the cultural borders. At base, San Francisco is a city of rich families, relatively few in number, despite its equally-deserved reputation as the capital for the rainbow coalition. The only advantage that we would have is its relatively small urban size and its vast area of plantable vineyards (say, 45,000 acres in Napa County alone). The introduction of a root louse like phylloxera (or a simple set of well-placed fires) would result in devastating costs, but any such operation was logistically unthinkable. Ditto an attack on Alcatraz. Unless the protesters were great swimmers or in possession of a fleet of aircraft, that portion of the tourist landscape would remain unscathed.

"You've forgotten the local universities," Mike said. "The destruction of some portions of Stanford, Berkeley or UC-San Francisco would not only make a political statement; it could also wreak havoc on the forefront of the medical, physical and biological sciences. Even the social sciences, in the case of Stanford."

"Thou shalt not commit a social science," I said.

"Point," Mike said. "Besides, the protesters might leave the local universities alone, as a kind of professional courtesy."

I laughed at that, in part as a defense mechanism to take my mind off of the other possibilities.

"Got something else for you," Mike said. "You were thinking that Ms. Carrie may be coming to San Fran to meet with Queen Noor…"

"Yes."

"She isn't, or at least not yet. She met with someone else at the airport, someone unexpected, at least by me…"

"And the mystery guest is…?"

"Larry Heinrichs."

"The Sociology grad student from Wisconsin. Fascinating. What in the hell is he doing in northern California?"

"That's the question, isn't it?" Mike said.

"Went to Oberlin as an undergrad," I said. "Probably from a wealthy family. One of the nice neighborhoods in Milwaukee."

"Brown Deer," Mike said.

"So he's not visiting home. He's in San Fran for an operation. Noor may not have been up for the task."

"She may now be completely off of their TO&E chart," Mike said. "They've whittled down the list to the people who are ready for real action…the street soldiers or commanders rather than the talkers and dreamers."

"Possibly," I said. "What else do we know about him?"

"Not a whole hell of a lot," Mike said. "He was swept up in a protest back at Oberlin…"

"Over that bakery thingie? Students were caught shoplifting. They admitted to being guilty but the proprietors were still accused of racism. Not the college's brightest moment. Long-established local store; people attempted to boycott…what was it called?"

"Gibson's. Cost the college a fortune for their recalcitrance. Just a second…almost $37 mil. Ouchy."

"That was awhile ago, Mike. More than ten years. Even if Larry was a senior at the time he's been in grad school a long time."

"Isn't everybody now?" Mike said. "Wait…give me a few."

Ten minutes later he was back. "He was a junior at the time of the protests at Oberlin, but he's only been at Madison for a few years. Where was he in the meantime?"

"You check; I've got to run out and get some groceries."

"Give me an hour or so," he said.

I went to the *Giant* store in McLean, picked up some bread, cheese, fresh fruit, milk and a box of Cheerios, gassed up the Director's car, and returned. Mike asked for a few more minutes so I made myself some tea and buttered toast.

"OK, sorry about the delay," he said. "I don't have the full picture yet, but I can tell you that Larry had some internships in DC after he graduated from Oberlin."

"How sweet it is to have wealthy parents. They probably picked up the tab for his rent, health insurance, subsistence, etc. etc. because it's very doubtful that he was drawing any kind of salary for his DC labors."

"No, it's a magnet for overachievers," Mike said. "They would pay the putative employer for a chance to add some lines to their resumés. I've got one specific so far."

"Don't keep me in suspense."

"I wouldn't think of doing that. Would you believe the civil rights division of the DOJ?"

"I most certainly would. This means that he and Carrie have done business before."

"There were also some other gigs that I'm running down. No NGO's, however."

"That would be too good to be true," I said. "It does say something, though…"

"Larry wasn't someone caught up in Allyson's net. He's Carrie's find."

"Someone was giving the Barry woman leads (or at least one lead)," I said.

"The good leads, the Glengarry leads," Mike said.

FORTY-SEVEN

"I'll let the Director know, ASAP," I said. "He may also have some thoughts on the San Fran operation, assuming that one is in the works."

"I doubt that Larry's there for the seafood," Mike responded.

"Good work on this, Gwen," the Director said. The only other cultural/institutional site that I might add to your list is the Emanu-El temple in Presidio Heights. Large, old, a Jewish landmark. If you're mounting an anti-semitic protest of some sort this would be a likely location."

"I'm sure there's adequate CCTV coverage there as well," I said.

"No doubt," he answered. "Do we have video of Muller actually meeting with Heinrichs?"

"They met briefly at the airport but traveled into the city separately. Unfortunately, Mike lost them while they were en route. Too many blurred license plates; too much traffic. We're waiting for them to surface again. There was no meeting per se in the airport…more like ships passing in the night…nods of recognition, but no coffee klatch or lunch."

"Where did they meet?"

"Luggage pickup; they came in on different flights."

"Right. She stopped in Chicago to meet with the bent congressman. Heinrichs would have flown direct."

"Yes, Sir."

"Let me know when they rally in the city."

"Will do, Sir."

I called him an hour and a half later. "They checked into the Hyatt by the Embarcadero. Separately. They're on the same floor but not in adjoining rooms. Correction: that's where they're *registered*. At the moment they're in the Ferry Building. They could be leaving town for a quick trip to someplace like Sausalito, but I doubt it. They don't have time for sightseeing and gawking. They're there to do business and if they wanted to make it more difficult to follow them the Ferry Building would meet that requirement."

"Right. It's filled with shops, restaurants, tourists, travelers and looky-loos. At this time of day it would be very crowded."

"Just got a text from Mike," I said. "They're at a place called *Boulettes Larder*, eating gourmet pizzas. They're not sharing."

"He's the best," the Director said. "They're plotting and planning."

"Seriously," I answered. "They have a map of the bay area spread across their table. I'd love to have a closer look but Mike is doing as well as he can. They're drawing red circles on the map. Several of the circles are close to one another."

"By their hotel in the north end of the city, along the water."

"Right."

"Gutsy of them to be staying nearby. Or stupid."

"Yes, Sir. Hard to see any specifics but it looks like the circles fan out along the shore, from the Embarcadero area to the Golden Gate area."

"Multiple targets or multiple protest sites? Or both?"

"I hate to say it, Sir, but we'll probably have to wait to find out."

"I have other assets in the area, Gwen. We have a lot of activity on the jungle tom-toms. Our primo CI predicts an event two or three days in the future. He and the other members of his rent-a-mob cohort have been given a headsup. The time is not yet firm, but the assembly point *is*: Laurelwood Park in San Mateo."

"Nice little jaunt, Sir. What—twenty-five miles or so?"

"Just under, if you're heading to the port area. The CI says that there will be changes of uniform. That means commando outfits, not granny gowns. We're past the chanting and dancing by this point."

"We'll be waiting and watching, Sir," I said.

He contacted me in a day and a half. "Early warning, Gwen," he said. "There's been a major development."

"Yes, Sir?"

"Thank God for security sweeps. *Cunard* operates a cruise from San Francisco to Sydney. Twenty-five nights aboard the *Queen Mary 2*. Mucho dinero (for those who are smart enough to figure out all of the upgrades and upcharges). *Cunard* is smart enough to check things out early and often. They found a limpet mine on the ship's hull."

"What kind of explosive, Sir?"

"Semtex. More powerful than TNT, waterproof, low-to-no odor."

"And where was it located?"

"Good question, Gwen. *The* question, I think. That ship utilizes a unique 4-pod propeller system, but the mine was placed on the front hull, the front being defined as the area closest to the cameras and pedestrian traffic on pier 27."

"So the purpose was not solely to disable the ship but to create a big bang that would attract the attention of the tourists, the media, et al. Perhaps even do some human damage."

"Yes, and that's not the whole story. The tidal fluctuations in the bay can be as large as 9 feet; the average range is about 4 to 4 and a half feet. The mine was five and a half feet below the water line."

"For a maximum sound and light show," I said. "With that level of precision someone or other was doing his or her homework."

"Yes, exactly. And someone who had access to the materials for the mine, the assembly process, the magnetic attachment process and a person capable of installing the device in the dark, without being discovered. And one other thing: an individual with little or no regard for human life."

"As you said, thank God that the cruise line does regular security sweeps. It may be that Carrie and Larry are staying in the Hyatt for the view."

"Possible," the Director said, "but there are also those other circles on the map. The city may be small but the 'port' is huge."

"And *you've* got all hands on deck from the locals to the federals searching for other potential sources of mischief, but you can't be too obvious about it."

"No, we don't want them to know what we already know. We've removed the explosive and rigged the mine to let us know when it receives the detonation signal but we've reinstalled the now-dummy device in the same position on the hull, just in case they're making routine checks to make sure its presence hasn't been detected."

"Spy vs. spy."

"Yes."

"What else can we do, Sir?"

"Just stay alert. I don't want to send you in, because your identity and reputation precede you. I trust the SAC but I want to keep him in need-to-know land. As far as the locals know, our actions are the result of a regular report from a CI. They don't need to know about our gang of four and their nationwide schemes with regard to protests and demonstrations, especially the involvement of the congressman. Too many tentacles, too many potential listeners and bad actors. All that the locals know is that the entire port area includes potential targets and that its inspection requires the highest degree of discretion."

"We'll keep thinking and checking," I said. "The placement of the device is really important. They're going for a demonstration of their skills, perhaps even their capacity for lethality, far more than the disabling of the ship. They want to headline the evening news now, not sink the ship off the Kona coast when they're out of camera range. This is coming from their marketing department as well as their ministry of war."

"Agreed," he said, "but it's still nasty. That ship has more targets on board than the tank, mortar and small arms ranges at Ft. Knox. It has a planetarium, for God's sake. You could put sand in their massage creams, salmonella in their kitchens or hoist the Jolly Roger over one of their outdoor swimming pools. There are dozens of ways in which you could embarrass them by demonstrating your unimpeded presence. They're putting a mine filled with Semtex on the hull of a ship that cost $800,000,000 to build, a ship that's 21 storeys high, a ship with just under 4,000 passengers and crew. This isn't the equivalent of making a statement; it's more like crying out to high heaven."

"Let's make them sorry they opened their mouths," I said.

"That would certainly be my preference," he answered.

FORTY-EIGHT

I brought Mike up to speed, decided against an insulated tumbler of coffee and instead raided the Director's bourbon stash. I would have felt guilty hitting his *Pappy*; besides, I much preferred one of his small-batch specials: *Corner Creek.*

I slept well that night but spent the next day wondering when the San Francisco event would actually occur. I had to wait another day and when it began it surprised everyone.

The three large buses dropped off a group of largely-young, largely-male demonstrators. The big jobbies contained a maximum of 56 passengers each and when the black-clad troops arrived there were at least 125 of them. They marched in front of the Ferry Building and formed neat lines. They reminded me of an Infantry company, divided into four platoons. They marched silently and then stood at attention, waiting for their commander to emerge from the last bus. He was dressed in the same black regalia, but without any captain's railroad tracks or other differentiating badges of office.

He carried a bullhorn, told his troops to be at-ease and then proceeded to deliver a Castro-length speech on the evils of capitalism, the evils of the current administration, the evils of the United States, the evils of its imperialist, colonialist and fascistic history and what to him at least was the obvious 'fact' that this would all be destroyed when the people rose up against their authoritarian jailers, the bulk of whom he identified as Jews, conservative Catholics, Aryan supremacists and, generally, white trash.

After a speech that seemed to last hours he led the troops in a chant that promised the end of America, the end of Israel, the end of Poland, Italy and any other state or nation that had recently elected conservative leadership. This was followed by some foot stomping and weird gesture that appeared to be some form of occult salute.

"They've upped the financial ante," I said to Mike. "Those boots alone cost a small fortune."

"I checked," Mike said. "They aren't Army surplus; they're Belstaff *Endurance* motorcycle boots. $425 a pop. Multiply that by 125 and you get a tab in the neighborhood of…"

"Over 50 grand," I said. "Imagine if they had gone for a designer brand…"

"You must be on the same site as me," Mike said. "I had no idea that you could buy boots like this from *Burberry*, *Jimmy Choo* and *Manolo Blahnik*."

"You left out *Saint Laurent*," I said.

"My bad," Mike responded.

"Did you enjoy the speech?"

"One of my college teachers once told us the meaning of the word *professional*. He said it was doing something you hated doing, but still doing it to the best of your ability."

"Works for me," I said. "Wish the camera angle provided a better shot for you. I'd love to know who Captain Blowhard is in his day job."

"Agreed," he said. "I'm trying to run some voice rec software, but that's much more of a shot in the dark than the face rec. I can tell you one thing; it's not Larry Heinrichs. The speaker is at least four inches taller, and that's adding an inch and a half for the boots, which is probably way too generous."

Finally, he finished chanting and saluting and ordered the black shirts to come to attention. "Looks like the show is over," I said. *Der Hauptmann* is directing his followers back onto their buses."

As the three buses pulled away from the curb the sky lit up with flames and smoke. "What?!" I said.

"That wasn't the cruise ship," Mike said.

"I hope not," I said. "If it was, we screwed up big time."

"I'm looking at multiple screens," Mike said. "In effect I can pan the whole port area. There was a small flash from the left, over by the Golden Gate; the big one came from Oakland--the port area, in the Oakland Estuary."

"Container ships," I said. "A jungle of stacked containers, visible from the bridge."

"Exactly," Mike said. "It's cargo container city. I'm homing in. There's a lot of dust and smoke..."

"Blowing up containers would be tantamount to making a comment on capitalism, international trade, globalism, modern technology...you name it."

"Yes, indeed. Wait a sec. Here...coming into focus. It looks as if the containers in one section were mined along the fronts of the bottom row, so that those in the rows above would collapse. There were probably also some incendiary devices, because I can see a lot of flames...they're working their way from container to container and destroying whole sections of humongous steel boxes."

"Probably few or no human casualties; we can be grateful for that," I said.

"Let me see what I can see on the left side of my screens," Mike said. "It's...yes...the Marina Yacht Harbor."

"Macro/micro," I said. "They're saying that the global shipping should be stopped as well as the concentration of wealth in the hands of individuals."

"The cruise ship would have covered the self-indulgence of all the little people. They hit Cunard because it's a top global brand, but a lot of the cruise traffic out of San Fran is small potatoes—a few nights to L.A., San Diego, Vancouver, etc. A couple hundred bucks. You buy the drinks package and go on a weekend bender. Blue collar vacation. Actually just a little bit more than a staycation."

"Anything specific on the burning yacht?"

"Trying to pick up the KPIX feed," Mike said.

"CBS affiliate."

"Right. There are at least a half-dozen reporters on the ground, trying to jockey for position among the lookies and the firefighters. They're throwing a lot of elbows, but one girl with a microphone is holding her own."

"The firefighters are worried about the fire jumping from ship to ship and pissing off the prominent and vocal taxpayers who own them."

"Yes," Mike said. "And if some eggs are broken during the omelette making, so be it…hold on…"

I reached for my coffee which was now cold, but not yet to the oil-slick stage.

"OK," Mike said. "It's a nice one. A raised-pilothouse Hatteras, possibly a *105*. Serious luxury, serious coin."

"Very deep pockets needed. No one else need apply."

"Always hard to say," Mike said, "because the pricing is determined by age, condition, number of miles, and so on. These are not like *Civics* rolling off the assembly line. You would need to know how much brass, teak and other good stuff went into the construction. You could be talking high six figures, low seven figures or…the stratosphere. Any way you slice it, however…"

"Megabucks."

"Right."

"Does it have a name?" I asked.

"Yes, the *Dolly*, with an image of the 15-state Dolly Madison flag adjoining the title."

"Your basic Star-Spangled Banner," I said.

"I don't have to translate their message," Mike said.

FORTY-NINE

"I wonder what they're asking themselves about the limpet mine on the cruise ship, Sir," I asked.

"Two out of three isn't bad?" the Director responded. "Probably not. They paid for the whole deal and they would have wanted the whole deal. In some ways it's good that we missed the other two detonations, because that limits the possibility that they're aware that we're bird-dogging them. They're probably thinking that their installer screwed up. If so, fine. In some ways, he did."

"Time for us to check obituaries, freshly-turned soil or bodies bobbing up and down in the Bay," I said.

"True that," the Director said.

"It's frustrating," I said, "particularly the waiting. It's not my normal state of being."

"Completely understood," he answered. "But you need to breathe out and leave room for a brief reality check: we're monitoring the activities of all the principals and all of the potential local operatives. Michael Liu is the best. If one of those under his observation coughs or sneezes out of turn he'll notice. However, we can't be everywhere 24/7/365, no matter how much we would like to be, and there are some modes of communication (particularly communication via third parties whose number could be endless) that we simply cannot track. In this case at least there appear to have been no human casualties.

"There's also the matter of prosecution. The fact that explosions followed their recent demonstration is convincing to us but not to the courts. It's the first rule you learn in Logic 101: *post hoc ergo propter hoc*. Just because an event followed directly in time is no proof that the prior action *caused* the latter. Their attorneys would throw that in our face in their opening statement to the jury. Even worse, they could claim that the fireworks were caused by the Aryan nation, whose actions their well-meaning, upstanding, concerned citizens were at pains to protest. Unfortunately, it's your bona fide non-starter. In the meantime, I've got some advice for you, Gwen."

"Yes, Sir?"

"After an operation such as this there will be a break in the action. Clear your head for a couple of hours. Drive up to the Galleria. Get a glass of wine; look at some unconscionably overpriced purses; put your feet up for a few minutes. You haven't had a serious day off in weeks. Come back refreshed."

"I can do that, Sir."

And I did. I checked out the overpriced purses, the overpriced scarves, shoes, watches and miscellaneous forms of jewelry and geegaws. I had dinner at *P. F. Chang's*, starting with a pair of Zombies that mellowed me out very nicely. One or two more and I would have had to be driven back to the Director's low-slung aerie. Anything beyond that and I would have to check in at Fairfax Hospital (on the aptly-named Gallows Road). I followed with a cup of hot-and-sour soup. I always think about switching to a *bowl*, but their idea of a bowl feeds four or five people. For main course I thought about some Orange Beef but instead talked them into making Governor's Beef rather than the Governor's Chicken which is their conventional menu offering. I followed with tea which, by itself, would be bland but which always pairs nicely with Chinese food (or should I say Chinese/American food).

When I returned to my above-the-garage flat I took a hot shower and climbed into bed. Ten minutes later I was awakened by a message from Mike.

"I know it's almost bedtime," he said, "but I thought you would want to know…"

"They found a body."

"Yep. A bad boy who washed out of Seal training, apparently for insubordination. One/each William Beauchamp. Pronounced *Beecham*. Nasty mess. His face appears to have been caught in the duel propellers of a new Chris-Craft. A *Catalina 30*; doesn't look like much but the MSRP is half a mil."

"Where was the body found, Mike?"

"Just outside a marina on San Pablo Bay, near Novato."

"Thirty miles or so from Oakland?"

"Right," he said. "Of course, it could be anyone, but in this case it wasn't. Billy Beauchamp was an associate of Carl Snyder, actually Carl Snyder's cousin."

"Snyder was Anderson's Cleveland cop pal."

"Succeeded by his brother Virgil, after Carl died from multiple myeloma."

"Who may have recruited Billy and may have eventually killed him, as well. Interesting that they didn't bury him on some local mountain side. I suspect they wanted to demonstrate the manner in which they would respond to ineptitude."

"Propellers in the face would be sure to *encourager les autres*."

"Whatever happened to honor among thieves, Mike?"

"Long out of fashion, I'm afraid," he responded. "By the way, I took the liberty of letting the Director know."

"As you should have. These people move quickly, don't they?"

"Yes. They've never heard of the old British expression, 'Softly, softly, catchee monkey.'"

"Remember that picture from Vietnam, the one in which the National Police Chief of South Vietnam put a bullet in the head of the Vietcong soldier?"

"Yes, hard to forget it."

"The hardened GI's called it an 'on the spot correction'; that's the style of the people on Anderson's team."

"Or is it his daughter-in-law's team?" Mike asked.

"Hard to say. I'm pretty sure that it's not his son's team. Beyond that it's unclear. We *can* say that they're not happy with incompetence and that they're aware of the pirate's truism that dead men tell no tales."

"Right," Mike said. "No loose lips; especially not in the case of people who are suddenly unavailable and unable to sink ships."

"One of your best, Mike."

"God knows I try," he said.

"Just when we thought we might have found a new lead that could take us back to the head of the snake…"

"Well, Billy Beauchamp's fate *does* solidify our assumptions," Mike said, "but he won't be a good witness for the prosecution."

"As Dr. Lecter says, after he persuades Multiple Miggs to swallow his tongue, 'not anymore'."

"When do you have time to go to the movies?" Mike asked.

"I don't. I just automatically go to my mainstays and standbys."

He laughed and said, "Get some rest. I have a feeling that our gang are going to strike again. West coast…Chicago…DC…what's the logical next target?"

"The smart money would probably be on Manhattan," I said. "It's where so many protests begin. What would you guess— Morningside Heights?"

"Maybe a little too tried and true," he said, "but they work that territory heavily and they're probably comfortable there."

"I had a friend who went to Columbia and raved about it as well as the area. I was never clear on why he would say that, particularly after he admitted that there was an occasional exception to its attractions."

"Yes?"

"He said he woke up one morning and there were several dozen gawkers on the street below his apartment. It seems that they were fixated on something floating in the gutter above a clogged sewer: a human arm."

FIFTY

So much for my half-day vacation, I thought, as I emerged from bed at 6:15. I brewed some coffee, buttered a pair of English muffins and pulled up a map of Manhattan on the Director's computer screen. The bad thing was that the city was replete with terrorist targets. The good thing was that there were nearly 40,000 uniformed officers there and they had been at their task since 1845. The second good thing was that the mayoral leadership had taken a recent right turn and was now prepared to utilize the elements of law enforcement at her disposal.

Mike and I went back and forth on a host of possible targets and operations, none of which came to fruition. Then, a week and a half later, we saw the unanticipated curve ball coming for our eyes. By the time we had adjusted to it it was already past us.

"I suppose we should have considered the possibility," I said. "Miami Beach…the *Fontainebleau…*"

"Your basic Jewish riviera," Mike said. "The perfect place for a pro-Hamas demonstration. Maybe Skokie was closed that day."

"I suppose that we should be grateful that it was non-violent," I said. "At least physically non-violent. The signage was ugly…"

"And very professionally done," Mike added. "What did you think of the later march through Biscayne Bay?"

"Not particularly antisemitic in its thrust," I said, "but it wasn't exactly a message of love. My take was that the demonstrators were saying that we can spoil both your vacation and your home life. Money won't save or insulate you; we'll find you wherever you are."

"Sounds about right," Mike said. "Curious that no one was in evidence that day from the gang of four, but it had their fingerprints all over it, even down to the more-civilian but still uniform garb."

"Yes, they were going for something like the march of the all-aged useful idiots rather than the teenage mutant ninja fascists."

"In Florida the age range would have been a constraint," Mike said. "I take it that the green and white shirts were an attempt to evoke the Hamas logo without going so explicit that they could have been subject to charges for supporting a terrorist organization."

"Again and always: not cheap to fund and not easy to organize. What's next…Manhattan?"

"I hope not," Mike said, "but I'm not laying any significant bets."

Which turned out to be wise, since the next statement was made in Denver, or, more properly, Aurora. A pro-drug demonstration was followed by some local manna—an array of illegal drugs dropped into the streets from an outsized drone. This was followed by howls and cackles, but the police were quick to intervene and warn the would-be consumers that they could be ingesting fentanyl in lethal quantities. This dissuaded the majority of onlookers from tempting fate but a few were unable to resist temptation and ended up covering themselves in vomit as they rolled in the available grass, gasping for breath and fighting the effects of seizures.

I didn't quite know how to interpret this one. On the one hand it could have been a message from an Old Testament deity, warning the decadent of the evil of their ways in enacting lax drug legislation. On the other (and more likely): a message that poison could be delivered early and often and that the children of the legislators would be the first victims in a war for the human soul which might well prove to be unwinnable.

Again, there were no gang of four reps on the ground that day and the drone (which was later commandeered and flown into the side of the Aurora Fox Arts Center) was unmarked and untraceable. Darvish could have delivered a squadron of them without any difficulty and Petrov could have furnished the cargo on a day or two's notice. The only thing missing from the scenario was some form of currency manipulation that might have benefited Vanzetti, but there was economic disruption aplenty, particularly with the next episode in their filthy little melodrama.

That came a week later when the homeless in both New York and Los Angeles were notified by broadsides that the city's restaurants were going to provide free meals that evening to anyone who would present themselves in the middle of the dinner hour. Suddenly the cities' struggling restaurants found themselves buried in malodorous and increasingly angry individuals, many of them drug addicts, many of them mentally-challenged and many of them spoiling for a fight when they discovered that they had been duped. Needless to say, the restaurants' actual diners were sickened by all of this and promptly left for home.

Again the same message: economic disruption such as this could happen at any time, in any place, at any degree of severity, and there was very little that could be done to prevent it.

"As we discussed earlier," the Director said, "the purpose (or at least one of the key purposes) is to create chaos. It's primal; we don't like it; we vote against it; we decry it; we resist it at all costs. Even if the government is doing something that will ultimately help us, the intervening disruption is hard to stomach. People are inherently conservative, even if what they're trying to hold onto is bad for them. Count on it…*chaos*…they hate it."

"Are you seeing a change in their mission, Sir? Mission creep, perhaps?"

"I wish I could give you an unvarnished answer, Gwen. It's probably the fact that the gang of four are profiting individually in some way. I think we can consider that a certainty. Whether or not they're footing the opportunity costs…? That's another issue altogether. We know that Curtis Anderson is not the head of a philanthropic organization; he'll be wanting to wet his beak big time, and it's a distinct possibility that he'll want to do that at other peoples' expense. That's what he's done all his life. On the other hand, this effort has expanded markedly and it's operating coast to coast. Their logistical costs are skyrocketing.

"And this is more than some rent-a-crowd operation. That sort of organization might be available for minor criminal purposes, but this one could mount (what would you call them—scaled events?) on a far larger stage. They can trot out some anti-semites in Miami, dose some crackheads in Colorado or blow up cargo containers in the Oakland harbor. Their pomps and works could attract the business of enemy governments, engage the interest of a gang or cartel or tempt some neophyte politician with no measurable following to rent a loud group of enthusiastic acolytes (assuming he or she could afford the cost of the organization's club dues)."

"We've talked about this before. It's like the entertainment services in New York that have long lists of individuals willing to fill seats at poorly-attended performances in an attempt to hoodwink the drama critics."

"Yes," the Director said. "They're borrowing the business model of a whole set of dubious but legal enterprises. Think of the practice of enlisting people who are famous for being famous and compensating them for simply showing up at an event with which they have no logical, personal or cultural connection. They breeze through a 90210 party, blowing air kisses at the social-climbing host and hostess…all for a fat fee for a five-minute appearance."

"Loving the alliteration, Sir," I said.

"Trying to keep my spirits up in the face of my frustration," he said.

"If they are going national and if their interests transcend the immediate needs of the gang of four…no, let's make that the gang of three, because Anderson's family is clearly directing the operation…who is their ultimate funding source? They're clearly attempting something on a far grander scale than a local rent-a-crowd outfit. At first it may have looked like they were trying to create a competing enterprise, but this operation is simply too large and they're skating too close and too often up to and across the edge of criminality. That criminality now includes murder and manslaughter, not just general mayhem."

"Someone who's not just interested in a one-off action; someone who's buying a larger product," he said. "My vote is that the purchaser wants something like, well, what I said before…*chaos* with a capital C."

"So it could be an uber-rich Soros-type who's trying to plug the hole in his own soul by creating fissures and crevices throughout society."

"Possibly," he said.

"Or possibly a foreign enemy?" I asked.

"The latter is increasingly becoming more likely," he said.

FIFTY-ONE

Mike and I mulled over these possibilities. "I'm going to increase my focus on Anderson," he said. "I'm figuring that he's one of the pivotal figures just below the guy with the cat on his lap."

"That would make him Number Two," I said.

"Yes, because Anderson doesn't have the money you would need to carry out these operations and because his entire life has consisted of grifting and skimming and ripping off other people."

"So far he's succeeded at it very nicely," I said.

"The son-of-a-bitch…that's what keeps me motivated, Gwen. I want to see his expression when he dips his dinner spoon in a bowl of rancid leftovers. Unfortunately, that will have to wait, because so far he's still working his way through his King of Kiwanis routine. This morning he turned up at the dedication of a playground for a local school. All very safe these days—huge, enclosed plastic chutes and plastic tree houses about three or four feet off of the ground. No monkey bars, none of those see-saws positioned above the hardpan; no swing sets with poles that rocked out of the ground when you swung high…all very safe and very dull."

"You men all have a longing for the days of dangerous playgrounds," I said.

"Back when boys were boys and the girls showed them they could do the same things that they could. Fearlessly."

"If you could survive the time on the playground you could survive the time when nuns carried big sticks, tested their rigidity across their palms and didn't speak softly."

"Damned right," Mike said, smiling.

"So what was Uncle Curtis doing this afternoon?"

"Well…continuing with the Kiwanis routine…he was attending the opening of a children's wing at the Cleveland Clinic."

"Noble," I said, "for a change."

"All face-time stuff," Mike said. "From what I could see he was just there to wave his own flag. He didn't participate in any of the significant fundraising for either project. This was all smiles and back pats. I did notice that he spent a lot of time on his cell phone."

"Love to hear with whom."

"Yep, sorry I can't tell you that. He's also smart enough to turn his head away from any fixed-CCTV or reporters' cameras when he's plotting and scheming. He loves to have his face on the front page, but most of the time he spends his life in the shadows."

"Anything happening with his son or daughter-in-law?"

"Nothing of note. The son picks up carry-out and sometimes chauffeurs daddy to dinners and other functions. I suspect he's a whiz at making coffee and assembling basic cocktails. Anything else would be above his capacities. Ms. Carrie, on the other hand, tries to keep a low profile, but whenever she comes into camera range she's on her phone, usually with an insistent look on her face."

"Her way or the highway."

"Right," Mike said. "Possibly her way or the cemetery."

"You think she's got that kind of authority within the organization?"

"She's certainly the heir apparent," Mike said. "You can see it in her eyes. She defers to the old man but when she speaks he nods a lot."

"You mean he nods in agreement."

"Right. He doesn't nod off. He's too careful for that. If he turned his back on anyone—especiallly the daughter-in-law—he might end up with one of those thousand-dollar Japanese carving knives lodged in it."

"Anything else going on?"

"Just one thing. Not sure what it might mean. Vanzetti turned up on an Italian news site. He was meeting with an economic minister, regaling themselves with some primo cuisine in a restaurant on Lake Como. And I'm not talking about *primo* as first course; I'm talking about it as a package that would be unaffordable for most mortals."

"What did the website story say?"

"It was mostly innocuous. It didn't describe him as an international criminal, if that's what you were thinking; the Italian words would have translated to something like 'mover and shaker', but not in a way that would instill confidence. The thrust of the story was: look who our Minister of Economy and Finance is breaking bread with…and washing down white truffles, pearl lobsters and Caspian-sea caviar with *Gaja's* best wines."

"A little cozy corruption."

"That was the inference."

"Northern Italy is a long way from home," I said.

"Yes, especially when so many other things are going down back in the U.S. of A."

"Maybe he's detaching from the larger operation? What do you think?"

"Impossible to say," Mike answered. "He could just be keeping his network in repair. Today the Italian economy, tomorrow the Greek…"

"But refocusing is a possibility."

"Always. And if that's what he's doing he should be very careful about it," Mike said. "If they no longer need him he should be aware that he's in the process of mutating from his role of founding partner of the illustrious gang of four to the barely visible position of a card-carrying useful idiot."

"How about Petrov?"

"Spending most of his time near Brighton Beach, sipping strong black tea with an occasional drug supplier. Never, of course, with street distributors."

"I wish we could march in and arrest the lot of them," I said.

"Yes. That would be very nice and very gratifying. Unfortunately they keep themselves insulated from the action and mask their criminal enterprises with legit businesses."

"He imports precious metals and stones, doesn't he?" I asked. "Also some agricultural products…"

"Sunflower oil," Mike said.

"And I guess some petroleum products before the sanctions…"

"Yes. Fertilizers," Mike said.

"But no indication that Petrov has been sitting on Anderson's lap when the various protest events went down?"

"No. None," Mike said. "He's been ensconced in Brooklyn for the duration."

"I'm not sure if that means anything, but it's a fact that we should probably keep in mind," I said. "What about Darvish?"

"Nothing much beyond a dinner with a member of the Iranian consulate in Manhattan. At *Jean-Georges*. No word on the specific menu, just some still photos of individual courses. Lots of caviar, wagyu beef, lobster…a lot of overlap with Vanzetti's tastes."

"And always at something like $300-400 a pop," I said.

"Right," Mike answered. "I'll say one thing about these guys. They know how to take care of their personal creature comforts."

"I'm always surprised by the Iranians' diplomatic presence, especially in DC. I know the maxim about keeping your enemies close, but if they're not roiling the middle east they're directing terror cells in our country and in those of our allies."

"They're probably one of Darvish's primary clients," Mike said, "so his keeping in touch with them should come as no particular surprise."

"True, and they're also Darvish's neighbors in New York, so this could be nothing more than routine fence maintenance. The bottom line is that we don't have anything fresh to report to the Director. That's not a criticism. That's simply a reflection of reality."

"Regrettably, yes," Mike said.

FIFTY-TWO

And then, finally, there was an event. Vanzetti disappeared from Mike's radar screen. *Lupara Bianca* the Italians call it: the white shotgun. An individual disappears without a trace and is never found again. In Vanzetti's case the white shotgun characterization was drawing the bulk of the smart betting money. He was scheduled to fly nonstop from Milan to Manhattan on the *Emirates* airline, but he never appeared for his $10K first-class seat. Nor did he check out of his lakefront-view suite at the *Villa D'Este*.

None of the cleaning staff had seen him, although his bed had been slept in. There was always the possibility that his body had been put in a laundry basket, covered with a dirty sheet and rolled to a loading dock, but the hotel was scrupulous in its organization and the CCTV cameras supported the conclusion that the hotel's baskets were all in place and accounted for, their visible number squaring precisely with their official allotment.

He must have walked out in inconspicuous clothing and used back steps and/or fire escapes. Still, there was no CCTV evidence, indicating that their system had been hacked in a very professional manner so that the filming could be disrupted in real time without leaving indisputable evidence of the rigging of the system. The most interesting detail was that his luggage had disappeared with him; there were no clothes hanging in a closet; there were no toiletries in the bathroom and no empty minibar bottles or snack wrappers. Indeed, the trash containers were all empty. The amateur might conclude that the abductor was a pathological neatnik, but the professional knew that the scene was being scrubbed to the point that it might even be difficult to find a fingerprint, much less an object capable of carrying traces of DNA. This was a Houdini-level action and an indicator that finding the actual body would be well-nigh impossible.

The lake itself (the deepest in Europe) was no puddle. Fifty-square miles in surface area, with depths reaching 1,400 feet, it was twenty-nine miles in length. Given the pains that had been taken to usher out the body from the hotel, it was doubtful that it would soon be found enwrapped in black plastic, chained to a set of cinder blocks. The water was uncommonly cold, the shoreline often pebbly and rocky, the winds (particularly in the north) challenging. The lake was also filled with fish; a skilled butcher could have cut Vanzetti into miniscule bits of chum that now resided in the bellies of the lake's perch, pike, shad, whitefish, lake trout, carp, tench, chub, bass, char, 'river monster' wels catfish, et al.

Throw in the local mountains, the adjoining seas and the endless array of metropolitan sewers, trash bins and alleyways as potential drop zones and the enormity of the salvage task was obvious. *Arrivederci, Signore.*

I shared these largely unsurprising observations with the Director. He acknowledged my efforts but regretted that they spoke loudly and clearly concerning the daunting task that they entailed. He said that he was not surprised that Vanzetti had disappeared, but that he did take heart in the cumulative knowledge that we were acquiring. Vanzetti had been thousands of miles away from the actions in America when they occurred and his liquidation had probably been fabricated to appear to be the result of his actions with his Italian associates. "From the perspective of the gang of three," he said, "he was also the most expendable. He was rich but not rich 'beyond the dreams of avarice'. And his reach was, ironically, far more limited, even though his financial maneuvering encompassed the entire globe." It was still, as the Director put it, a niche form of criminality. "Currency gonifs don't compete with one another in the way that drug dealers do. 'If you try to take over my corner you can expect to be reduced to blood splatter on the wall behind you.' If Petrov had been liquidated it would not have come as a great surprise. He might even have been eliminated in some gruesome way, *pour encourager les autres*, but Petrov is still among the living (as far as we know) because of the focus of his activities, the financial success that they consistently represent and (most important, perhaps) the players who are necessary partners in his enterprises. In other words, he's still useful, at least for the moment."

"So you think they're thinning out their own ranks because Vanzetti is no longer needed and their preference is for permanent silence rather than early retirement."

"For us, the evidence points that way," he said. "By the same token, his playing footsie with the Italian Minister of Economy and Finance had the benefit of deflecting attention from his former American partners *and* providing motivation for all manner of Italian criminals and politicians to keep him from sticking his nose in one or more of their businesses. They already *had* the means and opportunity."

"And he was eliminated in an Italian manner."

"Yes, that too," he said. "These people are serious planners as well as skilled assassins."

There was a pause in our conversation as we each sipped some coffee and pondered the implications of what we had been discussing.

"We're keeping an eye on Darvish and Petrov," I said, "and, of course, focusing heavily on the members of the Anderson family."

"Good. The big money would flow through Darvish and Petrov's hands and our congressperson always has his eyes on cash flow, particularly that which he might be in a position to intercept and commandeer."

"But he is unlikely to get too close to the ultimate source or sources," I said. "He'll want insulation, even if it has to be provided by his son or daughter-in-law. I like Darvish for his middle east connections. There's big money there, big hate there, big thirst for vengeance there. Plus there's that cozy dinner at *Jean-Georges*. Darvish is in bed with the representatives of the mullahs (or at least prepared for a one-night stand with them)."

"You're right to do so, Gwen," the Director said, "but drugs are linked to our closest neighbor and our most aggressive international adversary. Or should I be politically correct and say *competitor*?"

"Either one works for me. The Chinese have the money, but so do the cartels. We may have to be a bit more politic in the ways in which we describe the Chinese but they're not hosting any celebratory parties when we have the good fortune to succeed in our trade wars or our defense of the Taiwanese. We've been more confrontational with the cartels but that's because they're an easier target with far less ultimate risk. If we struck China the world would gasp; if we struck the cartels the world would cheer."

"Petrov, however, would not," the Director said. "Either way, the events in the middle east and the distribution lines for drugs, particularly fentanyl, are of global importance. We are the fly in the opposition's ointment on both counts and any damage that they can do to us is high on their list of desiderata, from the redistribution of our available resources to the general atmosphere of chaos that a nation of protests and demonstrations projects. The first undermines our efforts; the latter undermines the world's confidence in the reach and success of our efforts."

As he spoke I was taken with his ability to assess and describe our challenges. He could speak like a political scientist but command a battlefield with the technical skill and self-confidence of his heroes, Georgie and Abe. We signed off, agreeing to stay in close touch.

FIFTY-THREE

As I continued to remind myself, I lacked the technical resources and the engineering skills to do monitoring at Mike's level, but I did what I could, even as I wanted to get into some dark clothes, go into the field and sit silently in the darkness with my Leica binoculars, tactical knife and Sig *P320c*.

I began, however, by taking a break. Emptying and clearing my mind was my best strategy for preparing for highly-focused work. My default location is always Great Falls, where the Potomac gathers strength and plummets over mammoth rocks through Mather Gorge. I found an empty picnic table in a heavily-wooded area where I sipped from a 20-ounce double-insulated travel mug of fresh, black coffee. The irony was that the brewing and drinking of coffee is reputed to have begun in Yemen in the 15th century. These days the Houthis attempt to kill or bedevil us even though we are able to bomb them at will. If only we could establish some joint coffee shops and stimulate ourselves with caffeine rather than bloodshed....

I left my laptop in the car and instead jotted thoughts and notes on a small, lined, yellow pad. Unfortunately, nothing fresh and incisive sprang to mind. The Director and I were largely in agreement that we had succeeded in outlining the lineaments of our situation but unable to do little more than wait and watch and react as it developed. The good thing was that we were in agreement that the eventual reaction would be definitive. While we were not yet prepared to leave the battlefield a charnel house we were ready to insure that explosions and drugs falling from drones into the hands of children would not be tolerated, even if we had to respond in ways that straddled the line between acceptable and questionable.

I already had some thoughts in that regard, very partial and very tentative thoughts, of course, but thoughts that would entail a greater reaction than the fair and simple response predicted by Newton's third law of motion. The best cure for omnipresent chaos is the drawing of red lines and the reassurance of the public that any subsequent crossings of those lines will result in the deployment of strength of the shock-and-awe variety.

It was the old Colin Powell doctrine—the avoidance of war until other steps had been exhausted, followed by the violent application of overwhelming force. The military is not the field element of a School of Social Work. With regard to Operation Desert Storm his plan was crystalline in its clarity: "Our strategy to go after this army is very, very simple. First, we're going to cut it off, and then we're going to kill it."

Then, suddenly, I began to wonder if I had become too emotionally involved. Planning actions when your pulse rate is above 95 may not be the most prudent or, for that matter, the most effective of strategies. No matter how much we might enjoy utilizing advanced weapon systems it was always wise to remind ourselves of the fact that our most lethal and most important weapon (for deployment *or* reflection) sat between our ears. The world is a complicated place and one should think twice before beginning to blow it up.

Then I became wistful, thinking about the fact that while I loved what I did, my only connections (beyond those with my parents) were with my Bureau colleagues. I was floating in relative isolation and that can lead to precipitous action. It was not always so. When I first left Quantico for my initial assignment (in St. Louis) I had actually developed a romantic relationship with one of my classmates, a West Point graduate named Richard Ingle. That relationship had not yet devolved into the annual exchange of fruit cake, but the romance had mutated into distant friendship. The longer Richard was isolated in remote field offices the more he realized that he needed stability, perhaps even stasis, in his life. He had left the Bureau, taken a civilian position in military communication systems in western New York and married a special education teacher, named Kathy.

I wasn't ready for the porch swing yet but I was beginning to be more self-reflective in my approach to tasks. Perhaps it was because of my special, ad hoc relationship with the Office of the Director. The enlarged battlefield which that entailed had also enlarged my perspective and while I was always ready to charge forward I now did it with a greater sense of the potential consequences.

As I sipped and pondered I tried to put the current investigation into its most appropriate context. Someone was attempting to do great damage to our country and their reach and skills far exceeded the efforts of the mindless marchers they often employed. With the feckless placard-carriers as the public face of their operations our response would be expected to be a bit gentler in its dimensions. One does not, as the maxim reads, kill a mosquito with a howitzer. On the other hand, these mosquitos were likely seen by their betters as expendable fools who would be sacrificed without a moment's hesitation. They would be used and discarded in the same manner as commanders of totalitarian states would order barely-trained civilians into battle without any regard to their fate or the bottom line on the butcher's bill.

Instead of writing notes I found myself scribbling and drawing caricatures when I was suddenly approached by a little girl who had dared to leave the safety of her parents' spread of casseroles, chip and pretzel buckets, soft drink and beer bottles, paper plates, plastic cups and cutlery arrayed on a nearby table.

"What are you drawing?" she asked.

"Not really much of anything," I said. "I'm just taking some time off from my computer. Do you like to draw?"

"No, I sometimes draw but most of the time I prefer to play with my tablet," she said. "What's your name?"

"Gwen," I said. "What's yours?"

"Jenny," she said.

"That's a lovely name," I said. "That's my aunt's name."

"Does she live here?" Jenny asked.

"No, she lives in North Dakota," I answered.

"I've never been there," she said. "Is it pretty?"

"It's very pretty," I said.

"What do you do?" she asked.

"You mean what do I do for a job?" I responded.

"Yes."

"I try to protect people," I said.

"That's very important," Jenny said. "My uncle Will is a firefighter. He protects people."

"I bet he's a good cook too," I said. "When the firefighters are in their station houses they cook for one another. I bet he knows how to make great stuff like stew and chili."

"I'm not sure about that," she said. "When we get together with them my aunt does most of the cooking. She likes to barbecue things."

"So do I," I said. "Especially ribs. Would you eat ribs?"

"Sometimes I do," she said. "They take a long time to make."

"Good things are worth waiting for," I said.

"That's what my dad says." She then looked at her watch and turned its red plastic wrist band to gain a better view. "I better go," she said. "We're going to eat soon. It was nice to talk to you, Gwen."

"Be safe, Jenny," I said.

FIFTY-FOUR

When I drove back to McLean to the Director's garage apartment I felt refreshed, even though I hadn't really accomplished anything of note. I thought momentarily of Jenny, the bold one in the family, no doubt. She reminded me of an earlier incarnation of myself.

Or so I wanted to imagine. My thoughts instead turned to Carrie Muller. I thought of her as the linchpin for our investigation. She was not in charge; she was not the source of funding; she was unlikely to be involved in actual wet work, but she was Anderson's insulation. She was the organizing force, at least at ground level, and whenever something violent happened she always seemed to be nearby. She may have been expendable in the eyes of the ultimate puppet masters but she appeared to be essential for their ongoing tasks.

And so I focused on her and in doing so developed even greater respect for Mike Liu's abilities. He had covered much of the most important ground so I went to the less-likely nooks and crannies.

Carrie and Wayne had met in Rhode Island but Carrie's parents were from the north shore of Chicago. Her father James was a (very) young protegé of Chuck Percy's—the *wunderkind* CEO of Bell & Howell and later Republican senator from Illinois whose daughter Valerie's body was found bludgeoned and stabbed to death at their family home in Kenilworth.

Chuck, Jim Muller and Jim's daughter Carrie shared a high school— New Trier—a prominent institution on the north shore in Winnetka. New Trier had produced a host of famous graduates and attendees

(Ann-Margaret, Ralph Bellamy, William Christopher, Charlton Heston, Bruce Dern, Rock Hudson, Michael Shannon, Rainn Wilson, Archibald MacLeish, Scott Turow, Donald Rumsfeld, Virginia Madsen, et al.) but Carrie left little more than a trace: a simple black and white yearbook picture. Her grades must have qualified her for admission to Brown, but Brown lists a *James and Sarah Muller Scholarship Fund* among their larger student-support endowments, so there may have been some quid pro quo involved in what turned out to be a negotiated selection process.

Her mark left at Brown was perceptible but not dramatic. She was the member of a club sport team in some mutation of 'ultimate frisbee', but the standout member of her 7-player team was a woman named Rita Hansen, whose exploits were occasionally mentioned in the *Brown Daily Herald*. Carrie appeared twice in what were little more than addenda to footnotes.

She graduated without Latin honors but she *did* graduate. That may be why she ended up at AU law school (tied for 104th place out of 195) rather than one in closer proximity to the top tier. Doubtless her graduation speaker at Brown had enjoined her to 'follow her bliss' but it was very difficult to discern from the written record what that bliss might actually entail.

Putting on my psychobabble hat I attempted to draw conclusions from the faint footprints that had marked her past. Then I added the obvious, sad facts. From the existing images in the recent months and years she was not an attractive woman. Slightly overweight, she carried the remains of acne scars which even the most highly-skilled dermatologist would have been unable to expunge. My conclusions were stereotypical but inescapable. She was an average person with a below-average presence, even though she might have been the progeny of above-average parents.

Her financial and social status were sufficient to provide her admission to top schools but she had left no marks there. She married an equally privileged but perhaps even less-than-average young man, who may have been the single individual to ever express any interest in her. Together they had produced no children and each, ultimately, was beholden to a prominent but sleazy public figure, the sort of individual who would have been described in the 18th century as a 'great' man, an adjective laden with sarcasm.

She had, in short, never really *belonged* and she had failed to secure the external validation which we all inevitably seek--the perfect prerequisites for a position in the attention-seeking world of radical politics. Unfortunately, the group to which she finally belonged was one whose separate members had instead established careers in various realms of criminality. I felt a certain sympathy for her and for those, like her, who substituted impossible dreams and failed theories for everyday successes and achievements. What she most needed was probably a family reunion or picnic, surrounded with children like Jenny. What she chose instead (perhaps because of a lack of any other options) was a lead role in middle management of a group dedicated to the acquisition of wealth which would never be sufficient to provide fulfillment or the kind of food for the soul which her graduation speaker would have urged her to seek.

This was truly sad, but it was counterbalanced by the fact that in giving aid to our country's enemies and adversaries by organizing and directing events that would bring the kind of chaos which would ultimately end in human suffering, she was indulging in the practice of what many reasonable individuals would characterize, quaintly perhaps, as treason.

That fact alone put us on opposite sides of the red lines drawn in the sand and meant that if and when the moments of truth came I would have to remove her, with (as we say) extreme prejudice, no matter how large the residuum of pity or solicitude which I might be forced to face.

FIFTY-FIVE

Mike (not unexpectedly) was less conciliatory. "If she reaches for the red button or hair trigger I'd turn her ample body into red mist," he said immediately.

"I would have to as well," I said.

"Of course you would," he answered, "because when the air is suddenly filled with burning shrapnel you wouldn't think of the dreams and theories that bounce among the clouds; you would think of the innocent bystanders we are sworn to protect, the people who are raising the families, teaching the young, building the country and trying to worship their God."

"Beautifully said, Mike," I responded. "You should go into politics."

"I'm serious," he said.

"I know you are. I didn't mean the kind of politics that focuses on words and promises. I meant the kind that go against the DC grain and actually are designed to protect the citizens, the taxpayers, the dads and moms..."

"I could also do the word stuff," he said.

"Ninety percent of the job, unfortunately," I answered. "Anyway, what do you think of my psychoanalytic take on Ms. Carrie?"

"I think it's probably close to the mark, sadly," he said. "You should do the psych shtick more often."

"They say that 'everything is political' and that that is their warrant for action, but I believe the opposite," I said, "even though my job necessarily drags me into the maelstrom. Deep down I think that *nothing* should be political, or, well, *almost nothing* should be. When you drill down to the bottom of things it's a substitute for real life and a practice that brings everything to the level of morbid partisanship, the kind that destroys the soul by creating a restlessness there that is the opposite of the peace and reflection which should be the business of the civilized."

"Wow," Mike said. "We should have these kinds of discussions more often. But maybe not too often."

I laughed. "I'm serious," I said.

"I know," he said, "but you don't want to overdo. What are you doing for dinner tonight?"

"Haven't decided fully, but I know it will involve red wine."

"My girl," he said.

I fulfilled my promise at *Café Tatti* with some *Coq au Vin* (the evening special) and some Willamette Valley Pinot (also special for that evening). I consciously kept my phone in my purse, resolving to occasionally concentrate on enjoying life rather than working 24/7. It worked, for awhile, but I kept coming back to my thoughts of Carrie Muller and the mess that she had made of her life. It was just as I had discussed with the Director. The thoughts of power and personal significance had driven her into the waiting arms of Satan and the possibility of escaping them had now dissolved into distant mist. She had passed the point from which she might have been able to return and he (whatever or whoever his current earthly incarnation) now owned her. Completely. Her choices were to remain under his rule and (probably) be eliminated when she was no longer useful or to reject his rule outright and be eliminated immediately. If she had ever entered the world of dominance and power with a smattering of authentic idealism those thoughts and beliefs had long ceased to matter.

What do the Brits say--in for a penny, in for a pound? It was now all a great pity, but what could I do except line up—fully armed—on the other side. A clever man was once disputing with a partisan government hack over his administration's actions. He defended the policy which the wise man abhorred by arguing that their purposes were pure. "Whatever you're claiming…that was not our intention!" the hack said. The other man responded immediately that "God judges intentions; men judge results."

Whether or not there was still some well-meaning intention at the bottom of her actions, I could only respond to Carrie's thoughts and feelings by considering their impact upon the real world—Jenny's world—where innocent children should be able to play and talk, sing, learn and grow up without fear of becoming an anonymous statistic on a collateral damage chart.

"Did you enjoy the special?" the waiter asked, momentarily distracting me from my own musings.

"Yes, very much," I said.

"Chef Carlo actually uses the French Burgundy for the dish. The Oregon wine is—what would you say?—tasty, but not for him. He is a purist."

"Tell him that I thought they worked well together; both were delicious."

"I will tell him that," the waiter said.

The next morning I received a text from Peggy, the Director's assistant, telling me that he would be incommunicado for the next two days. "Meetings," she said, "doubtless a waste of time, but if there is an emergency we can always reach him. Just let me know if anything pressing turns up."

"I will do that," I said. "Thanks for staying in touch."

"Always," she said. "By the way, he's frustrated as well…on your case. I'm not privy to all of the details but I know that your suspects are quite clever and that you're being cast in a reactive role. He hates that. He misses his tank divisions, roaring over the ridgeline. What does he say—engaging and destroying?"

"I've only ridden in one once," I said, "but I think I can feel what he feels. The midges and mosquitos are annoying you and you're sitting within a 70-ton armored vehicle, unable to strike back."

"That sounds like something he would say," Peggy responded.

"We'll have our day," I said.

"I don't doubt that you will," she said. "Stay safe out there."

Three days later he called. "It just happened," he said. "I wanted you to know immediately."

"Sir…?"

"East 161st Street."

"That's…Yankee Stadium."

"Yes. Just outside. Fortunately there weren't 40,000 civilians there at the time. Remember Jesus Cabrera, the drug trafficker?"

"Big fentanyl dealer, in the Bronx. Doing what now…30 years?"

"Yes. Sentenced in 2025. Succeeded by a guy called Chucho. A nickname; actually a diminutive form of Jesus. Anyway, Chucho was caught in the middle of a firefight this morning at dawn."

"Don't tell me. Petrov was on the other side."

"He was indeed. The NYPD has a CI in their DTO. He's saying that one of Chucho's dealers was told that the Brighton Beach DTO was inviting him for a meeting. The purpose was to develop joint operations—which would produce a tidal wave of money--but this turned out to be a ruse, a simple trap. Petrov's people (the story goes) held out this carrot but they actually wanted to apply some stick, a lot of stick. Their intention was to move north and invade Chucho's turf. Unfortunately, we don't have any CI's in Petrov's group, but our working hypothesis is that it was actually Petrov who was invited to meet with Chucho to discuss some form of partnership, but Petrov took a platoon of people with him, just in case. Chucho sussed that he could be outgunned and he took a small army. The bullets took out Petrov the moment he arrived, as well as four members of a family of five, going to open their bodega. One was only 9 years old. It's entirely possible, of course (and most likely), that Chucho's people were manipulated and funded by Anderson's, who were pulling the strings from the get-go."

I held back any comments, waiting for him to continue.

"Anyway, they made what appeared to be a very odd decision with regard to the shootout. The street was covered with 9mm shells but Chucho himself caught a 7.62 between the eyes."

"NATO round, common in sniper rifles," I said.

"Yep. Whoever was masterminding this wanted to insure that it appeared to be an actual drug war rather than a spontaneous shootout, so they had positioned a sniper somewhere in the shadows. Ultimately, they wanted both leaders dead. With the sniper round, however, the NYPD quickly leaped to the conclusion that this was a carefully-planned confrontation, not a business meeting. They concluded that this was the B team, leaving evidence like that behind. Of course, they're not aware of all of the facets of the case. We know (or certainly believe we know) that the Anderson group is playing to several audiences. What do you think happened next?"

"With Petrov out of the way the mice immediately began to play."

"How did you know that?"

"Just guessing."

"You guessed correctly. As I said, we didn't have a CI in Petrov's DTO, but Chucho must have. His people looted Petrov's stash and shopped a large portion of it at Coney Island, at bargain-basement prices."

"Undiluted?"

"Yes, unfortunately. Several dozen overdoses so far, 5 demonstrable fatalities."

"Message to those in Brooklyn: don't ever buy product from this guy again."

"So we believe," the Director said. "And whoever's left among Petrov's people will suffer supply chain problems for months, if not years. If they attempt to restart the business they'll face the effects of public awareness of their damaged goods, assuming that users would notice or care about the fatalities they've left in their wake. Meanwhile, the Anderson group's maneuverings continue apace. Their motto: damn the collateral damage; full speed ahead."

"Complicated story to concoct."

"Yes, and we're still working on the details. Petrov could have simply been assassinated on the street. The planners went to a great deal of trouble to fabricate the drug war scenario."

"Good insulation, though," I said, "perhaps worth all of the effort and risk. Plus, they accomplished their mission—the elimination of Petrov."

"They're not stupid," the Director said.

"With their string of successes they may be developing a false sense of security," I said. "That could be exploited to our advantage."

"I'm counting on that," the Director said.

FIFTY-SIX

The only good thing about this development was that the number of founding members of the gang of four had now been reduced by 50%. The horrific thing was that the civilian body count was rising, along with the gang of two's obvious indifference to the numbers. From the point of view of the Anderson gang (if that was now its most appropriate title) they were sticking their thumbs into plum pies and saying 'look what a good set of boys we are'; for their newest exploit they had demonstrated that they could take out a major NYC drug trafficker, an almost-major NYC drug trafficker and, simultaneously, instill fear in the heart of the populace. I could see the Times's headline already: "From Brighton Beach to the Bronx, from Coney Island to the House that Ruth Built."

They were gaining the high ground and the momentum and we simply could not allow that to happen. I contacted Mike, brought him up to speed and asked him to focus as intently as possible on Darvish and the Andersons. He had already heard the outlines of the news and confirmed his agreement with my tentative interpretation of the case.

Mike and I connected the next morning but quickly began bouncing off of brick walls. We decided to break for a 'recap and rethink' timeout. "I don't want to waste your time thinking out loud and meandering all over the map," I said. "Let's reconvene in an hour."

In the meantime I made fresh coffee and doodled on my mini-yellow pad, drawing connecting lines, encircling names, adding question marks and exclamation points. Fifty-five minutes later he texted "I'm ready when you are" and our faces appeared on our secure zoom screen.

"Want me to start?" I asked.

"Sure. You're probably sufficiently wired by caffeine that you could carry us well into the afternoon."

"True that," I said. "Anyway, this is what I'm thinking: Both Vanzetti and Petrov were expendable. They could provide startup funds and a bit of street cred to the overall operation, but they didn't have sufficiently deep pockets to carry the group to the sunny uplands and they had become distinct liabilities because they simply knew too much. Think of them as bishops or knights, maybe rooks on a good day, but it was time for them to be taken off the board.

"Darvish remains and, of course, so do the Andersons, who are administrative lampreys, putatively civilian figures motivated solely by greed (Daddy, at least, with Carrie undergoing a mandatory conversion and Wayne playing office boy). Think of them as 'system navigators'— those people in an organization who know how to make things happen while remaining as anonymous as possible. After awhile you awake to realize that they're the ones who are actually in charge.

"Darvish has the means (ordnance, money) to be of use, even if he doesn't have enough of the latter to fund the operation and leave enough lagniappe to keep Curtis at his desired standard of living. He does, however, have contacts. His favored turf is the middle east but most recently he's been seen dining with a suspicious Chinese person. If you think of an ultimate adversary who would like to see us falter and fail the circle is fairly small. They boil down most often to China and Iran. The North Koreans would like to make mischief but they're too invested in weaponry to feed their people or deliver enough electricity to light up a miniscule portion of the night sky.

"The Cubans are nothing but tiny proxies and the Russians who traditionally supported them have been decimated by the fluctuation in oil prices and the U.S.'s energy independence and newly-regained role as replacement supplier for Europe. What did old John McCain say? Russia is a gas station masquerading as a country (while conjuring with vast corruption). The Chinese are monkeying around in the Caribbean and utilizing Cuba as a prime site for intelligence gathering. Whether or not they unleashed Covid to create their own form of medical and economic chaos is still subject to debate in some circles. Their preeminence as our major adversary/competitor, however, *is* no longer in debate.

"My view is that Darvish stays put within the organization, both because he affords the Andersons some insulation and because he can pick up the phone and set a dinner date with the Chinese and the Iranians. He's sold weapons to the Houthis, Hezbolla, Hamas, the Palestinian Islamic Jihad, et al. but that's all Iranian money that's simply passing through their proxies' hands."

"The mullahs have their own financial problems," Mike interjected, "as do the Chinese."

"True," I said, "but the Andersons are probably looking for a mere hundred million or so. My guess is that they want to endow the family business and then stand by to stir up any on-demand trouble that their Final Boss (or bosses) want to fund. They've now demonstrated that they can whip up a protest here or a protest there, leave no perceptible evidence beyond and create public anxiety at a high level. They can take out two drug kingpins on legendary ground and escape unscathed. That may bring more relief than a sense of chaos to the general populace, but it also conveys the message that that populace could easily be caught in the crossfire. They're willing to spill civilian blood and they've shown that they could operate from one end of the country to the other. They are now the go-to company for crowd-and-mob rental and within their ranks they have an individual (Darvish) with whom all of the bad guys have traded before."

"In short, they're fully open for business," Mike said.

"Big time," I added.

"But we lack the hard evidence to dress them up in chains and zip-ties and welcome them to their 6'x8' steel-barred apartments."

"Or the narrow beds with needles, tubes and lethal-injection cocktails."

"So we have to get creative," Mike said.

"Exactly," I answered. "Perhaps we start by rattling cages, but we can't rattle so hard that they become aware of how much we know and how little we can prove."

"Works for me," Mike said.

"You think my analysis holds water."

"Gallons," Mike said, "but it will evaporate the moment that Anderson's lawyered up and Gonif, Gonif, Gonif and Gonif turn the heat lamps up and focus them on our evidence."

"And there are other wrinkles with which we would have to conjure," I added. "For starters, we couldn't be certain how many of our possible judges spend their works and days in Anderson's pocket. For that matter they wouldn't even have to be friendly to him. All that they would need is a visceral distaste for our country and the elements of law enforcement who spend their time trying to protect it."

"Unfortunately, that's true as well," Mike said. "You're going to have to be *very* creative."

"*You*, not *we*, Kemo Sabe?"

"I'm with you in spirit," Mike said, "but my field experience is pretty much limited to an occasional trip to the grocery store or the service station. You need to talk to someone who knows real strategy and tactics."

"He's next on my call list," I said.

FIFTY-SEVEN

"I agree," the Director said. "First and foremost with your analysis, but also with the fact that we need to be very creative in fashioning our response. We'll need to do much more than shake down a Virgil Snyder, Larry Heinrichs or Paula Vestry—one of those people on the periphery. They'd squeal like a stuck pig and alert the Andersons to our intentions. Ditto a drone flight or two. Anything that let's them know that we're getting close could scuttle our efforts."

"I have a thought, Sir," I said.

"I thought you might," he answered.

"It will require some prior preparation."

"What do you need, Gwen?"

"It's more a who than a what, Sir."

"Name?"

"Someone who is already anonymous enough to escape internet detection."

"That would be possible; we could also jigger the existing information there."

"Someone with a pleasant demeanor but gray enough to fade into the wallpaper," I added.

"Our traditional specialty," he responded.

"Someone with state-of-the-art training and experience in the use of certain forms of weaponry."

"Specifically?"

"I think we should go full-dark on the rest of the conversation, Sir."

"Understood. Drinks at mine…say 9:00 p.m.?"

The drinks were an array of liqueurs. The Director went for the cognac; I chose B&B. The chill in the living room air was counterbalanced by the heat from the fireplace. The drapes were closed and the light was provided by the grate fire and reflected light from the kitchen.

"I have the guy you need," he said. "Some call him the Doc, because he's attended so many training schools. His actual code name is Ben."

"Mossad?"

"No, he's actually home-grown."

"SEAL?"

"Army."

"And don't tell me… he served with you…"

"No comment," the Director said, smiling. "ROTC grad, actually, so he doesn't turn up in any USMA records or yearbooks. Distinguished Military Graduate at his college. Fairly select club."

"Gold fourragère guy."

"Yes. He chose Infantry as his initial branch and over the course of his first six years he completed Airborne, Ranger, and Pathfinder training. Eventually he switched to the Combat Engineers and completed Sapper training at Ft. Leonard Wood."

"Sounds very lethal, Sir."

"He is that."

"Still on active duty?"

"In a sense…"

I didn't pursue that any further, since it appeared that he was in some sort of highly-classified status whose existence was best left unspecified.

"I understand," I said. "He sounds perfect."

"And you want to use him in Darvish's Manhattan townhouse."

"Yes, Sir. We see Darvish as the major conduit to Anderson's funding source or sources and we doubt that Anderson would ever risk the exposure of hosting a confab at one of his own residences. The city is big and bustling and crowded; the upper East Side is filled with private security firms as well as street traffic. Lots of distractions; lots of cover and concealment."

"That's certainly true," he said. "So the plan is that you would move in Ben to dress the set and then start poking at the players to precipitate a meeting."

"Yes, Sir."

"You'll need to meet with Ben first, of course. He'll need to hear the details of your plan directly from the horse's mouth. No offense on the metaphor."

"None taken, Sir."

"We're going to have to be very careful in controlling the narrative," he said.

"Understood, Sir."

"Give me a day or two; I'll get back to you with a time and location."

"How will I recognize him, Sir?"

"He won't look like what you expect."

FIFTY-EIGHT

Thirty hours later we reconnected. The Director told me that our rendezvous point would be a safe house in Selby Bay, Maryland, a blue collar community with some pied `a terre cottages for people with sailboats and motor yachts on the Chesapeake.

The house was a little weather-beaten; the paint could have used a systematic touchup and the roof shingles were spawning some green and rust-colored growth. I gained access via a coded rear-door lock. Inside it was simplicity itself: a galley kitchen, attached dining area, living room with a couch and three chairs, a bathroom and two bedrooms. Ben arrived on time. I noticed that he made some adjustment to his watch as he entered the house.

He was balding and slightly overweight, with wisps of nose and ear hair. He was wearing a tee shirt advertising a towing service that looked as if it had been washed in bleachy water.

"Gwen…Ben," he said. "How do you like my non-threatening disguise?"

"Effective," I said. "No offense intended…"

"None taken. I was going for something between Smurf and Munchkin." Before he settled into one of the chairs he reached behind himself and removed his sidearm, setting it carefully on the coffee table to his right. It was a .50 cal *Desert Eagle* with a black tiger stripe finish. MSRP: $2,500+.

"Great safe house," he said. "You can escape by land or by sea, but you have to know what you're doing. You look out over the bay and everything looks peaceful and calm, but you have to slalom through the crab pot floats. If you come in too close the crab pot lines wrap themselves around the screws of your boat and you're locked in place, a perfect target for anyone wishing to do you harm."

"Nasty," I said.

"This is one of the major launching spots for a tour of St. Michaels— the 'town that tricked the British'. During the War of 1812 the locals hung lanterns in the trees beyond the town and fooled the British into misdirecting their fire. Chicanery is still our watchword," he said.

"The protection of a warrior archangel never hurts either," I said.

"*He* always gave Satan hell," Ben said. "I gather that that's the nature of *our* current enterprise."

I couldn't help but smile.

"The problem is that we've got to prep the site but we don't know when the site will be fully occupied."

"Exactly," I said.

"So we should move quickly. We don't want to create any suspicions by intimating linkages between the prep and the operation proper."

"Definitely not," I said. "Did the Director tell you the location of the site?"

"Upper East Side of Manhattan," he answered. "That's in our favor. Big money…arrogance…the perp will see me as below the level of hired help and say, 'Do what you have to do and get the hell out of here.' That's exactly what I'll do."

"How long will it take for you to assemble the needed materials?"

"A couple days," he said. "I'll work through several intermediaries for the purchases. We'll also need to dress the truck. That might take a day or two longer."

"Sounds good. By the way, the Director speaks very highly of you."

"And you as well," he said. "We'll make a great team. Unfortunately, if we do our jobs well nothing will ever be recorded in the history books."

"The nature of the task…" I said, "just like the national parks and Smokey's advice. We may take some pictures but we won't leave anything but untraceable footprints."

FIFTY-NINE

We rallied four days later by phone. Two days after that Ben drove to NYC, while I took the Acela. Our departure point in the metro area was in the Ironbound section of Newark. After we completed our last-minute planning we drove into Manhattan at 3:00 a.m.

The Upper East Side was quiet. The few stairwell hookers who made their way through the upscale neighborhood had all gone home for the night and the residents were tucked in their beds with visions of sugar plums and stock prices, dancing in their heads.

"I'll put on my LED head lamp, assume my most bored look, and set out some safety cones," Ben said. "I'm sure that I'll be the subject of multiple CCTV surveillance cameras, so I'll enter the tunnel a block or two from Darvish's house. Do you have the line map on your laptop?"

"Right here," I said. "You'll be entering about 1/10th of a mile from Darvish's address."

"Doable, no problem," Ben said.

Four minutes later, I helped him slide the manhole cover open and closed it behind him. Fortunately, it was located near the curb and we could mask our activity by parking the truck directly behind it. We didn't need the safety cones. "This could have been easier if we had done a recon earlier," Ben said, "but I don't like to show up in the same place twice. I treasure my anonymity."

"I understand," I said. "How soon will you be back?"

"Probably in around twenty minutes, allowing for an unexpected issue. Hopefully sooner."

He was back in fifteen.

"I'm going in for the wakeup call. I'll have my mic on, so you can hear the interchange and I'll let you know if there are any problems. If there are I'll use the word *snafu*."

I handed him the large toolbox; it was shaped like a standard, two-suiter piece of luggage, on casters. "Good luck," I said.

"Hopefully I'll be back in about forty minutes," he said.

I could hear the casters rolling over the sidewalk joints and, eventually, the old-school ring of Darvish's doorbell. It was silent for a full minute until the door opened and I heard the sound of a husky voice.

"What the hell are you doing here at this time of night?" the security guy asked.

"Inspection and, hopefully, help," Ben said.

"The Con Ed guy was just here," the disembodied voice said.

"That was for the required inspection of the gas line," Ben said. "Just now our sensor system detected an interruption in your service. Is it getting cold in Mr. Darvish's townhouse?"

"Hell, I don't know. I sleep with the fucking window open. Just a second…"

He returned in several minutes. "The thermostat's set at 68; it's 66 in the house."

"It'll be a lot colder than that when Mr. Darvish is getting ready to enjoy his breakfast."

"So what is it that you want to do?"

"The gas line is open from the street, so I want to check on the inside. It's probably a corroded pipe. If so, you've got a gas leak in the house that won't get better on its own."

"These fuckers cost millions but they're still money pits," he said.

"If you'll show me how to get to the basement I'll turn off the gas and repair the piping, assuming that that's the issue."

"And then charge the shit out of us for the middle-of-the-night call."

"The charges are based on the nature of the problem; we work around the clock with no upcharges; we're here because your safety is our paramount concern. You want the bottom line? We don't want a series of gas explosions in your house and your neighbors' houses. It's bad for our branding."

"I get it. Just take care of the problem as soon as you fucking can."

"The basement?"

"Follow me."

"I'm gonna get some fucking coffee," the security guy said. "Tell me what you find." He didn't offer any coffee to Ben.

For the next twenty minutes Ben worked silently. I heard the buckles on the toolbox open and close and I heard some items being placed on the table. When he was finishing up I heard several wooshes of air from a canister.

Five minutes later I heard the voice of the security guy. "Jesus H. Christ," he said. "That gas smell is awful."

"The scent is added to the natural gas," Ben said. "I'm sure you knew that. The natural gas is odorless, but we want any leakages to come to our customers' attention immediately."

"Yeah, yeah, I get it," the guy said. "I guess I should thank you for coming out as quickly as you did. We don't want that shit coming through the house and we sure as hell don't want it to explode."

"Understood," Ben said. "Don't give it a second thought. We don't advertise the fact, for obvious reasons, but this kind of thing happens all the time. In Manhattan and Westchester we've got almost 4,000,000 customers. Do the math."

"So it was a corroded pipe?"

"Yes, but in a place where you wouldn't automatically see it. Up in the basement's rafters. Probably dated from the building's construction. The pipe will look new but there's a scorch mark or two from the mini-welder. Nothing to worry about. You can go back to sleep."

"OK, thanks buddy," he said.

I heard the townhouse door close and the sound of the casters on the sidewalk. A few seconds later Ben said, "All done at this end. Back in a few."

"One more trip through the tunnel and we can go," he said. "I have to reconnect the gas line."

This time it took a few minutes less.

When we arrived in Newark we found an all-night diner where we bought some coffee, bacon and donuts. "Sugar and grease," Ben said. "Homo sapiens' favorite food, mostly because it was both satisfying and rare."

"Always works for me," I said. "Glad that our visit went well."

"Easy peasy," Ben said. "Much harder to do that sort of thing when you're underwater or when the bad guys are shooting at you."

"What did the security guy look like?"

"Not quite as handsome as your average Silverback, but nearly as big and half as intelligent."

"Rent-a-goon," I said.

"Straight from central casting," Ben responded. "I do, however, have a confession to make."

"What's that?" I asked.

"I couldn't resist a little head game with him."

"Yes?"

"When he came to the door I left my LED head lamp on and shined it in his eyes."

"Did it fluster him? I remember hearing a lot of mumbling."

"Noticeably. I turned it off and smothered him in apologetic gestures but that little moment of dominance may have taken the edge off his initial, angry response to my presence."

"I love it," I said. "I'll have to add it to my repertoire."

"With my blessing," he said.

SIXTY

"All set, Sir," I told the Director

"Ben's the best," he answered, "and I always know that I can count on you."

"Even-tempered, highly-skilled and dangerous as all hell," I said. "Ben, I mean."

"What does Wyatt say, 'you called down the thunder, so you tell them I'm coming and hell's coming with me'?"

"All we have to do now is assemble the cowboys and remove their red sashes," I said.

"That may be tricky," the Director said. "Let's wait a few days before we begin the cage rattling. I don't want them drawing lines of connection between Ben's visit and our next step."

"Virgil Snyder's in Cleveland," I said. "The 450+ miles of distance between him and Manhattan will help us. Plus, the murder of Allyson Barry is, in a way, self-contained. With the Columbus cops doing the interview it would be less likely for the Anderson team to suspect Bureau presence in their lives."

Five days later Frank McConnell knocked on Virgil's door. It was 6:30 a.m.

"Good morning, sir," he said. "Sorry about the early call but I have a busy day ahead, as I'm sure you do." Frank showed Snyder his shield. "My name is Detective Sergeant Francis McConnell, from the Columbus Division of Police."

"Columbus? That's a long fucking way out of your jurisdiction," Snyder said.

"We're liaising with the Cleveland PD, sir; they're aware of my presence here."

"What do you want?"

"I want to ask you some questions. If needs be we can go down to the station and complete the interview."

"Come on in," Snyder said. He pointed to the least comfortable chair in his living room and didn't offer to make coffee.

"The question is actually quite simple," Frank said. "A short time ago there was a murder in the parking lot behind the Polaris Hilton. As you probably know, that's a northern suburb of Columbus. The victim was a young woman named Allyson Barry…"

"Never heard of her and never heard of any murder in Columbus."

"You work for Congressman Anderson…"

"Among other people."

"Congressman Anderson met with the victim shortly before her arrival in Polaris. We have CCTV footage of the meeting. It took place at a restaurant just west of Columbus, adjoining route 70."

"I don't know anything about that," Snyder said.

"Ms. Barry's head was crushed by a tire from a large vehicle. The tire size at the murder scene matches the tires on your *F-150*."

"Wait a minute, wait a minute. Do you have any idea how many fucking *F-150's* there are on the road?"

"Yes, sir. Around sixteen million, but your tires have recently been cleaned with bleach. A lot of bleach, sir."

"So what? I hit an animal on the highway and my truck was covered with blood and shit. I cleaned it up because I didn't want any fucking rabies or other diseases in my garage. Is that all you got?"

"That and your past record, sir."

"That doesn't mean a damn thing and it's probably inadmissible; my lawyer would laugh that out of the fucking court house."

"My question, sir, is what did you have to do with the death of Ms. Barry?"

"Not a fucking thing. And I don't appreciate your coming here and making those kind of allegations. Have you got anything else or are we done here?"

"Final answer?"

"Yes, it's my fucking final answer. I'll repeat myself. Are we done here?"

"Yes, sir, for now. The case is developing. We'll be back in touch. Please contact us if you have any plans to leave the state."

Snyder walked him to the door and closed it without speaking.

Frank communicated all of this to the Director and me on a zoom call.

"Very interesting, Frank. Thanks so much for your help. There's one thing that jumps out at me, but let's hear Gwen on this…"

"Yes, thanks so much, Frank. The one thing that strikes me is that Snyder went for the blanket denials. He never said a word about taking the 5th, even though you gave him enough evidence (evidence that he knows is accurate) to make any normal person pee down his pantsleg. He's probably still wondering how you knew about the bleach on his tire."

The Director nodded in agreement. "He probably thinks Anderson can protect him. I'm sure he has in the past."

"True, sir," Frank said, "but this is capital murder and Ohio has the death penalty. That would normally focus a perp's attention."

"He's probably assuming that he has a brief window of time before the next shoe falls," the Director said, "time for him to sit down with Anderson and make some plans. That means both will be peeing down their pantslegs, which was precisely the purpose of our mission."

"They'll also want to huddle with their lawyer," I said. "He'll probably assure them that he can beat the state's case (or call in some markers from the players in the court system). There's a small bit of light at the edge of the door that could enable a gullible jury to have reasonable doubt. The question is: knowing what he knows, will Virgil Snyder expect Anderson to save him or to leave him twisting in the wind? The latter could loosen his tongue a bit. Most important, it will alert Anderson to the fact that he's already implicated in the murder and he'll wonder how many other things we have in store for him. Bottom line: mission accomplished."

"What do you want me to do at this end?" Frank asked.

"Sit tight for a few days," the Director said. "Let Snyder stew while we tighten our focus on Anderson. And thanks again, Frank."

The Director was careful to leave Darvish, Carrie Muller, et al. out of the conversation. 'Need to know' and all that stuff. After Frank signed off we continued our conversation.

"Not sure who he'll call first," the Director said. "Probably his lawyer, but then Darvish and Carrie (unless he decides to cut them all loose). We'll ask Mike to keep a close eye on each of them and then talk again as soon as there are any developments."

"I'll stay in close touch," I said.

SIXTY-ONE

I contacted Mike, who had already received a text from the Director. "I'm already on it," he said. "Sounds like things are coming to a head."

"Time to exfoliate," I said.

"Oozy white stuff," Mike said. "Poke, squeeze and collect. It's the newest clickbait on *Facebook*."

This stuff will be red, I thought to myself.

In the next several days the local police interviewed both Paula Vestry and Larry Heinrichs. They were asked about a nationwide network of demonstrators and protestors for hire. What was their role in it? Who was their contact there? And (with Larry), why did he travel from Wisconsin to California for the Embarcadero event?

Each was visibly surprised by the questioning but each recovered quickly. Paula said that she was an aspiring journalist and that any event that was newsworthy was worth attending. It was, in effect, part of her academic training. Larry said that he was a doctoral student in sociology and that any event that 'spoke to social activity' in a significant way was possible material for his research.

He was then asked how he knew so early about the event in San Francisco and he waffled, saying that he heard about it on the student grapevine. "Madison's always been an 'energized' place for social activism," he said. "All of the graduate students have a good idea of the location and likelihood of political activity."

When they were pressed about their possible recruitment to the national network they each said that they had been approached but that each of them were reporters/scholars/observers, not direct activists, and that it was essential that they maintain their independence and stay above the fray. When they were asked about Allyson Bond they pretended not to remember her name. "The woman who contacted me was simply trying to elicit interest," Larry said. "I thanked her and then told her I didn't go in for that sort of thing."

Each of the interviewers were surprised by their resourcefulness in having 'bullshit answers' at their fingertips. Perhaps they had been rehearsed, particularly after the Columbus Police's contretemps with Virgil Snyder.

Finally, they were confronted with the fact that each had indeed been involved directly in demonstrations/protests in the past. They responded that these were youthful actions which seemed important to them at the time but now were an admitted source of embarrassment. When Paula was presented with the fact that her direct involvement took place less than a year and a half ago she replied that she was an 'old soul'.

"Slick perhaps, or at least oily, but the answers were pure and unadulterated bullshit," I said to Mike.

"That's for sure and certain" Mike responded. "They were no doubt advised on their answers but the facts are so much in our favor that they couldn't help but look as if they were making it all up as the interviews proceeded."

"Nothing was said about Carrie Muller," I continued. "They weren't even asked about whether or not they had 'handlers'. That was the whole point, of course. We weren't really interested in their answers, just the degree to which they actually had been 'handled', the ultimate purpose of the interviews being our hope that they would now be so enveloped in fear that they would contact Carrie and Carrie would turn to her daddy-in-law for fresh orders."

"The walls are closing in," Mike said. "They don't know what we know but they know we know more than they want us to know. Does that sound too much like Donald Rumsfeld?"

"No, I like the analysis," I said. "The question now is whether or not this leads to a pow-wow among the principals."

"They're all on candid camera," Mike said. "The moment I see any activity I'll let you know."

Two days later he contacted me. "Nothing new with Vestry and Heinrichs and Carrie is staying put for the moment. Curtis is holed up in Cleveland. He was seen at the West Side Market buying cottage hams. Usually that's a southern Ohio thing. Very tasty."

"I've heard of them," I said. "They're actually not hams but shoulder butts. You cure them in brine, I think, and then boil the hell out of one of them in a big pot with some potatoes and green beans. Peasant food, perhaps, but really, really good. Add a 22-ounce bottle of cold beer and I'm there."

"Yes. Well, he didn't do anything at the Market besides buy the hams. The butcher knew him and they exchanged pleasantries. One or two constituents came up and gave him shoulder pats but there were no significant interactions beyond the blow-by kisses."

"So that's it?"

"No, that's not it," Mike said. "I haven't had lunch yet and I got distracted for a moment. We have actually had some serious action, but with Darvish."

"Going out to dinner again? Who with this time, the Chinese or the Iranians?"

"The Iranians. Well, an Iranian. Darvish's dining companion looked like a functionary (their form of insulation, again) but they were eating like the Shah when he took temporary leave from the Peacock Throne."

"Recently?"

"Last night," Mike said. "They ate at *Eleven Madison Park*. Maybe I should say 'lived' rather than 'ate'. They were there for almost four hours."

"Bring your MasterCard and your VISA," I said.

"Yep. Eight-to-nine course tasting menu. A cool $365 each. Three Michelin stars but you don't get any meat. You don't even get any 'animal products'. It's all plant-based."

"You'd have to *pay me* to do that," I said. "I'm a peasant. I'll take the cottage ham with the beans and potatoes."

"Roger that," Mike said. "Important point: Darvish picked up the tab. Demonstrably. He also bowed and scraped a lot, kissing up as best he could."

"They're worried," I said. "This is fence-mending, or at least some form of reassurance that there's still a steady hand on the tiller."

"Everything's heading down the crapper, but they don't want their banker to go wobbly."

"That would be a reasonable inference," I said.

I thanked Mike, felt guilty about compartmentalizing him, and contacted the Director.

SIXTY-TWO

"I was worried for a second," I told him. "You mean that they had already held their meeting, set up their plan and were beginning to execute it."

"Right, Sir, but I'm having second thoughts…more positive thoughts. With our interviews of Vestry and Heinrichs, Carrie Muller should be drawn into that discussion. The higher muck-a-mucks will want to talk to her at length and tease out any details that they can. Moreover, the meeting between Darvish and the character from the Iranian consulate would probably have required a day or two to arrange. The consulate people would want to coordinate with Tehran before they made any commitments or cut any ties. When you look at the timeline you have to come to the conclusion that the dinner was a finger in a leaky dike, not the signing of a final agreement."

"I think you're right, Gwen," the Director said. "There's too much at stake here, too much of a prior investment. The gang of two (two and a half?) is trying to protect their opportunity costs and the banker (assuming that's Iran) is seeking to be reassured that their mortgagor can meet his monthly nut."

"But the mortgagees are not known for their patience."

"No," the Director said. "They'll put a rope around your neck, attach it to a crane and hoist you in the air before you can begin to beg for mercy."

"Let's hope that their impatience leads to some sort of summit conference."

"And that they'll use Darvish's townhouse for the event. Wait and watch, Gwen."

Later that day I heard from Mike. "Ms. Carrie is in the Chicago suburbs. Sorry I missed her departure and landing. She may have flown private. That would indicate to me that there's urgency in the air."

"Hearing Vestry's sob story, probably."

"Just so, this time over burgers and an onion 'brick'."

"At *Hackney's*? That's pretty public."

"The place is jammed," Mike said, "even this early in the day."

"Which location?"

"Evanston."

"Interesting. Carrie comes to her. Carrie takes her out for comfort food. Carrie's trying to calm her down and reduce her fears."

"The cold beers are also helping to soften the blow," Mike said.

"I love those so-called 'bricks' of onions," I said.

"What better way to ingest a bazillion calories?" Mike asked.

"How about demeanor?"

"Carrie is all mom and cuddles. At one point she even put her hand on the back of Paula's. As best I could lip-read she was saying 'it's ok; it's ok'."

"So we have Paula's full attention."

"And now Carrie's."

"Target acquired," I said, "and mini-mission accomplished."

"There's more," Mike said.

"She's ticketed for Madison next?"

"Flying commercial this time. First thing in the morning," he said. "Again, I'm sorry I missed the first leg of her trip."

"Maybe it's a small bit of obfuscation on their part," I said. "Don't worry about it."

"Larry's showing some spine," Mike said. "No tears, no whimpers. Carrie seems a little surprised. Anyway, she shot for the same kind of ambiance for lunch, a place called *State Street Brats*. In this case the favored side is cheese curds. Larry is picking at his. He's all anger and frustration. No fear, no way."

"Those sociologists think they're badasses," I said. "They think they know the law and are always ready with some stupid response like 'charge me or release me'."

"They're surprised when you charge them," Mike said.

"Yes," I responded, "so he's probably trying to convince Carrie that they should stand their ground and fight."

"Yes, but he's expressing it via clenched fists rather than wordy paragraphs."

"I love it," I said. "Just when Team Anderson wants to pee on the fire, retreat, and hide in a dark corner he wants to pour gasoline on it."

"He should be more guarded," Mike said. "They (or their final boss) could send him into permanent retirement."

"They may have to," I said.

"Interesting side note: she isn't touching her beer and he's drinking ice water."

"That says it all," I responded.

She left on a late afternoon flight to Cleveland, with a stop at O'Hare. Mike lost her briefly as she changed concourses, but picked her up at the gate area. She was sitting empty-handed: no book, no laptop, no coffee. She was stewing, no doubt in anticipation of her upcoming debriefing with daddy-in-law.

I sent the Director a brief summary of the day's activities.

"Trouble in paradise," he texted. "I like it."

The next day I heard from Mike. "Interesting development at the Iranian consulate, They've brought in a big gun."

"Name?"

"Bijan Ghasemi."

"No relation to the clothier on Rodeo Drive, I assume."

"The 'make an appointment and I may serve you' guy? No, not hardly."

"What's his actual gig?" I asked.

"Go-fer for the mullahs," Mike said, "sometimes doing diplomatic work, sometimes darker stuff. Senior officer in the Quds force, under the general umbrella of the IRGC, the Islamic Revolutionary Guard Corps. Originally one of Soleimani's acolytes."

"How did he arrive?"

"Chauffered limo, not an Uber or NYC cab."

"How serious does he look?"

"Very serious," Mike said. "I hate to sound as if I'm stereotyping, but…"

"What's he look like, Mike?"

"Ready for this?"

"Sure."

"He's a dead ringer for the Iron Sheik."

"The old wrestler?"

"Yep. No longer with us. Built like a fireplug. Short in stature but something like 250 pounds of muscle. Bald head. Fulsome mustache. Handlebar-type with little twisty things at the end. No keffiyeh on his head, but a beautifully-tailored Savile Row suit."

"With a little room for a sidearm?"

"I think so. He was out of the limo and into the building in a matter of seconds. Fortunately, he turned for a second and looked over his shoulder. I was lucky to get a facial shot."

"Sounds like the mullahs have called in the A-team, at least one member of it."

"Yes," Mike said, "but remember…the Iron Sheik…Hulk Hogan took him down in a little over ten minutes."

"I had forgotten that," I said, smiling.

"There's more news," Mike said.

"I hope it's good," I said.

"I think it's significant," Mike said. "Curtis' *Mercedes* just turned onto I-80. Virgil Snyder is driving. Carrie Muller is in the back seat."

"Which direction?"

"East."

"Seven hours out," I said.

SIXTY-THREE

"This could be tight timewise," the Director said. "We have to move quickly. Ben is inside the beltway, just leaving. He'll pick you up on the way."

"I'll be ready," I said.

Ben was driving an unmarked Bureau sedan; we drove to Dulles, where the Bureau *Gulfstream G550* was idling. "No *Cessna* today," Mike said.

"This is important," I said.

"Roger that," Ben answered. "We should make it to Newark in under an hour, perhaps as quickly as 45 minutes. We need to go to our hidey hole in the Ironbound section of the city and pick up our marked truck. This time we'll actually use the traffic cones."

"We probably have a little time before they actually meet. If Anderson has any brains he'll want to send Snyder ahead to check out the scene. He probably knows who he's meeting with (certainly the level of the participants) but he doesn't know whether the meeting will begin with a preemptive strike. He may also want to talk to Carrie when Virgil's out of hearing range. Again, if he's smart he won't have shared the complete details of their enterprise with a potential loose cannon."

"Fully agree," Ben said. "Have you got a good observation point for us?"

"Yes. There's a passageway just down the street, catty-cornered from Darvish's place. We won't need binoculars but we'll still be a safe distance away."

"Then let's sit back and enjoy the flight," Ben said.

Except that he didn't. He was on his phone the whole trip, coordinating with a man from the New York field office. He wanted to make sure that the battery was charged on our putative *Con Ed* van and that there was a 'uniform' for me as well as for him. This had all been checked out earlier but Ben was a measure twice/cut once guy. He also checked on the availability of traffic cones, other signage and small tents that would cover manholes.

"All ready," he said to me, as we landed. "And no troubles anticipated. Newark is one of the top 25 sites for private jet traffic."

I nodded approvingly, knowing that the airport had had its problems in the past due to outdated control systems, but we were now on the ground and that was our only concern. An unmarked Bureau sedan was waiting for us. The driver was Ben's contact from the New York field office. 'Circumscribed intelligence'; strictly 'need to know' was the order of the day, a necessity given the results that were likely to follow.

Everything was copacetic at our Ironbound departure point; I had already engaged with Mike.

"Darvish is in place," Mike said, "as is his pet gorilla. Each was seen on the sidewalk outside Darvish's home on East 64th. They appeared to be looking up and down the street, checking sight lines. They were probably just expending nervous energy. Anyway, no worries for you. The Anderson car is at least twenty minutes outside of Montclair, so you've got world enough and time to beat them into the city."

"Much appreciated, Mike. What's happening at the Iranian consulate?"

"In a word, nothing, but they're only 24 blocks south of Darvish's house. They probably plan to be fashionably late anyway, just to reinforce who's boss of the local peons."

"I'm looking at the map on my phone," I said. "It looks as if there's a

Shake Shack right across the street from them. They could hang out there with the 12th Imam, if he ever shows up."

"I believe they would consider that to be very politically (and religiously) incorrect," Mike said.

"No doubt," I answered, "but if he has any access to our plans he would best be advised to continue to hunker down in the place where he's presently residing."

"You're incorrigible, Special Agent Harrison."

"Guilty as charged," I said. "You stay in touch now."

"Will do," he said.

Ben's response was to estimate the joint time of their arrival at two hours. "As we said before, the Anderson party will want to stretch their legs and gather their thoughts, not simply drive to the townhouse with full bladders and bodies that feel as if they're still in motion."

"Plenty of hotels in the area," I said, "especially if you like to pay $800+ per night."

We arrived at our site, parked the van three blocks south, broke out the large thermos of black coffee, and waited.

"As soon as they arrive we can set out the cones," Ben said. "I want to reduce any possible collateral damage to civilians."

"Right," I said.

An hour and a half later the Anderson group pulled in front of the *Pierre*.

"Going for the high-priced spread," Ben said.

"They're probably going to walk to Darvish's place," I suggested. "They would be the suspicious types and would want to do a little recon before they expose themselves."

"Maybe they've met Darvish's gorilla before," Ben said. "Maybe they think that this time he'll be accompanied by some playmates."

"Anything happening at the consulate?" I asked Mike.

"Not really," he answered. The lights are all on and I can see some heads and shoulders pass by the windows, but otherwise nothing."

"The Andersons are moving," Mike said. "Walking north on Madison; Snyder is walking point, a few yards ahead of Curtis and Carrie. Each of them looks apprehensive. I only caught one or two good facial shots; most of the time they were looking down, dodging whatever might be waiting for them on the sidewalk. When they did look up they each had an expression that said they would have preferred to be someplace else. Anyplace else."

By now Ben was in the back of the van, lining up his materials for dressing the set. Mike checked in ten minutes later. "The Andersons are a block from the townhouse and a Caddy *XTS* just pulled up in front of the consulate, very long and black and intimidating, not goofy like some high roof Mercedes *Sprinter*. This is for Mr. Serious, not a prom party."

The Andersons arrived at Darvish's townhouse; the door opened before they had a chance to ring the bell. They were greeted by the Silverback, who was now arrayed in a gray suit that left enough material below the left shoulder to accommodate what Wyatt would have described as a sizeable smokewagon. None of the members of the Anderson party made eye contact with Darvish's goon.

Twelve minutes later the Caddy limo arrived. Two men emerged, one looking west, the other east. Ghaseni got out and walked toward the door, which immediately opened. Ghaseni didn't make eye contact with the goon but he looked him over, from his shoes to his shoulder. From what we could see from the partial image, Ghaseni's look was one of utter contempt. As soon as he entered the building the Caddy drove west toward the park and abruptly turned left. "Let's go to work," Ben said.

The first step was to put cones across 3rd Avenue and Lexington Avenue, along with two 'road closed' signs. The next was to erect the tent a few doors west of Darvish's townhouse and surround it with 'road closed' and 'men working' signs. Finally, we put 'sidewalk closed' signs at either end of the street, in an effort to keep pedestrian traffic blocked on the north side of East 64th.

Driving north and south in Manhattan is always a challenge, but driving east and west is a five-star shaggy bitch, so we would need to move quickly before the anxious and inconvenienced local citizenry would begin to call the NYPD, city hall, the governor's office, the White House, and the palace of the resident lord of the galaxy.

"The group is fully assembled," I told the Director. "Anderson, the daughter-in-law, Snyder, Darvish, his goon and the Iranian muscle."

"How's the pedestrian traffic?" he asked.

"Nonexistent for the moment, Sir," I said. "A family was walking on the south side of East 64th, but they entered a townhouse and currently remain there."

"Vehicular traffic?"

"A few parked cars, but no occupants."

"Put the phone to Ben's ear, Gwen."

"Ben…"

"Sir?"

"Gwen…"

"Sir?"

"Proceed with the operation."

Just then the door to Darvish's townhouse opened and the gorilla came outside for an unexpected look-see. Ben had just sent the second electronic message to the property's basement. From that point on everything happened in milliseconds. There was a cracking boom and a huge shock wave. Darvish's thug's body was propelled from the north side of the street to the south and smashed across the steps and iron hand railing of the opposite building. It looked like the remains of the proverbial puppet whose strings had been severed with a giant scissors. A series of flashes dotted with fragments of stone and brick and glass and smoky-black dust followed the hurtling man as if they were poking him in the back and directing his movement.

This was all followed by a secondary explosion which shattered the remaining intact windows and set the entire building ablaze. Less than five minutes later we could hear the sound of police sirens and the air horns of, probably, two to three fire trucks. We were already in our van, Ben had peeled the plastic *Con Ed* livery markings from both sides of the vehicle and we were driving comfortably toward the Lincoln tunnel.

SIXTY-FOUR

The line for the Tunnel was shorter than we expected; Ben's contact from the field office was waiting for us at our rallying point. He had opened the left side of the large double doors, pointed to our parking place and exchanged keys with Ben, all without uttering a word.

We got into an unmarked sedan with New Jersey plates and in a little more than an hour were on 95, halfway to Philly. The drive south was completely uneventful. Everyone was driving at least five miles above the speed limit and none were looking in our direction. When we returned to the DC suburbs we decided to split up and have dinner separately, so as not to tempt fate or anyone with a curious mind and an iPhone camera.

I went to *Rocco's*, taking a small table in the rear of the restaurant. I did a cup of Minestrone, some pasta and either two or three glasses of Chianti. It wasn't that I was woozy and lost count so much as I was decompressing and coming down from the operational high. Ben said that he would probably have bourbon with his steak, but he didn't indicate where that would be happening. "The Russians have neat little personal splits of vodka with their dinner; I'll do the same thing, American-style." It was as close as he would come to something like 'whew, glad that's over'.

I passed on dessert but did a glass of *Sambuca* with a double number of dark coffee beans drifting toward the bottom. The coffee was designed to keep me awake while complimenting the taste of the liqueur. Fifteen minutes later I was back at the Director's aerie. His home was dark, but as

I entered my room I felt my phone twitch with an incoming message. The headline was 'call me with your thoughts'. The material was as follows:

(from their website)

The New York Times

Explosion on East 64th Street

2 MIN READ

At 2:16 this afternoon a townhome on the upper east side was destroyed by the detonation of a powerful explosive, believed to be Semtex, a plastic material invented in Czechoslovakia in the late 1950's. The event is being compared with the Weathermen bomb-factory explosion on March 6, 1970 in Greenwich Village. Three Weathermen were killed in that blast while two survivors fled.

Bomb-making equipment was found in the basement of the home on East 64th Street (between Lexington and 3rd Avenues). These included initiators, switches, containers, fragments of explosives and such 'enhancements' as nails and ball bearings. Law enforcement officials are speculating that the bomb makers accidentally detonated materials, taking their own lives in the process.

The occupants of the house are still being identified. The owner was Hassan Darvish (birth name: Azimi), an Iranian businessman, believed to be a major arms dealer. A second man, believed to be an employee of Darvish's, was propelled across the street by the blast. The NYPD has not yet identified him. Also killed in the explosion was retired Ohio congressman, Curtis Anderson and a young woman believed to be the possible bomb maker. Her identity has not yet been verified, though there is speculation that she may be Congressman Anderson's daughter-in-law. Another individual—believed to be one Virgil Snyder—was a longstanding employee of the Congressman's. Finally, the NYPD has identified the remains of Colonel Bijan Ghasemi, senior officer in the Iranian Quds force.

There is unverified speculation that this group was responsible for a number of recent events involving demonstrations and protests, their purpose being to create an atmosphere of chaos across the United States that would both result in unrest, the undermining of confidence in its government and the masking of other activities, such as the construction of terror cells, the assembling of intelligence-gathering units and, potentially, the importation of drugs, including fentanyl. The NYPD will work with elements of federal law enforcement as the investigation proceeds. The section of East 64th Street in question was cordoned off by *Con Ed*, which appears to have been working in the area. The NYPD is investigating the possibility that the traffic cones and other signage were installed by associates of the group destroyed in the blast, the purpose being to redirect pedestrian and vehicular traffic in the hope that the individuals assembling there could resist identification.

I called the Director immediately.

"Perfect," I said. "The Weathermen analogy defines and fixes the narrative. The story corresponds with almost all of the known facts and settles some scores with the Iranians for past mischief. The fact that the story appeared so quickly reinforces support for the NYPD, exhibits a surprising degree of transparency and offers comfort to the local residents. Since the site of the event is somewhat iconic it will draw positive public attention from across the country. Seeing villains hoist on their own petard is always a gratifying story line. Do I detect a leak from the Bureau's new headquarters, Sir?"

"We have friends in many places, Gwen, some high, some low."

"It will be interesting to see how this develops," I said. "The old pols used to say that it's better to see yourself exposed on the front page and then gradually move to the back of the paper as other interests develop; far better than to turn up in the back of the paper and then slowly but inexorably move to the front. My guess is that this will start on the front page, probably above the fold, and then dissolve into a succession of human interest stories about the people found there, both because it *is* a fascinating group of individuals and because the core narrative fits together so nicely that it resists challenges to its veracity."

"I think you're right," the Director said. "At least we are all counting on the fact that you are."

"Darvish's goon's body being hurled across the street was very lucky. We were past the point of no return on our countdown when he appeared. Pity that there was no one on the scene to take a picture of him, because the imagery is wonderful. Not to sound ghoulish, Sir, but it has a way of summarizing all of the narrative."

"I never liked him anyway," the Director said, "and I never met him."

"When the papers begin to probe his past (assuming that they actually do begin to probe) we will doubtless discover an unsavory life that will add ripples and echoes to the original story. Virgil's rap sheet (equally unattractive) will remove any vestiges of respect for Anderson. The only thing missing from the story is the reason for the meeting. As a disinterested reader I would infer that the principals were there to inspect the premises and see some of its newest products. Unfortunately, as Robert Burns would say, the best-laid plans of mice and men often end up in the crapper (or words to that effect)."

"Agreed," the Director said. "I think he said something about the plans going 'aft agley', but your version makes the point with greater rigor. Now you get a good night's rest and treat yourself to a day off. That's an order."

"Understood, Sir. I can do that."

"We'll reassemble in a couple of days. I'll be back in touch with a time and place."

"I'll look forward to that, Sir."

"As will I," he said.

SIXTY-FIVE

After a late breakfast of English muffins and peach preserves I filled a thermos with black coffee and drove to Great Falls. I found a vacant table near a copse of river birch and sipped my coffee. I didn't think of anything in particular, but checked my email and some websites on my phone. I tried to listen to my own breathing as the river crashed across the boulders in the falls.

After the first cup of coffee I took out a mass market paperback that I had carried in my purse and read for forty-five minutes. When I returned it there I had to first move my Sig to the side. As always, its weight gave me comfort. Individuals who are unfamiliar with sidearms are always surprised by their weight. I suppose their muscle memories extrapolate from their recollections of the plastic toys that they had as children. A full magazine contributes several ounces to the overall impression. The fact that I had a full load but didn't have a chambered round was a positive indication of my current comfort level.

When I finished my coffee and my pseudo-meditation I returned to the apartment above the Director's garage and waited for his instructions. They came at 4:00 in the afternoon.

"Dinner tomorrow at 7:00. *Ritz-Carlton*, Tysons. Check in with Club level (floor 24) concierge, who will direct you to our room. Specify the 'Patton party'. Casual dress. Skip lunch."

The 'Patton party' was the Director's idea of a joke. He idealized Georgie, of course, but he was also aware that the *Patton* name was one which entailed anonymity. Patton's ancestor, the surgeon Hugh Mercer, was at the Battle of Culloden in 1746. He was a friend of George Washington's and a Brigadier General in the patriot army. His son-in-law Robert (Georgie's great-grandfather), was a Scotsman who had assumed that (common) Scottish surname because he was a wanted criminal with a substantial price on his head. In Gaelic the name Patton means *king's pensioner*, which indicated Robert's loyalties. Assuming the common name *Patton* also made it easier for Robert to lose himself in America. Hence we do not know Georgie's actual surname.

The concierge directed me to a suite which had been rearranged in the form of a private dining room. When I entered the Director handed me a very dry martini on the rocks with a lemon twist that looked as if it had been fashioned by a senior chef. Ben arrived five minutes later, just ahead of the hotel staff who brought in our food. Each time that they served a course they left the room to give us privacy.

"Not to worry," Ben said. "I swept the room a half hour ago, right after we had changed rooms to insure the absence of bugs."

The first course was a leek and potato soup accompanied by a *Chateau Montelena* chardonnay.

"Tell me about the biggest challenges," the Director said.

"Getting the dimensional charges set properly in the hundred year-old basement rafters," Ben said. "They had to be functional but also out of sight. Also positioning the unexploded blocks of Semtex and the miscellaneous parts for the bomb fabrications. They had to be discoverable after the blast but invisible to the naked eye."

"Gwen?" Ben said.

"Always the timing," I said. "The right planets had to come into the right alignment. We wanted to lock the participants in a tight box but preserve the health and well-being of any innocent bystanders. That meant closing down a very busy street and insuring that no one accidentally stumbled into the line of fire."

"The goon in the air was an unexpected blessing, a gift from the Almighty," Ben said.

"Yes, indeed," the Director responded.

The second course was Wagyu ribeyes, medium-rare, with the largest russet potatoes I had ever seen. The perfectly-parallel grill marks on the asparagus were a signature move. We all sat in silence as the servers offered us an array of toppings for the baked potatoes, sauces for the ribeyes and hollandaise for the asparagus. Before leaving they removed our first-course wine glasses, substituted the Riedels for claret, poured each of us a third of a glass of *Chateau Leoville-LAS Cases*, and left. "They've been making this crystal since the middle of the 18th century," the Director said, as the door closed behind the servers.

"So," he said, "any second thoughts or regrets?"

I began. "I keep thinking about the scenes from *The Exorcist* in which the younger priest (Fr. Karras?) wants to talk to the old, experienced priest, Fr. Merrin, about the nature of the 'case'. Fr. Merrin will have none of it, for one simple reason…"

"The demon is a liar," the Director said. "Closed quotes. The gist is clear: this is a battlefield, not a hospital room. He must be driven out. His presence cannot be tolerated."

"We started with that, didn't we?" I asked. "Allyson tried to deal with the devils. Carrie actually did deal with the devils. Not a good career move, especially when we had seen the extent of their designs. When Ben and I were at Selby Bay we talked about St. Michaels in Talbot County and how nice it was for the residents to have a warrior archangel on their side. I was thinking…why does God actually *need* an army of angels? I know the standard answer. Milton says that if Adam hadn't had free will he would have been an empty fabrication—like a puppet in a children's show. No free will, no moral achievement. The kicker is that when you introduce free will (even in heavenly beings) you introduce the possibility of evil. That means that you have to have an army of angels, just in case.

Now I guess He could have constructed the universe in such a way that we'd trade off moral achievement for eternal peace and joy, but he went another way—the constant possibility of evil and the necessity to have the good guys available to combat it, from archangels to…yes…soldiers and G-men."

"And G-women," the Director said. "Sometimes we have to remind ourselves that we're at war. So much of our work is desk work: we check records, scroll through computer screens, build cases, fill out forms, anticipate legal counterattacks…but sometimes we're in the field and we realize that thousands of lives are ultimately in our hands. We're not clerks then; we're soldiers. We don't hand the enemy subpoenas; we attack. It's a fine line, I know, and it puts us in a difficult position. Maybe we end up utilitarians, trying to do the greatest good for the greatest number, no matter the costs to our treasury or our personal psyches. Maybe we're vigilantes of a sort, even though we carry badges. What do you think? Is everyone sleeping well?"

"Always," Ben said. "I've seen the disfigured and dismembered bodies that they leave behind. I also know that everyone who offers us death in return for personal gain and self-aggrandizement knows that there can always come a time when we remove the cotton gloves and reveal the iron fists. Those that always expect politeness and paperwork are seriously deluded."

"Gwen?" the Director said.

"There's a spectrum of evil," I said, "and I feel bad—a little bad—for those like Carrie who may have begun as idealists before sliding into the dark, but she was never an innocent bystander. She didn't turn up at the wrong place at the wrong time; she was (if you'll pardon the expression) along for the ride. She chose the valley of death and now remains there, in small pieces."

"Whenever I feel bubbles in my stomach I think of the potential victims," the Director said. "Usually I think of a single individual. Someone young, someone innocent, someone who deserves a long life of joy and opportunity. You come at someone like that with a bomb in your hand and I'm not going to call up the legal department. I'm coming at the bomb thrower with a 120 mm smoothbore cannon, a .50 cal Browning, two 7.62 M240's and, if necessary, my tank tracks carrying 68 tons of weight."

"That would certainly fix their attention," Ben said.

"And there's always the final option," I said, "the 9mm round between the eyes that turns Beelzebub into the cyclops."

Dessert was a platter of miscellaneous pastries, the principal choice a trio of miniature rum babas with fresh whipped cream inside and atop them. "I passed on the raspberries," the Director said. "A little too chichi for my taste. I hope you weren't disappointed. I also wanted to leave room for…"

"Whatever you're hiding in that paper bag beneath your feet, Sir," I said. "I'm betting on something old and French."

"Cognac," the Director said. "A simple *Rémy Martin*. I was going for *festive* but I didn't want to go over the top and show off."

We each clinked glasses, looked in each other's eyes and relished the generous pours.